CECILIA GALANTE

The World from Up Here

Scholastic Inc.

Copyright © 2016 by Cecilia Galante

This book was originally published in hardcover by Scholastic Press in 2016.

All rights reserved. Published by Scholastic Inc., *Publishers since 1920.* SCHOLASTIC and associated logos are trademarks and/or registered trademarks of Scholastic Inc.

The publisher does not have any control over and does not assume any responsibility for author or third-party websites or their content.

No part of this publication may be reproduced, stored in a retrieval system, or transmitted in any form or by any means, electronic, mechanical, photocopying, recording, or otherwise, without written permission of the publisher. For information regarding permission, write to Scholastic Inc., Attention: Permissions Department, 557 Broadway, New York, NY 10012.

This book is a work of fiction. Names, characters, places, and incidents are either the product of the author's imagination or are used fictitiously, and any resemblance to actual persons, living or dead, business establishments, events, or locales is entirely coincidental.

ISBN 978-0-545-84846-6

10 9 8 7 6 5 4 3 2 1   17 18 19 20 21

Printed in the U.S.A.   40
First printing 2017

For my Sophia—Everything you need
is already inside of you.

Chapter 1

Mondays are hard.

Mondays at school are even worse. But kicking off the first ten minutes of a Monday at school with a fire drill is my definition of insanity.

I'd barely gotten settled at my desk when the fire alarm went off, blaring so suddenly from the speakers in the room that I almost fell out of my seat. You'd think I'd be used to the sound, since we have at least three drills every year. But no. That shrill, ear-splitting noise shoots through me every time and leaves me trembling all over.

"All right, boys and girls!" Mrs. Danforth, my sixth-grade science teacher, clapped her hands together as we rose from our chairs. "You know the drill! Everyone in single file!" This was the first time I'd been in science class when the drill sounded, and while I was unsure where we needed to go when we got outside, I also knew I wouldn't have any trouble finding out. At Sudbury Middle School, Mrs. Danforth was known for two things: her love of all things green and her megaphone-mouth. "We will be heading for the side door," she hollered now, "and then lining up outside on the south side of the building! Everyone hear me? The *south* side of the building! All right, let's go now! No talking, please!"

My heart, which had begun to slow down a little, sped back up again as I got in line behind Charlotte Reinert, who was braiding her waist-long hair. I leaned forward as we traipsed down the stairs. "The south side?" I whispered. "Isn't that where . . . I mean, can't you see . . ."

"Wren Baker!" Mrs. Danforth's voice tipped toward the dangerously annoyed–sounding zone. "What did I just say about talking?"

I pressed my lips together as Charlotte pushed the door open ahead of me and tried to concentrate on the backs of her blue sneakers, which were worn and scuffed. It wasn't even nine o'clock yet, and the chill in the autumn air made me shiver. The sun hung low in the sky, and I could smell wood smoke somewhere in the distance. "This way!" Mrs. Danforth shouted. "Right over here by the chain link fence, everyone!" I pulled the sleeves of my sweater over my hands and tried not to look up.

"All right, boys and girls, let me take roll and then you may talk quietly until it's time to go back in!" said Mrs. Danforth. "When I call your name, please say 'here!' Janie Answel?"

Even with my eyes on the ground, it was impossible not to feel the enormity of Creeper Mountain looming in front of us like a gigantic ship. People who didn't know better might have thought the mountain was beautiful,

2

with its thousands of trees, each one splotched with the colors of fall: pomegranate red, brilliant orange, warm yellow. But I knew better.

"Wren Baker?"

"Here." My voice was barely a whisper.

"Carmela Callahan?"

"Here!"

"Everyone look up at the mountain!" I squeezed my eyes tight as Jeremy Winters hissed to the rest of us. "Holler if you see anything witch-related!"

Charlotte's now neatly braided head swiveled in Jeremy's direction. "My dad saw the raven last week!" she whispered. "He was on his way home from work, and all of a sudden he saw this big shadow above him. When he looked up, he saw a flash of red, and then it disappeared."

"She sends it out at dusk." Jeremy nodded. "It guards the whole mountain—" He stopped abruptly and pointed. "There! You see it? Right at the top! A tiny thread of smoke!"

"Where?" Carmela Callahan pulled a finger out of her ear. "I don't see . . ." She gasped. "Oh, there it is! I see it!"

A flash of heat spread through the center of my chest as the excitement began to build among the rest of the students. I took a few steps back, hoping I didn't seem too obvious, and willed myself not to listen. Next to us, another line of students was forming. Silver Jones stood in the middle of the line, her blonde hair shimmering like gold strands in the morning light. She and I were first cousins, but I'd never actually met her before she and her mom showed up in Sudbury. In fact, until she moved here from Florida a few months ago, I wasn't even sure how old she was. Now, all the boys strained in her direction, clamoring for a glimpse of her. Even Jeremy, who was in my line, leaned forward as she came into view. "Hey, Silver!"

Silver looked up at the sound of her name. Her eyes were pale green and set inside a face that was so pretty it made my teeth hurt. *Someday*, I thought, *if I get very lucky, and all the stars align themselves just right, I might end up looking a little bit like her.*

"You know about Creeper Mountain, don'tcha?" Jeremy seemed giddy to have Silver looking at him. "Witch Weatherly and all that?"

Silver's eyebrows narrowed. "Witch who?"

Jeremy pointed. "You see that smoke coming out of the top of the mountain?"

Nathan Billings and Dylan Fisk, who were standing on either side of Silver in line, seemed to explode simultaneously. "Holy cow, there it is! There she is!"

"There who is?" Silver tucked a stray strand of hair behind one ear and pulled out a tube of coconut lip-gloss from her back pocket. "What are you guys talking about?"

"No one's told you about Witch Weatherly?" Dylan's brown hair looked like it had been cut with a pair of Popsicle sticks; shaggy wisps stuck out all over his head.

"She lives right up there on that mountain. Look! You can see the smoke coming out of her chimney."

I reached up slowly and pressed in the little nub of cartilage on my left ear as hard as I could. I would look like an idiot if I stood there with both hands over my ears, but I knew what was coming, and I didn't want any part of it. Even one blocked eardrum would help a little.

Silver squinted at the mountain as she rolled the gloss over her lips. "I think I see it," she said. "Kind of on the left?"

"Yeah!" The excitement in Dylan's face seemed to fade as he looked around the group. "Man, I wonder what she's burning up there," he said.

"Or cooking," Nathan said ominously.

"Anyone hear of any missing people lately?" Jeremy asked.

"Or pets?" Charlotte chimed in next to me.

The single eardrum block was not working. I started to hum "My Country Tis of Thee," softly at first, then louder as the conversation continued.

"Missing people?" Silver capped her lip-gloss and slid it back inside her back pocket. Her lips glistened like the inside of a peach.

"Oh man." Jeremy shook his head. "We gotta tell you the whole story. It goes way back. Like all the—" He stopped suddenly. "What's that noise?" All eyes turned toward me as he took a step in my direction. "Wren, are you humming?"

"She's blocking her ears, too!" Dylan hooted. "She doesn't want to hear about the witch!" He shook his head. "Geez, Wren, how can you be twelve years old and still act like such a baby?"

"I'm not." I lowered my finger as my face flushed hot. "I was just humming a song I heard on the radio this morning. Go ahead, tell her the story."

The kids in both lines seemed to come alive all at the same time. The flurry of competing voices bubbled and swelled—words like *fires* and *ravens*, *pits* and *snakes*, flew in all directions.

Silver crossed her arms over her chest. "I can't hear anything!"

"I'll tell it," Jeremy said, holding up his hands. "Geez. I brought it up in the first place." He cleared his throat and glanced warily up at the mountain, as if whoever lived up there might hear him. "Okay, so there was this lady named Bedelia Weatherly who lived here in Sudbury a really long time ago."

"Like a hundred years ago," Carmela Callahan chimed in.

"*Over* a hundred years ago," Jeremy continued. "But even way back then, before she was old, people could tell this lady was really, really weird. Like, she never got married, and she never talked to anyone and she spent all her time in the woods digging up plants and stuff. Then one day her house caught on fire, and she went totally cuckoo."

"Yeah, she blamed us!" Dylan interjected.

"Why'd she blame you?" Silver asked.

"He means the town." Jeremy sounded impatient. "She blamed everyone in Sudbury for what happened."

"Why?" Silver looked confused.

"Probably because she got stuck in the house when it was on fire and most of her face got burned off," said Jeremy.

"Her *face*?" Silver's eyes widened.

"Yeah. And she thought the people of Sudbury did it on purpose. You know, to get rid of her."

"And then she disappeared." Dylan's voice was ominous. "No one knew where she went. It wasn't until a few years later that people realized she'd gone to live on Creeper Mountain. And that she'd haunted it to get back at everyone."

"Haunted it?" I could see Silver's eyes roving over the trees ahead, taking it all in. "It doesn't look very haunted to me. Actually, it looks pretty nice."

"It *was* pretty nice," Jeremy said. "It was one of the nicest things about the whole town. Big, wide hiking trails, picnic spots, little streams all over."

"And Shining Falls!" Nathan added.

"And Shining Falls," Jeremy repeated. "One of the most beautiful waterfalls you've ever seen. Crystal blue water, rock steps on the side, a huge pool at the bottom where you could swim . . ." His voice drifted off.

"So what happened?" Silver asked.

"I already told you," Jeremy said. "She haunted it."

"How?" Silver was eyeing the mountain suspiciously.

"Well, first, she made these huge, invisible pits all over the mountain. People would be walking along one of the trails, and all of a sudden, the ground would just swallow them up."

"And they were filled with pointed sticks!" Dylan said. "My dad told me. Sharp as knives!"

"Have you ever heard of a guy named Ray Bradstreet?" Jeremy asked. Silver shook her head. "Well, he fell into one of those pits." Jeremy sliced the air with the side of his hand. "Completely broke his back. That was twenty years ago. He's still in a wheelchair."

Silver's eyebrows narrowed.

"Then there's her hornet-head snakes," Jeremy continued.

"What's a hornet-head snake?" Silver asked.

"Oh, they're deadly," Jeremy said. "There only used to be a few around here, but then Witch Weatherly started breeding them and setting them loose all over the place. They've got little horns right above the tops of their eyes and fangs that stick out on either side of their mouths. If they bite you, those fangs go right to the bone. Supposed to be one of the most painful things ever."

"Plus, if they bite you, you'll die," Dylan added. "No one's ever found a cure for their venom."

"And then there's Shining Falls," Jeremy went on. "Witch Weatherly did something crazy to the water. Now there's lights that shoot up from the bottom and the surface gets this crazy, eerie glow across it at night. Some people say she's turned it into her own personal cauldron. You know, like for casting spells."

"And cooking body parts!" Nathan raised a single eyebrow.

Silver cocked her head to one side. "Come on."

"It's true!" Annie Billing said. "And you haven't even gotten to the creepiest part yet." Annie was in my line, near the end. She wore overalls every day and had short black hair that made her look like a boy. "Tell her about the raven."

Was there a way to hum inside my head so that no one would hear? Could I block my eardrums using only the muscles in my neck?

"She has a pet raven." Jeremy's eyes were practically glittering. "She caught it in the wild and trained it. It's huge, like as big as a dog almost. But the really freaky thing is that it's not black like other ravens. It's bloodred."

"It circles the mountain every night at sundown, looking for trespassers," said Nathan.

"And its favorite meal is human eyeballs," Annie said. "For real. It can peck out a person's—"

A whistle sounded suddenly, slicing through the conversation like a shriek. I jumped and then screamed a loud, short sound, and everyone laughed as I clapped my hand over my mouth.

"All right, guys!" Mrs. Danforth yelled. "Time to go back in!"

"She thinks the witch is gonna come down off the mountain and get her!" Jeremy snickered as we filed back in.

"Or the raven!" Dylan hooted.

I didn't laugh.

I'd probably heard the Witch Weatherly legend a hundred times since I was a little girl. Even Momma and Dad had mentioned it once or twice during dinner.

Still, Witch Weatherly had always just been a story. A scary story, sure. Maybe the scariest story I'd ever been told. But this was the first time I'd seen anything close to actual proof that she was, in fact, more than that.

Somehow, despite all my efforts not to, I'd just seen that thread of smoke that Jeremy had pointed out to everyone.

Which meant only one thing.

Witch Weatherly was much more than a story.

She was real.

She was alive.

And she lived less than ten miles away from my front door.

Chapter 2

The back of the bus is the absolute worst place to sit, since there is a huge emergency exit door that can fly open at any minute and the exhaust pipe is right underneath the window. Still, I forced myself to sit there on the way home from school so that I could have a clear view of Creeper Mountain. I pressed myself up against the window, and stared as hard as I could, but there was no sign of the smoky thread I'd seen that morning. Not even a wisp. Maybe I hadn't really seen it all. Maybe I'd only imagined, it, especially considering all the things everyone had been saying about Witch Weatherly earlier. Was it possible I'd gotten confused, mistaking a wayward cloud for a trail of smoke?

I peered out the bathroom window the next morning, even though the only part of Creeper Mountain I could see from our house was the very tip-top. Still no sign of smoke. Below me, two squirrels raced through our backyard like wind-up toys. I paused, my toothbrush still in my mouth, and watched uneasily as they darted this way and that, making little figure eights across the grass. *Shoo*, I thought to myself. *Go away.* I hate squirrels. I think they look like big rats. Plus, they're jumpy, unpredictable, and can carry rabies, which, according to Mrs. Danforth, can only be treated by six very large, very painful shots in your stomach. I mean, like, *no, thank you.*

I waited until both squirrels disappeared up the huge oak tree on the far side of our yard before I bounded downstairs. Momma was sitting at the kitchen table in Dad's brown bathrobe, fiddling with the little bird charm at the end of her silver necklace. My little brother, Russell, was slurping the rest of his milk out of a bowl of Cheerios, while Dad stood in front of the counter, putting bread into the toaster. Momma's teakettle hissed lightly on the stove, and the smell of coffee hung like fog in the air.

Without warning, Russell jumped up as the copper teakettle began to whistle, and reached out to turn the flame off.

"Russell, no!" Momma lunged for Russell's arm and snatched it back from the stove. Her face was white, and her fingers, clutched around Russell's wrist, were trembling.

"Hey, let go!" Russell shouted, pulling away from Momma. "Don't grab!" Russell has a thing about being touched, especially if it startles him. It doesn't matter who it is, either; if you catch him off guard, he'll bite your head off. He has something called Asperger's syndrome, which isn't the end of the world, but does make him act a little goofier than other kids his age. He doesn't like to talk to people he doesn't know, for example, and he has a serious temper. Sometimes he'll even hit or punch someone when he gets really mad. He has to take medicine every night to help calm him down, and even though he's eight years old, he's still afraid of the dark. Needless to say, he is not the easiest person in the world to live with.

Momma dropped his wrist as Dad took a step toward both of them. "All right now, everything's okay," Dad said. "No need to yell, buddy. You know you're not allowed to touch the stove."

"I don't like the whistle noise!" Russell bellowed. "It hurts my ears. And it's annoying."

"I know it's annoying," Dad said, watching Momma. "But you know the rules, Russell. Momma or I will turn off the kettle when it starts whistling. Now calm down."

"I am calm!" Russell glowered.

Momma, who was standing off to one side, suddenly held out her arms. "Hey," she said softly. "How about a family sandwich?"

I looked at her strangely, not because of the request itself, which she hadn't made since I was at least ten years old, but because she had made it all. For the past two weeks, Momma had been sitting at the kitchen table, dressed in Dad's ratty old bathrobe and staring out the window. Some days, she would make some tea or nibble on a few slices of apple. Most days though, she barely even talked.

Two months ago, Grandpa William died. And although none of us saw him more than once a year, because he lived so far away, Momma hadn't been the same since taking the train out to Arizona for his funeral. I could see the difference after we picked her up at the train station a week later. Usually, it was hard to get Momma to stop talking. If she'd been gone for a few days, her stories could go on for weeks. But that day, after she hugged and kissed everyone hello, she hardly said a word. She looked tired, too; the circles under her eyes were almost violet. She was noticeably thinner and she walked slowly, as if something inside her stomach hurt. She commented on the weather once or twice on the way home, her fingers fiddling with the little necklace around her throat. After a while, she laid her head back on the seat rest and closed her eyes.

Dad said to give her time; that she was hurting because Grandpa William was gone, and that she would snap out of it. But two months passed, and she didn't snap out of it. Instead, she started to do things more slowly. Folding a basket of laundry would take her an hour. Making dinner became impossible. And then, two weeks ago, she stopped doing much of anything at all. Since then, I've come downstairs every morning, hoping I wouldn't see her in her usual place at the kitchen table, staring out the window in silence, but so far, it hadn't changed.

Until today.

Momma gestured again with her arms. "Come on, guys, family sandwich."

I've always thought Momma was beautiful, but now even her prettiness seemed to be worn out. Her hands were still covered with the red blotches that came and went with her spring allergies, and her long hair, which had started turning gray in high school, hung messy and loose around her shoulders.

Russell dropped his spoon. "Family sandwich!" he screamed, barreling so hard into Momma that she almost fell over.

But I rolled my eyes and hitched my backpack up my shoulder. I may have been taken aback by Momma's request, but twelve was still way too old for this silly game. Family sandwiches were definitely not my thing anymore.

"Hey, hey, hey!" Dad said, as I headed for the door. "Where are you going, Wrennie? You heard your mother. Family sandwich!"

"Come on, Wren!" Momma called, her voice still shaky.

"Yeah, don't be a poop-head, you dumb old poop-head!" Russell buried his face in the front of Momma's bathrobe.

I rolled my eyes again, then suddenly Dad was pulling me over to join the family huddle.

"Let go!" I yelled, but my giggles began as he pushed me in flat against Russell's back and then squeezed the stack of Momma, my little brother, and me with his long arms. It always amazed me that he could still get his arms around all of us, especially as Russell and I kept getting bigger. And that he could still hold us all so tightly.

"Fam-ly sand-wich!" The four of us jumped up and down, chanting loudly as Dad squeezed tighter and tighter. I could smell toast cooking behind us. Jackson, our golden retriever, barked happily from the other side of the kitchen. The sun peeked out behind the yellow gingham curtain over the kitchen sink, and Dad's aftershave, which smelled something like gingerbread and dry leaves, drifted over the top of us.

And then the bus honked outside.

"Okay," Dad said, dropping his arms. "Come on, you two. I don't need any of Mrs. Watkins's cross looks this morning." Mrs. Watkins was our bus driver. Dad liked to say that she should have been driving a big rig instead of a school bus, since she was crabby and impatient, the opposite of a morning person.

Russell's eyes grew wide. "Bye, Momma!" he screamed. "I have to go or Mrs. Watkins will be evil to me!"

"She's not evil, Russell," Dad said. "She's just a little rough around the edges. And please, buddy, don't say anything to her today about the hair on her chin."

"It's long, though." Russell paused for a moment, considering this. "It's real long. She should cut it off before it gets stuck inside something."

"Russell!" Momma's voice broke as she said his name. "How about a kiss, sweetheart?"

Russell rolled his eyes and then ran to her, turning his head dutifully to one side so that Momma could kiss his cheek. She ran a hand lightly along the back of his neck, and then, as he tore away from her, let her arm drop.

"See you later, Russellator!" Dad said, holding open the front door. "Come on, Wren, let's go! Mrs. Watkins is starting to look at me sideways!"

But I couldn't stop staring at Momma. She was staring at the door where Russell had disappeared, as if she might never see him again. The gnawing sensation in the pit of my stomach began to grow. "Momma?" I asked. "Are you okay?"

She blinked at the sound of my voice and then nodded. "Yes, sweetie." Her voice drifted over the top of my head, soft as cotton candy, as she drew me in for a hug. "You know I love you, Wren, don't you?"

"Momma." I took another step away from her. "You're acting weird. What's wrong?"

She shook her head and dropped her eyes, tracing one of the red splotches on the top of her hand. "Nothing's wrong, Wren."

"She's okay, honey," Dad said, putting an arm around my shoulders. "She just didn't sleep well. I'm going to make sure she gets back into bed before I leave so she can rest up, okay?"

I listened to Dad's words, but I watched Momma's eyes. They had a hollow quality to them, as if the very middle of her, the part I knew and loved best, was missing somehow. Momma is a worrier like me. She frets about things that have already happened—like the scar Russell got under his chin when he fell out of our tree in the front yard; things that are happening right now—like the cavities growing in Russell's and my teeth; and things that haven't even happened yet—like Iceland disappearing from the planet because of global warming. But at that moment, I couldn't even see the worrying part of her. I couldn't see anything at all. It was like something inside of her, the part that made her Momma, had vanished.

The bus honked again, slightly longer this time.

"I have to go," I said, still watching Momma's eyes.

"Yes," Momma said. "Okay. I love you, Wren."

"Bye, Momma." I blew her a kiss from the doorway. "Get some rest, okay? I'll see you later."

Afterward, I replayed that conversation a million times over in my head, trying to think of all the things I could have said or done differently. Why did I have to say that she was acting weird? Why couldn't I have just not said anything, the way I usually did? What was I thinking?

Maybe if I had waited that morning, she would have tried to work up the nerve to tell me what was really bothering her. Maybe she would have told me the truth about what she was thinking about as she stared out the kitchen window for fourteen straight days, or why she'd asked for a family sandwich after so long.

Or maybe, at the very least, she would have told me good-bye.

Chapter 3

My third-period class is history, which is in Mr. Tunlaw's room on the second floor. I watched the small commotion as Silver came into the room. I always took a peek at Silver when she arrived, not just because history was the only class we had together, but because I still thought it was so weird that we were related. I think it was in July when Dad told me Aunt Marianne (who's Momma's older sister) and Silver were moving back to Sudbury after Aunt Marianne got divorced. They came over to our house twice for dinner, which was a nightmare, since Momma and Aunt Marianne disappeared so they could talk privately, and Silver spent the whole time sitting in the living room, texting her old friends from Florida. It might not have been so bad if I'd had my own cell phone to text with, but thanks to Dad, who thinks that kids today have way too much electronic stimulation as it is, I won't be getting a cell phone until eighth grade. So I sat there like a dork and pretended to read a book. It's not that Silver's ever been outright rude to me; we just don't have anything in common. And we might have been related at home, but we were already in completely different leagues at school. And you know how things like *that* go.

Now, her usual gaggle of male admirers, including Jeremy, Dylan, and Nathan, followed behind, practically tripping over each other to sit next to her. I couldn't blame them, really. Her heart-shaped face, wide hazel eyes, and long neck looked like something out of a magazine. Even her outfit—white V-neck T-shirt, black jeans rolled up at the ankle, and purple, patent leather flats— was perfect. Personally, I thought Silver should have been named Sparkle. Or Shimmer. She was all light and air, almost as if she had swallowed a piece of the sun. There was nothing silvery about Silver Jones. She was one hundred percent golden.

"All right, class!" Mr. Tunlaw, who had been standing just outside the door, moved across the room to his desk. "That's enough talking for now! Let's get started!"

He clapped twice to get our attention, and then smoothed a hand over the front of his brown-and-pink polka-dotted tie. "It's time to talk about our final semester project. As we discussed before, it must include a two-page paper. But instead of assigning you a general topic, I've decided to narrow things down. This year, I want you to pick any historical topic regarding our state to write about."

"You mean about Pennsylvania?" Dylan asked.

I rolled my eyes. Dylan was cute, but boy, was he dense.

"Yes, Dylan, that is where we live." Mr. Tunlaw, who had settled himself in his chair, leaned back against the blackboard, propped his blue cowboy boots up on his desk, and began to unwrap a Twinkie. "I'm sure you all know that Pennsylvania is rich with history, from William Penn's founding of it, to Philadelphia, which is where its founding fathers met to sign the Declaration of Independence. Let's start with a little brainstorming to come up with some topics of your own. Just throw out ideas. Anyone."

"The Liberty Bell?" asked Mandy Dunkin.

Mr. Tunlaw nodded, taking a bite of his Twinkie. "Good, good. What else?"

"How about coal mining?" Randy asked.

"Definitely," said Mr. Tunlaw. "Keep going."

"William Penn!"

"The Amish people!"

I looked out the window and thought about the daily writing assignment I still hadn't finished for English class yesterday. Miss Crumb had asked us to write a few lines about two wishes we'd most like to have granted. My first one was easy. I wished that I were braver. Aside from worrying a lot, I am also the biggest scaredy-cat you will ever meet. Honestly, sometimes even *I* get annoyed by how much of a chicken I am. Aside from squirrels, I'm also scared of spiders, planes, horses, mean old ladies, and thunderstorms. Sometimes I wonder if I was just born scared, if the little brave gene inside everyone else just didn't make it inside me. Whatever it is, I wish I didn't have it. It's exhausting, worrying so much and being afraid all the time. It takes the fun out of almost everything.

Anyway, that was my first wish. Miss Crumb, however, had asked us to name two wishes. I thought and thought, but I could not come up with a second wish. If I stopped being such a chicken all the time and could become brave and confident, I could do just about anything. And if I could do anything, what else was there to wish for?

"The Pittsburgh Steelers!"

I drifted back to the class, which was still yelling out topics.

"The Gettysburg Address!"

"Harrisburg!"

"Witch Weatherly!"

The class turned, gasping collectively, to see who had uttered such an insane suggestion. Even I sat up a little straighter.

It was Silver, who was perched on the edge of her chair, her pretty face cocked a little to one side as she looked eagerly at Mr. Tunlaw and the rest of the class.

"Witch Weatherly?" Mr. Tunlaw repeated.

"Yeah!" Silver nodded.

Dylan drew back in his chair, his lips curled in disgust. "Did you even *hear* what we told you yesterday during the fire drill?"

"Well, yeah." Silver shot a sidelong glance in my direction. "But my mom told me that no one really knows if any of that stuff is even true. It might just be made up."

"How does your mom know?" asked Mandy boldly. "She's not even from here."

"She was born here," Silver contradicted. "And she might not have spent a lot of time in Sudbury, but she heard all the stories growing up."

"So why would she say it's made up?" For the first time since she'd arrived, Jeremy looked annoyed with Silver. "Has she ever been on the mountain?"

"No." Silver bit her lower lip.

"Has she ever talked to Ray Bradstreet about his legs?" Jeremy scooted forward in his chair, eager to defend his position.

"Well, no," Silver said. "But . . ."

"Yeah." Jeremy waved Silver off with a flick of his hand. "I didn't think so."

Mandy decided to try a different approach. "There's no way you could do a report on Witch Weatherly, Silver. You couldn't get anywhere near her without getting killed first."

"I don't want to do a report on her," Silver said.

"Oh?" Mr. Tunlaw uncrossed his cowboy boots and sat up straight. "What did you have in mind then?"

"I want to interview her," Silver said. "Ask her what it's been like, living in Sudbury for over one hundred years."

For a moment, the room was silent, except for a faint buzzing sound somewhere. Mouths dropped open, and eyeballs skittered from side to side. "Are you out of your *mind?*" Dylan said finally.

Silver didn't seem to hear the question. "Think about it, Mr. Tunlaw. Sudbury is a part of Pennsylvania. And Witch Weatherly is probably its oldest living citizen. Which makes her a perfect person to interview about the history of the town. It would make a great paper, don't you think?"

Mr. Tunlaw seemed to be at a loss for words. A few nervous laughs erupted around Silver. Jeremy and Dylan exchanged a bewildered look.

"You're new." Jeremy sounded almost angry. "You don't get it, Silver."

Silver's eyebrows narrowed. "What don't I get?"

All three boys were turned around in their seats, talking to Silver now as if they were the only four in the room. "Witch Weatherly doesn't just live on Creeper Mountain," Jeremy said. "She *haunts* it. She's totally evil. No one's been up there for the past twenty years because of the pits and the snakes and—"

"All right," Mr. Tunlaw protested. "I don't know about . . ." He paused, flicking his hand at something in the air. "What I mean is, I just don't know how accurate . . ."

He broke off all at once, leaping out of his chair like a startled cat. His cowboy boots made a loud thud as they landed on the linoleum floor. With a hoarse shout, he grabbed at the front of his shirt. "It's a bee!" he gasped, whipping his hand back and forth in front of him. "Go away, now. Shoo!"

Witch Weatherly was forgotten as Mr. Tunlaw continued to yell. I giggled nervously along with the rest of the class. It was hard not to. Mr. Tunlaw did look a little funny, hopping and squirming and slapping and grunting, his brown-and-pink tie flopping in front of him like a little flag, the hems of his pants hitched up along his boots. The giggles in the room turned to shrieks as he kicked his legs out wildly, and one of his boots flew off his foot and sailed across the room. Mr. Tunlaw's face got more and more red as he began to slap at his legs. "There's two!" he yelped, twisting violently in an attempt to slap his back. "No, three!"

And then, before any of us could register what he was doing, Mr. Tunlaw wiggled out of his pants and kicked them across the floor. A Twinkie wrapper flew out of one of the pockets, hovering in the air for a brief second before landing again. Mr. Tunlaw hopped up and down in front of us wearing only a pair of blue-and-white-striped boxers, black knee-high socks, and one cowboy boot. "Oh!" he screamed. "Oh, no! No, no, no!"

And then he ran out of the room.

Except for a few horrified gasps, the class fell silent, too stunned to move. Mandy sat with her hands cupped over her mouth. Above them, her eyes were wide as quarters. I had scooched as far back into my corner of the room as possible, still looking around fearfully. Were there any more bees? Would they sting me? I'd been stung only once before by a bee, but it hurt. Bad. Dad had to put a poultice on it made of baking soda and spit until the sting went away.

Suddenly, Jeremy stood up and pointed to the wall behind the blackboard. "Look! There must be a nest!"

I peeked over, rising a little bit out of my seat. Sure enough, a thin stream of wasps was floating up from behind the blackboard. Wasps were way worse than bees. One by one, they rose in single file, as if following orders from an unseen captain.

Pandemonium erupted.

Girls stood up, knocking over their chairs as they headed for the far corner. Mandy Dunkin, Rachel Gerrity, and Nicole Randolph began to scream, swatting the air around them. The boys ducked down as the wasps swooped overhead, and began rolling up their notebooks, ready to smack them flat. Justin Sanders ran over and opened a window. Dylan joined him until all the windows in the room were open.

But the wasps did not seem to notice their portals of freedom. They rose higher and higher, toward the fluorescent lights in the ceiling, until at least twelve of them clustered in a loose group just beneath the bulbs. Everyone stood there, heads thrown back, watching and waiting to see what they would do next.

Except for Silver Jones.

Silver had not moved from her seat in the back one iota during the entire incident. I watched, dumbstruck, as a lone wasp made its way over to her. She kept her eyes on it, not wavering once as the insect flew just inches from the front of her shirt. It made a faint droning sound, like a tiny machine far in the distance.

"Silver!" Jeremy yelled. "There's one right—"

"Shhh!" she whispered, not taking her eyes off the wasp. "Be quiet!"

By now, everyone had stopped staring at the swarm overhead. Silver and the wasp had taken center stage. The tiny insect moved closer to her and veered upward. The students gasped as the wasp hovered near Silver's eye, inches from her left cheek. Still, she did not move. The wasp hung there for a few seconds, just under Silver's cheekbone, and then swung lazily around her head.

"What're you *doing*?" Jeremy insisted, taking a step toward her. "Do you want to get stung?"

A muscle pulsed along Silver's jawline. Instead of answering Jeremy, she extended her right arm as the wasp flitted back around to the front of her, and opened her palm. Mandy and Rachel made small whimpering sounds in the corner. I held my breath and bit the inside of my cheek. With a honey-like slowness, the wasp made its way over to Silver's hand. Its slender, reddish body drifted above it for a few seconds, as if deciding whether or not it wanted to land. A pair of long papery wings fluttered back and forth. Silver sat motionless, her eyes still riveted on the insect. Without warning, the wasp descended lightly into the middle of her palm.

Silver smiled. Cupping her other hand over it carefully, she stood up, walked over to one of the open windows, and shook the wasp free. As if hearing secret directions, the other wasps followed suit, first lingering above the window and then finally disappearing out of it.

Two janitors rushed in then, followed by Miss Crumb. "Is everybody okay?" Miss Crumb asked. She bolted over to the corner where Mandy and Rachel and the rest of the girls were still cowering, clucking in her high-pitched voice.

But I didn't hear her. I was still staring at Silver, who had just walked back from the window. Other than a slightly dreamy expression on her face, she looked normal, as if nothing unusual had just happened.

And right then and there, I knew what my second wish would be.

Chapter 4

Since it was a nice day, we got to sit outside for lunch. The school's "patio" was basically just a bunch of picnic tables lined up in a little grassy patch behind the cafeteria. The tables were so close together that all you could hear was everyone talking about Mr. Tunlaw's freak-out session, from his dimpled knees and ugly black socks, to how his cowboy boot went sailing through the air.

And of course, the fact that he had pulled off his pants in front of the class and showed everyone his underwear.

Everyone wanted to know about *that*.

Nora and Cassie, who I sat with every day at lunch, were no exception.

"You mean, he actually took his pants *off*? Like all the way? As in he was totally just standing there in his underwear?" Cassie was pressed as close to my arm as possible without actually sitting on it. I leaned back a little, and tried not to inhale through my nose. Cassie didn't have very good dental hygiene. Even at seven o'clock in the morning, there was food stuck all over her braces, which meant that her breath usually smelled like old meat loaf and sour milk.

"Yup." I took a bite of my pizza. "But he was getting stung all over his legs. I probably would've done the same thing."

Nora snorted. "That makes just you and Mr. Tunlaw. No one else would take their pants off in front of a whole class. Like, ever."

I looked over toward the chain link fence around the perimeter of the patio, wondering for maybe the hundredth time why I was friends with these girls. Maybe it was because I didn't have any other ones. Maybe sometimes having people in your life who weren't really that nice to you was still better than not having anyone at all.

I stood up and took my lunch tray over to the garbage can. Then I headed over to the little maple tree by the chain link fence and sat down. I took out a pencil from my back pocket, and spun it along my knuckles with one hand. Up, down, over the tops of my knuckles, and back again. Up, down, over the tops of my knuckles, and back again.

I started the pencil trick by accident, after I saw a guy in the waiting room at the dentist's office doing it. His fingers moved so fast they were almost a blur, and the pencil itself looked like a spinning propeller. I'd never seen anything so cool. It seemed pretty easy, too—except when I tried it. Then I realized that it was almost impossible. In fact, it took me almost three whole months just to figure out how to get the pencil from my index finger over to my pinky finger without dropping it. Getting it over the tops of my knuckles and then back through my fingers again took me another two weeks. But after I got the hang of it, I started doing it all the time. Now I do it so much that it's become something of a habit.

Up, down, over the top, and back again.

Up, down, over the top, and back again.

I could feel my breathing start to slow as my fingers raced through their familiar contortions, and my heart settled a little inside my chest. *It's going to be okay*, I told myself. *Things will be okay.*

Behind me, I could hear Nora and Cassie getting up and following me.

"Come on, Wren." Nora glanced around behind her. "We want to know what else happened in Mr. Tunlaw's class. And would you stop doing that thing with your pencil? It's so . . . *weird*."

I didn't answer. But my fingers slowed. The pencil stopped moving. I stared at it for a minute, still balanced on top of my knuckles like a miniature log, and then slid it back into my pocket. Nora and Cassie had no idea how long it had taken me to get this good at pencil spinning, or what it did for my nerves. They'd never asked.

"We want to hear the rest of the story about Mr. Tunlaw," Cassie said. "Like, all of it."

"That *is* all of it," I said. "Nothing else happened."

"He's probably going to die," Nora said dramatically. "I heard Mrs. Hoban talking to Mrs. Bertoli. She said something about the hospital not having the right kind of medicine. And if a hospital doesn't have the right kind of medicine after you've been stung by something you're allergic to, you can totally die." She made a squirting sound with her mouth. "Done. Just like that."

"He's not going to die." I paused, watching as Silver stood up across the other side of the lunch tables and navigated her way toward the trash can, tray in hand. Jeremy and Dylan were right behind her.

"You never know." Nora fiddled with her earring. "Anything could happen." That was Nora's pet phrase—*anything could happen*. It drove me crazy. Of course anything could happen. After anything, what else was there?

"Wren?" Nora poked me in the arm. "Did you hear me?"

"Yeah," I answered, without taking my eyes off Silver.

"What are you staring at?" Cassie raised herself a few inches on her toes so that she could see for herself. "Oh, Silver Jones," she said, making no effort to hide the disgust in her voice. "Did you hear what she did?"

"You mean letting that wasp sit on her hand?" Nora nodded, slicking her lips with a strawberry-banana lipgloss. "I know! What an idiot."

I frowned. "Why does that make her an idiot?"

Cassie and Nora looked at me incredulously. "Seriously, Wren," Nora said. "If you didn't get such good grades, I might think *you* were an idiot." I turned away from her, not letting her comment settle inside where things were the softest. Nora elbowed me. "I don't mean to be *rude* or anything. But, I mean . . . who goes and lets a *wasp* sit on their hand? What if she had gotten stung? I don't know how they teach people to act down in Florida, but up here, Silver Jones is seriously about as dumb as they come."

Cassie laughed out loud. "My dad would say that she's two sandwiches short of a picnic."

"Yeah," Nora snorted. "Definitely not the sharpest knife in the drawer." The two of them giggled. Nora twisted the end of her empty honey-roasted peanuts bag and then popped it.

"It didn't, though," I said.

"What?" Nora asked.

"It didn't sting her. You said *what if the wasp had stung her* or something. But it didn't. Actually, I think Silver might've known exactly what she was doing when she opened her hand and let it sit down on her like that."

"Oh, please." Nora rolled her eyes. "She had *no* idea what she was doing. She was just showing off in front of Jeremy again—like she's been doing every single day since she got here." Her eyes got big, as if she was suddenly remembering something. "Oh, and get *this*. Mandy told me that Silver said she wanted to go interview *Witch Weatherly* for the history project."

Cassie inhaled audibly. "Witch *Weatherly*?" Her voice was a squeak. "Didn't anybody tell her the stories?"

"Oh yeah." Nora shook her head disgustedly. "All the boys, of course. But she thinks it's all a big joke apparently. Whatever. You know she'll never do it. My dad wouldn't go up that mountain if you paid him a million bucks, and he's not afraid of anything. No one would. I'm telling you, that girl is just an attention hog." She sniffed. "Little Miss High and Mighty from Florida. I mean, please."

"Like she *needs* any more attention," Cassie said. "Especially from Jeremy."

"Exactly," Nora said. "It's so annoying."

If I'd been braver, I might have turned around right then and told Nora to shut her mouth. Cassie too. They didn't know Silver Jones was my cousin. And while I didn't have any particular family loyalty to Silver, the things they were saying were mean. *Cassie* and *Nora* were mean.

But I didn't say anything.

Instead, as the bell rang, I put my hand inside my pocket and wrapped my fingers around my pencil. Sometimes, when things got hard, it helped just knowing it was there.

Chapter 5

I kept my eye on Silver after lunch, watching from a distance as she ambled down the hall. Jeremy, whose overly gelled hair looked like a plastic cap on top of his head, was on her left, talking a mile a minute. Dylan and Nathan struggled to stay in step on her right. Silver's large brown purse, slung across her chest, swung back and forth along her hip. Cascades of hair tumbled down her back, and I could see the outline of her cell phone in the back pocket of her jeans. The soles of her purple flats were bright red. She nodded at something Jeremy said, but as far as I could tell, she was not doing anything out of the ordinary to get his attention. If anything, Jeremy was struggling to get *her* attention. And I might have been wrong, but from where I stood, it didn't look like Silver was all that excited about giving it to him.

Mr. Pringle's voice came over the loudspeaker, making me jump. "Wren Baker, please report to the office. Wren Baker to the office."

"Ooooooooooo!" Everyone in the hallway turned to look at me. The principal had never called me to his office before. I could feel the skin along my neck getting hot, the heat spreading up to my ears. Inside my chest, my heart hammered like a snare drum.

"What'd *you* do?" Cassie asked.

I shrugged and shifted my backpack along my shoulder, trying to appear nonchalant. "Nothing." But my brain was racing. The last time I got called down to the main office was when I forgot my lunch in fifth grade and Momma brought it over for me. I hadn't forgotten my lunch today, and I couldn't think of anything else that would require my presence in the main office. In fact, I wasn't even sure if I remembered what the main office looked like.

It came back to me, of course, as I went inside. Mrs. Pool, the head secretary, was still sitting behind her desk, with the same collection of rubber trolls lined up behind her keyboard. Tufts of electric-blue hair stuck up like flames from the tops of their heads, and their naked, miniature bodies were smudged around the edges, as if someone had been squeezing them. There was the same collection of glossy posters on the wall behind her— ATTITUDE IS EVERYTHING, THIS IS A NO-BULLY ZONE, and KEEP CALM AND STUDY ON!—as well as the teachers' mailboxes on the opposite side. In fact, the only thing that seemed out of place was the person sitting in one of the red chairs outside of Mr. Pringle's door.

I blinked. *"Dad?"*

He turned toward me and got up out of the chair. "Hi, sweetheart." He smiled—a great big smile that stretched across his face and crinkled the corners of his eyes. I knew right away that something was wrong. Dad never smiles like that unless something bad has happened.

"Dad? What's going on? Why're you here?"

"I have to talk to you, honey." He was still smiling, but his green eyes told a different story. I could feel the little hairs on the back of my neck start to rise, and something inside my belly flip-flopped.

Mr. Pringle came out of his office then, and nodded when he saw me. "Hello, Wren. Thank you for coming down so quickly. Why don't we all go talk in my office?" He stepped back as Dad and I walked into the small, air-conditioned room. I brushed against Mr. Pringle's large belly as I moved past him through the doorway, and prayed that he didn't notice. Mr. Pringle adjusted his suit jacket as he sat, and leaned forward slightly. "So I asked you to come down here, Wren, because your father has some news for you!" He was using that brightly cheerful voice, too. It was as fake as Dad's smile, and totally unnerving.

"Wren," Dad said, turning in his chair so that he faced me. "I want you to listen carefully to what I have to say."

My heart did a double flip-flop. "Okay."

Dad took both of my hands in his. There were deep, dark shadows beneath his eyes. "Momma's in the hospital."

The double flip-flop turned into a squeeze. "Why? What happened?"

"She went in this morning for a check-up, and they found out that she was sick. She needs special medicine and special doctors. She's on her way to a hospital where they can give her that. It's far away, though, in Ohio. I'm going to go stay there for a while until she gets better."

My brain was swimming with information. I tried to backtrack to the chain of events that had occurred this morning, but the first thing that came to mind was the family sandwich. Thinking about it now, I started to cry.

Dad pulled me toward him and hugged me close. "It's going to be okay, Wren. It really is. I promise."

"But wait, what actually *happened*?" I pulled away. "She was okay this morning, wasn't she? You said she was just tired. Did she get hurt?"

Dad shook his head. The expression on his face was grave. "No, she didn't get hurt. I don't even know all the details yet, honey, but it has to do with something inside her head."

"Her *head*?" I repeated. "Like a brain tumor?" I'd known a girl named Wendy Titans in the third grade whose mother had gotten a brain tumor. Wendy said they'd done an operation on her that lasted fourteen hours and she *still* died.

Dad shook his head. "No, Wren. Nothing like a brain tumor."

"Cancer?"

"No, honey, not cancer, either. Like I said, I'm not sure what it is exactly, but that's why she's going to a special hospital. They're going to find out. And then she's going to get better." He ran his arms up and down the length of my arms. "Now, listen to me. Aunt Marianne is going to take care of you and Russell while I'm away."

Dad's words sounded far away, like he was talking to me from another room. Nothing was registering. My brain was still stuck back on Momma. What could possibly be wrong inside her head? What could have happened to her between the time I left this morning and now? Why didn't Dad know? "Wait," I said. "What hospital is Momma in?"

"It's a hospital in Akron, which is a town in Ohio," Dad said. "The doctors took her down this morning. I'm going to drive there tonight. It'll take me most of the night to get there."

"Ohio?" I repeated. "How long will you be gone?"

"Two weeks at the most." My eyes widened. "Maybe not even that long," Dad said quickly. "I'll know more when I get down there."

"Why can't Grandma come up to stay with us?" My breath was starting to come in little spurts. I felt light-headed.

"Grandma's on her around-the-world cruise," Dad said. "Remember?" He fingered a piece of my hair, twirling it between his first two fingers. He seemed lost in thought. "She won't be back until Thanksgiving."

"But . . . why . . . I mean, Aunt Marianne . . ." My voice was barely above a whisper.

"I know you still don't know her very well yet, honey," said Dad quickly, "but she is family, and I really think that—"

"And Silver . . ." My eyes filled with tears.

"What about Silver?" Dad dropped my strand of hair. "Is there a problem with her?"

"You don't have any issues with her here, I hope." Mr. Pringle's bushy eyebrows arched up along his forehead. "I've talked to her a few times since she arrived. She seems to be a very pleasant girl."

I shook my head. "No. It's just that . . ."

"Just what, honey?" Dad touched my arm.

Just what? Just . . . *everything*! Sure, she was my cousin, but it was still Silver Jones, for crying out loud! The most beautiful, most popular, most everything girl in the whole school who, as far as I could tell, didn't even remember my *name*, much less that I existed in the same hemisphere! I was going to have to *live* with her? And not just me—but my little brother Russell, too— who was easily one of the most annoying people on the *planet*?

"It's just . . ." I started again, and then shook my head, thinking of Momma. This was no time to be selfish. "It's nothing."

"You sure?" Dad pulled me in for another hug.

No, I wasn't sure. I wasn't sure of anything. It felt as if the rug I was standing on had just been pulled out from underneath my feet. As if my arms and legs were up in the air, and any moment now I was going to come crashing back down. "Yeah," I inhaled with a shaky breath. "Yeah, I guess."

Dad squeezed me tight. "Mr. Pringle here has been nice enough to make all the arrangements for you while I'm gone. You can call me if there's an emergency, but he's here, too, in case anything comes up." He stood up and rested his hand on top of my head. "I have to go talk to Russell now, honey. And then they'll bring him over here after school. You'll both go home with Aunt Marianne this afternoon."

I nodded dumbly, but my head was spinning. It was too much information to take in all at once.

Dad leaned over and kissed me on top of my head. "Oh!" He dug into his front pocket. "Before I forget. Momma asked me to give you this." He took out a silver necklace and placed it in my hand. "She wants you to keep it safe for her. Just until she comes back."

I held out my hand, watching the slinky chain coil into a pool in the center of my palm. The charm on it was really only half a charm, broken long ago, Momma said, after a bike accident. On the front of the medallion, half of the tiny bird that was left stared out at me, its wing and body already worn smooth from Momma's fingers. Below it were the letters GR, part of a word or a name, the other letters gone forever.

Dad squatted down next to me and put a hand on my knee. "She's worn that necklace since she was a little girl. I don't know if she's ever taken it off before."

I shook my head, the necklace blurring through my tears.

"I think it's Momma's way of giving you a little piece of herself while she's gone." Dad squeezed my knee. "You'll take good care of it, won't you?"

I nodded. I knew Momma was trying to be nice. But I didn't want her necklace. It scared me. What if this was the last part of her I would ever have? And what if, instead of keeping it safe for her, she really wanted me to have it to remember her by, in case she never came home again?

Chapter 6

The rest of the afternoon rushed by in a blur of science facts, reading comprehension skills, and the history of Wolfgang Mozart. It was impossible to hear anything my teachers said; instead, I spun my pencil so many times across the tops of my knuckles that the skin started to turn pink. It didn't help. My worry-meter, as Dad calls it, was off the charts.

What could possibly be wrong with Momma? And why was Dad being so vague about all of it? I could understand him not wanting to tell Russell all the details, but I was twelve now. Next year I'd be an honest-to-goodness teenager! I could handle it. Besides, I deserved to know. It was Momma we were talking about here, not some neighbor or friend of the family. Her well-being was the most important thing in my life.

Then there was the whole living arrangement. There was no way Dad could have known living with Silver Jones might add the tiniest bit more stress to the situation. She and Aunt Marianne *were* family, after all. And Grandma certainly wasn't to blame for going on her around-the-world cruise. But I found myself wishing, as I sat in one of Mr. Pringle's big red chairs, that one of them would come to their senses and stop all of this madness right in its tracks.

"Hello again, Wren!" Mr. Pringle strode into the office, swinging his arms along either side of his enormous belly.

Russell was behind him, walking on his tiptoes, which is the way he always walks, and staring wide-eyed at everything.

I jumped up and grabbed his hand. "Hey, buddy. You all right?"

"Momma went to the hospital." Russell wrenched his hand out of mine, and then kicked the side of the wooden chair where I had been sitting. "She's sick."

Across the room, Mrs. Pool stopped typing. People who don't know about Russell's Asperger's get very nervous around him.

Mr. Pringle put a hand on Russell's shoulder. "Let's go talk about it in here, guy." He tried to steer Russell into his office, putting a hand on his shoulder and directing him into the room. It wasn't Mr. Pringle's fault. He didn't know Russell doesn't like to be touched. Especially by people he doesn't know.

"Hey, get off!" Russell said, twisting out from under Mr. Pringle's arm. "Don't touch!"

Mrs. Pool, whose fingers were hovering a few inches above the keyboard, rose slightly out of her seat. But Mr. Pringle, who had released Russell's shoulder, shook his head. "It's all right, Janet." He opened his office door. "Wren, would you bring your brother into my office, please?"

"Come on, Russell." I took him by the hand and led him inside. "Mr. Pringle just wants to talk to us. It'll be okay."

Russell let me pull him into the office. I pointed to one of the two chairs in front of Mr. Pringle's desk, and told him to sit down. "Momma's sick," he said again, glowering at the floor. "Damn it."

I gasped as Russell cursed and then elbowed him in the side. "No blankety-blanks," I hissed. "Now, come on, Russell."

Blankety-blanks was Russell's term for a bad word. And I was pretty sure he knew by now that he was not allowed to use them. Especially in public. But if he had heard me, he didn't let on. His eyes were fixed on the floor.

"Your mother's going to be *fine*, Russell!" Mr. Pringle boomed, using another voice that adults use when they're trying to convince kids to believe something they know isn't true.

Russell's head shot up. "How do you know? Did you talk to her?"

Mr. Pringle picked a piece of lint off the front of his blue jacket and watched it flutter to the floor. "No, but I talked to your father for a good while this afternoon and he told me that there was nothing to worry about. He said your mother needs a little time to rest and get the right medicine, but that she is going to be absolutely fine."

"That's not what he told me." Russell's eyebrows narrowed.

I turned in my seat. "What'd he tell you?"

"He told me Momma was *sick*," Russell answered. "And that means she's gonna die."

Before I could stop him, he drew his leg back and kicked the side of the chair so hard that it scuttled across Mr. Pringle's pale brown carpet and almost toppled over.

"Russell! Don't!" I pulled on his arm as he drew his leg back again.

"I want Momma!" he yelled, kicking the chair again. This time, it went sailing into the wall, and plunked over on its side. "I want Dad!"

I pulled harder at Russell's arm, trying to move him away from the chair. Instead, he turned, slapping at me, trying to loosen my hold on him. When that didn't work, he kicked me in the shins, and then hauled off and socked me in the stomach.

"Oof!" I folded over, holding my belly. Tears sprang to my eyes, and for a moment, I thought I might vomit. Russell has a serious right hook.

Mr. Pringle darted out from behind his desk, knocking over a picture in a silver frame. "Hey, hey, hey!" He grabbed Russell from behind, holding him by the tops of his arms so that Russell could not swing his fists. "Let's take it easy now, guy! It's going to be okay! Just take it easy!"

Russell's arms may have been pinned back, but his legs were still free. And before Mr. Pringle knew what was happening, Russell had back-kicked him right in the groin.

"Ohhhhhhhhhhh . . ." Mr. Pringle gasped, letting go of Russell and sliding down toward the floor. A sound like air being squeezed out of a balloon came out of him. "Ohhhhhhhhhh . . ."

I was horrified, but there was no time to worry about my principal right now. Russell had dropped to his knees, and was banging his fists off the floor. I'd seen him get violent like this before. Pretty soon, he would start flinging other things in the room, even pulling at his own hair. It was like some dark thing inside him took over, as if he had no control over what he was doing. There was only one way to calm him down.

I grabbed both of his wrists and leaned in under him. Russell's face was bright pink. Beads of sweat dotted his upper lip as he tried to wrench himself from my grasp. "Russell!" I said. "Listen to me! Jackson's coming with us! He's gonna stay with us the whole time!"

Russell stopped. The features of his face, which had been squeezed up into a knot, relaxed, inch by inch. He straightened up a little and stared at me. "Jackson?"

"Yeah!" I didn't know yet if Jackson could come with us, but right now, it was all I had. Aunt Marianne had to let us bring our dog. She just had to. "You can hang out and play with him all weekend. He's probably already at Aunt Marianne's house, waiting for you."

48

Mr. Pringle pressed one hand on top of his desk, struggling to get back up on his feet. "Who's Jackson?" he groaned.

"My dog," Russell said importantly. "After me, he's the smartest animal in the entire universe."

"Oh yeah?" Mr. Pringle sank back down into his chair and ran his hands down the sides of his face. His skin had an odd grayish tinge to it. "And what makes him so smart?"

"He can read my mind," Russell answered.

I held my breath as I watched Mr. Pringle. I didn't know if Dad had told him about Russell's Asperger's, but I hoped by now he at least understood that Russell was a little different than most eight-year-olds.

Mr. Pringle took out a handkerchief from inside his pants pocket. "Well," he said, blotting his face. "That must be some dog."

I exhaled.

There was a tap at the door. It was Mrs. Pool. "Everything all right in here?" She craned her neck around the doorjamb, staring at me, then at Russell, and finally over at Mr. Pringle, who was still panting in his chair.

"All good." Mr. Pringle raised his hand, as if to ward Mrs. Pool off. "We're all good, Janet. Thank you."

"Marianne Jones is here for the children." Mrs. Pool looked relieved. "Should I send her in now, or do you need a few more minutes?"

"Yes!" Mr. Pringle stood up, pushing his chair behind him. "Yes, send her in now, please."

Aunt Marianne stepped into the office. I'd forgotten how small she was, not much taller than me, actually, with blonde hair that was soft and curly on top and fastened into two small pigtails in the back. She hugged me tightly, and touched Russell's arm. "Hi, guys!" Her teeth were white and crooked on the bottom, and when she stretched her arm over the desk to shake Mr. Pringle's hand, a silver bracelet tinkled around her wrist. "Thank you for helping us out with this, Mr. Pringle."

"My pleasure," he said.

I studied Aunt Marianne carefully out of the corner of my eye. She was dressed in dark denim jeans, a pale yellow shirt with long sleeves, and brown sandals that crisscrossed over her toes. Her toenails had been painted a brick-red color, and she had tiny silver hoops in her ears. Except for a few lines around her eyes and forehead, she looked like a carbon copy of Silver.

She turned toward me all at once, smoothing her hand over the top of my head. "How are you, Wren?"

"I'm okay." I looked at the floor.

"I know we still don't know each other very well, but I'm hoping we can change that. I'm really glad you're going to be staying with us."

"Thanks."

"And Russell, too," she said.

I poked Russell in the side of the arm.

He poked me back.

"Russell's a little uncomfortable right now," I said, trying to smile. "You know, with everything going on."

"That's perfectly understandable," said Aunt Marianne, watching him over the top of my head. "I would be a little uncomfortable myself, if I were in his shoes."

"You're not allowed to touch my shoes!" Russell growled.

Aunt Marianne laughed and then caught herself, covering her mouth with one hand. "Of course not, Russell," she said. "I wouldn't dream of it."

"Is Jackson at your house yet?" Russell's voice was too loud.

"Jackson?" Aunt Marianne inquired. "Who's Jackson?"

Something tightened in the pit of my stomach.

Russell's eyes narrowed. "My dog."

"Oh, the *dog*!" Aunt Marianne's whole face brightened. "Of course, of course! Your father dropped him off just a little while ago! He's at the house, Russell, waiting for you."

I exhaled again. Thank goodness Dad had remembered.

"Well." Mr. Pringle placed his palms flat on the desk. "I just wanted to make sure that everything was squared away. Wren and Russell, Mrs. Jones will be picking you up from school now every day until your father gets back. Are both of you all right with that?"

Russell stared at the floor. I hesitated for a split second. Of course we weren't all right with it. This was the strangest, most mixed-up situation we'd ever been in. But what choice did we have? We were just kids. They were the adults. This was the way it had to be—at least for now. And so I nodded for both of us.

Aunt Marianne put her arm around me. She smelled citrusy, like flowers and oranges mixed together. "Do either of you need to get anything before we go?"

I shook my head, and rubbed my fingers, which had started to itch, for some reason.

She squeezed my shoulders. "Well, let's get going then. My car's out front."

Chapter 7

Aunt Marianne's rusty blue truck was parked next to a black Lexus. I remembered the surprise I'd first felt when I saw her pull into our driveway a few months ago with the old vehicle. For some reason, I hadn't thought that anyone related to Momma, who was relatively prim and proper for the most part, would drive a truck. Momma herself still drove the same blue Toyota she'd had since I was a baby. Still, seeing the truck again filled me with a vague sense of comfort.

"You okay riding up front?" Aunt Marianne opened the passenger door and waited while I peeked in. Thick pieces of duct tape had been patched over a rip in the driver's seat. In between the duct tape, chunks of light brown foam stuck out, like mounds of dried oatmeal. The clutch rose up from the floor, bare and black as a weather vane, and five different colored air fresheners—all in the shape of pine trees—swung from the rearview mirror.

"You drove this all the way up from Florida?"

"Sure did." She grinned and patted the windowsill.

"Old Betsy's my other right-hand girl, after Silver. Hop in. There's plenty of room."

I slid inside the car, scratching my leg on the duct-tape-foam mess as I went, and beckoned for Russell to follow. He scrambled in next to me and fastened his seat belt. I looked around, but there was no sign of Silver. Was she coming?

"Silver has cheerleading practice," Aunt Marianne said, as if reading my mind. "So she won't be home until later. Are you okay with that?"

"Sure." I shrugged, my heart plummeting a little as I realized yet another ridiculous difference between Silver and me. I would sooner try out for cheerleading then I would walk up Creeper Mountain at night by myself. Which pretty much meant never.

Aunt Marianne hopped into the driver's side of the truck, rolled down her window, and turned the key. The engine rumbled awake. She smiled when she saw the look on my face. "I know she sounds and looks a little beat-up, but Old Betsy's a trooper. She's been around a long, long time. Never lets me down." She patted the dashboard. "Do you, old girl?"

As if in response, the truck made a low growling sound. Aunt Marianne threw back her head and laughed.

I winced and looked out the window.

I couldn't remember the last time I'd heard Momma laugh about anything.

Aunt Marianne drove through downtown Sudbury at an alarming speed, veering in and out of traffic with the ease of an experienced—or crazy—driver. I flattened myself as far back against the seat cushion as I could, and prayed that we would not get into an accident. We passed the library, with its bright orange READING IS FREE! banner strung up across the front, and the Wendy's restaurant, where Dad sometimes took Russell and me for double cheeseburgers and Frosty shakes. I slid down farther in the seat as she gunned past the Mobil station on the corner, where a bunch of high school kids always stood around after school and smoked cigarettes. And I gasped out loud when she went through a yellow light at the main intersection. It would be a miracle if we got to wherever we were going in one piece.

"Wow!" Russell yelled. "You go *really* fast!"

Aunt Marianne laughed and tugged at one of her little pigtails. "I can't help it sometimes. Old Betsy here's got a transmission that used to belong to a racecar. She's built for speed."

Russell nodded appreciatively. "Captain Commando is super speedy, too."

"Captain Commando?" Aunt Marianne repeated.

Russell nodded. "He's the fastest superhero in the universe. He's even faster than Superman!"

"Wow," Aunt Marianne said. "That *is* fast."

I tried to hide my annoyance as they continued to talk about Captain Commando. Neither of them seemed to notice that I was halfway on the floor, hanging on to the edge of my seat for dear life. I wondered if anyone could hear the way my heart was banging around in my chest, or the faint gasps that darted out from my mouth whenever Aunt Marianne screeched around a corner.

Finally, after what seemed like an eternity, Aunt Marianne pulled the truck onto a long, narrow dirt road. "Hold on," she said, easing up a little on the gas. "This part's a little bumpy." The road was not a *little* bumpy, I realized a few seconds later. It was a *lot* bumpy. Russell and I clutched one another as the truck dipped and bounced, sliding us up and down and across the front seat like two flopping fish. A few times, the truck lurched so hard against a rut that our heads bumped the ceiling. I was horrified. We were going to have to take this road every day for the next two weeks? Our heads would be permanently bruised!

Russell, of course, thought it was hysterical. He screamed with laughter every time the car dipped, and clapped his hands. "This is awesome!" he yelled at one point. "It's like being on a bucking bronco!"

It occurred to me that I had never asked where exactly Aunt Marianne and Silver lived. I tried to look out the window in an attempt to decipher where we were headed, but I had never seen this part of Sudbury before. Except for the occasional house, which appeared through the trees like a mirage, there was no sign of life anywhere. Cassie had told me a rumor once that the Joneses lived on the rich side of town. Nora said that her mother had told her they owned a gigantic house with a three-car garage and an indoor swimming pool. She was also pretty sure they had a maid. But the houses out here were just medium-sized, and the only swimming pool I saw was a wading pool covered with pink baby dinosaurs in someone's front yard.

I held my breath as we continued on, staring at the pack of air fresheners as they swung beneath the rear-view mirror. After another ten minutes, Aunt Marianne turned Old Betsy onto another, much smoother dirt road, and pointed out the windshield. "Look over there," she said. "Home sweet home."

I squinted through the bright sunlight, and then visored my hand over my eyes. The only thing I could see was Creeper Mountain, which was so close I could actually make out individual leaves on the trees. The inside of my mouth felt cold as the truck sped closer and closer, and my heart beat so loudly I could hear it in my ears. We couldn't possibly be staying here. It just couldn't be. There was no way.

Aunt Marianne made a sudden, sharp turn and brought the truck to a stop. "Well, what do you think?"

Russell was leaning up against the window, both hands pressed against the glass. "Cool," he breathed.

I turned a little to look in his direction. Unless I was mistaken, we were parked in front of Mr. Rawlins's old horse farm. Dad had taken me here a few times in third grade to look at the horses, but he'd gone a different way, which must have been why I didn't recognize it until now. He'd made me sit on an old gray mare named Traveler, even though I was scared to death that the animal would turn its head and bite my leg, and we'd strolled the grounds afterward, throwing corn to the chickens and licking ice cream cones. There was the rolling patch of pasture, fenced off by split posts and some heavy wire, which sat just in front of Mr. Rawlins's small two-story house, with its bare windows and sagging porch.

Except if I remembered correctly, Mr. Rawlins's house had been light brown.

This house was bright purple.

New white shutters flanked each of the four windows, and the door—which was also white now—had an enormous wreath of dried sunflowers on the front.

Russell edged his way to the rim of the seat. "Where's Jackson?" he demanded.

Aunt Marianne pointed past an empty henhouse. "Look over by the pear tree, Russell."

Russell scooched even farther along the seat, the upper half of his body hanging out the window. "Where? I can't see him!"

I put my hand out, pulling him back gently. "Russell, just hang on. We'll get him."

He swatted my hand away. "I can't *see* him!" he yelled, kicking the bottom of the dashboard with his feet. "Lemme out! I wanna see Jackson! I need to see Jackson!"

"Russell!" I yelled. "Don't kick!"

Aunt Marianne looked startled for a moment but then regained her composure. "Hold on, Russell," she said. "That door sticks on the inside. I have to let you out on my side."

"Lemme out!" Russell yelled. "Lemmeoutlemmeout!"

Aunt Marianne pushed her side of the truck open and stepped back as Russell scrambled out. Jackson barked as Russell raced toward him, and strained against his leash.

"Jackson!" Russell yelled. "Jackson, I'm here!"

"Go ahead and untie him!" Aunt Marianne called. "Now that we're back, you can let him run wherever he wants!" We watched as Russell collapsed against his dog and buried his face in the animal's fur. Jackson licked Russell's face over and over again until Russell started to laugh. For the first time all day, I could feel something loosen up inside.

Aunt Marianne turned back around. "Boy, it's a good thing your dad remembered Jackson. Otherwise, I think we would've been up the creek without a paddle."

I nodded, avoiding her eyes. Aunt Marianne was a little too—what was the word?—*friendly*—for me. It wasn't that I wanted her to be unfriendly; I just wished she'd slow down a little.

"Your father already brought your things," she said, slamming the driver's side door. "Your suitcase is up in your room. Let me show you around downstairs, and then you can go up and get settled. How does that sound?"

I nodded, still keeping my eyes on Russell, who was

heading our way. Jackson trotted next to him, licking his hand.

"Why's your house purple?" Russell yelled. Jackson barked, as if he, too, were demanding an answer. "I've never seen a purple house in my whole life! It's crazy!"

I turned away so that Aunt Marianne wouldn't see me smile. Dad told me once that part of Russell's Asperger's meant that he was missing the stop-and-think-before-you-say-it filter the rest of us have. He didn't realize he was being rude. It was just the way he was. And as embarrassing as this part of him could be sometimes, it could also be kind of great. Like just then, for instance, when he asked the very first question that popped into my head the minute we drove up to the house—and which I never would have had the guts to ask.

"Why's our house purple?" Aunt Marianne asked, repeating Russell's question. "Well, I guess because we like the color purple." She paused. "And because Silver and I decided recently that we wanted to start living out loud."

"I like living out loud!" Russell shouted. "I like to live out *very* loud!" He paused. "What's living out loud?"

Aunt Marianne grinned. "It means we're doing things our way, whatever way that might be. You know all the rules that say houses have to be white with green shutters, or that you have to eat dinner at six o'clock every night in the dining room? If Silver and I feel like taking some peanut butter sandwiches out in the field and eating them while the sun goes down at eight o'clock, then that's what we do. And when Silver said she thought this house would look great in purple, I told her to do it."

"You let *Silver* paint the house?" I asked.

Aunt Marianne laughed. "Well, we did it together. But she picked out the color. And frankly, I wasn't the least bit surprised. Purple has been her favorite color since she was in first grade."

I looked around, dumbstruck. When Dad had worked on our house last year, putting on a new roof and adding more siding, he had never once asked my opinion about any of it. But the thought of him asking me to help had never entered my mind, either. Having to go up on a ladder was dangerous, and everyone knew that if you slipped and hit your finger with a hammer, your nail would turn black and fall off. But now the possibility of being able to choose a color for a family house, and then going ahead and painting it, sent little shivers of glee up and down my spine.

Russell started to pick his nose. "Does Mr. Jones like the purple house?"

I swatted his finger away from his nose. "Russell. Don't."

"Well, does he?" Russell asked, examining the finger that had just been inside his nostril. There was a booger on it.

I looked away, mortified.

Aunt Marianne didn't seem fazed by the booger or the personal question. "Actually, Mr. Jones doesn't live

61

with us anymore. He stayed back in Florida, where we used to live. Just Silver and I live here." She paused. "And the horses, of course."

"You have *horses*?" Russell and I asked the question simultaneously.

"Two of them," Aunt Marianne said. "Roo is mine and Manchester belongs to Silver. They used to be Mr. Rawlins's. But they came with the property when he passed away, and neither of us could imagine not keeping them." She looked at me. "Do you know how to ride a horse, Wren?"

"Not really." I paused, remembering how high off the ground I'd been that day when Dad had taken me. Just thinking about it now gave me goose bumps. The horse had looked big from the ground, but sitting on top of him felt as if I was at least three stories up. I'd cried and cried until Dad had taken me off, and then clung to his neck until I stopped shaking. "I sat on one, once," I offered.

"Well, if you can sit on a horse without falling off, you're already halfway there," Aunt Marianne said. "If you want, while you're here, you can try again."

I smiled politely and looked at my shoes.

Russell grabbed Jackson's collar. "Come on, Jackson, let's go watch *Captain Commando*." He looked up at Aunt Marianne. "Do you guys get *Captain Commando* on your TV?"

"Of course we get *Captain Commando*," Aunt Marianne said, pointing to a room through the kitchen. "The TV's in the living room, Russell. Help yourself."

"Yesssss!" Russell pumped his fist in the air. "Let's go, Jackson!"

"Wren?" Aunt Marianne looked back at me. "What can I do for you, honey?"

Maybe it was because Aunt Marianne was being so nice to me, or maybe it was the fact that Russell and Jackson were getting ready to watch *Captain Commando*—which, before she started spending all her time sitting at the kitchen table, meant that Momma would have been starting dinner soon—but just then, I felt like crying. "I think I'm going to go upstairs for a while and lie down," I said. "Russell should be okay as long as Jackson's with him."

"Of course," Aunt Marianne said softly. "Let me show you to your room. You rest as long as you'd like. I'll call you when it's time for dinner."

Chapter 8

The bedroom that Aunt Marianne showed me to did not belong to Silver. When I realized I was not going to have to share a room with her, I almost sank to the floor in relief. Now I could get undressed, and do my pencil-spinning and squirrel-checking every morning in private. Plus, what if Russell needed to come in during the middle of the night the way he sometimes did with Momma and Dad at home? I would die if Silver saw Russell climb into bed with me.

I sat down on the bed next to the window and looked around. It was a nice enough room. The bed had a wrought-iron headboard with swirls and curls that met in the middle. It was covered with a blue-and-yellow quilt, and had a matching pillowcase with lace on one end. The floor was hardwood, and except for a little throw rug next to the bed, the rest of it was bare. There was also a dresser with a mirror on top, a closet, and a straight-backed chair next to the window. Aunt Marianne had put my brown-and-red suitcase on the chair.

I lay down on the bed and rolled over so that I was facing the window. Momma's bird necklace caught against the buttons of my shirt and I reached up, fingering the smooth edges with my thumb. Beyond my curtains, the strange landscape stared out at me. Old Betsy was parked sideways a few feet from the pear tree. At this angle, I could see a bumper sticker on the back, which read FLORIDA GIRLS ROCK!

Past the truck was a small stable with a riding ring behind it. The soft earth in the middle was tamped down with fresh hoofprints. Behind the ring was an enormous pasture filled with tall yellow grass, and beyond that was the base of Creeper Mountain. We were much too close to see any trails of smoke that might have been weaving their way up through the middle of it, but that just meant we were too close, period. Leave it to Aunt Marianne and Silver to buy the only place in Sudbury that afforded them a front-row seat to Witch Weatherly's personal place of residence. I wouldn't make a huge fuss right now, of course, what with Momma in the hospital and everything, but as soon as I was able to talk to Dad again, I'd tell him about it—and why we had to go stay with someone else immediately. Until then, I'd spend every waking moment staying as far away from that mountain as I possibly could.

I rolled away from the window and tried to think things all the way through again. When exactly had Dad called Aunt Marianne? Before Russell and I left for school? Or after? Was the answer he had given me this morning about getting Momma back into bed just a lie, or had she really gone in for a check-up? I squeezed my eyes, thinking about what Russell had said in Mr. Pringle's office about Momma dying. It had sounded ridiculous, but the truth was that I had thought the same thing.

Even before Grandpa William died, I knew that Momma carried a heaviness inside her, something that was always there, like an invisible stone in the middle of her stomach. I could see it when she was doing the dishes after dinner, when she would stop suddenly, and lean her whole weight over the kitchen sink, as if something was pressing down on her shoulders. I could see it when I glanced over at her while the four of us were watching TV, and caught her staring at something else across the room—the bookcase, maybe, or the family portrait on the wall, a million miles away from the rest of us. And a few times I caught her crying while she was sitting in Dad's big easy chair, or folding laundry on top of her big bed. There was no reason for it; nothing had actually *happened*. It was just as if the sad heaviness inside had leaked out a little, as if she could not bear to keep it in for one more moment.

But there were plenty of times when the heavy part of her seemed to lessen, like when she told us stories, when Dad or I made her laugh, or when Russell crawled into her lap while she was knitting and fell asleep against her chest. Those moments were the best, when her eyes lost that glossy look and it felt as if all of her was really there—right there—with us.

They just didn't come around that often.

And now that I thought back, I couldn't even remember the last time she'd been like that at all.

I reached inside my pocket for my pencil. My heart began to slow down a little as I started spinning it across the top of my hand. Some of the tightness inside my chest eased up as I moved it around my thumb and started over again. That's the thing about pencil spinning. It was more than just a cool trick. It also helped me to stop thinking so much. At least for a little while.

The slam of a door downstairs startled me. I blinked as the edges of the pencil came back into focus, and then shoved it back inside my pocket. I could hear Silver's voice downstairs.

"So she's here? Right now?"

"Shhh!" Aunt Marianne said. "Yes. She's upstairs. I think she's sleeping."

"Why didn't you tell me they were coming?" Silver sounded annoyed. "Geez, Mom."

"I didn't have time," Aunt Marianne answered. "And please keep your voice down."

"But . . ." Silver's exasperation was rising. "Did you even stop to think how awkward this might be? I mean, we barely even know them. Why can't—"

"You're being rude, Silver." Aunt Marianne's voice was solemn. "Stop it."

"I'm just saying," Silver said.

"Well, don't." Aunt Marianne sighed. "We're still family, whether we know them well or not. Besides, it's not like anyone planned for this to happen, honey. Uncle Bill called me this morning. You were already in school. Russell and Wren didn't even know anything until a few hours ago, the poor things."

Silence. And then:

"Is Aunt Greta going to be okay?" Silver sounded less aggravated.

Uncle Bill. Aunt Greta. That was what Silver called Dad and Momma. I stared at the ceiling as Aunt Marianne lowered her voice, and then I sat up, straining to hear her answer. But it was no use. She was speaking too quietly.

I got up off the bed then, walked over to the door, and slammed it as hard as I could.

They could talk about me all they wanted.

But when it came to Momma, well, that was a different story.

Chapter 9

Dad had packed several pairs of my jeans, a bunch of my favorite T-shirts, an extra pair of sneakers, and my two best hoodies. He had, however, forgotten a few other very important items. I snatched clothes out of the suitcase, looking frantically for my bras and underwear, but there were none. Zero. Zilch. I sat down on the edge of the bed and tried to slow my breathing.

The truth is that I'm pretty sure I could get away without wearing a bra to school. If I had to, I mean. It's not like I have much there yet, and I am so skinny that no one would really notice. But I draw the line at going to school without *underpants*. Besides being gross, it would also be majorly uncomfortable. But what could I do? It wasn't like I could go across the hall and ask Silver if I could borrow a pair of her underwear. That was just weird. Plus, she'd probably tell Jeremy about it, which meant that in less than two hours, I'd be dubbed with some horrible nickname like Zit-Pit, which is what he calls Carmela Callahan whenever her face breaks out.

Like I wasn't dealing with enough already. Maybe I could just wash the pair I had on now every night and hide them in the closet to dry. People did that sometimes, didn't they? As long as they were clean, who would ever know?

I froze as a knock sounded outside my door. "Yes?"

"Let me in!" It was Russell.

My insides relaxed again. "Hey, buddy. You doing okay?" I watched as he strode into the room, walking on the balls of his feet, taking everything in. His eyebrows sat high on his forehead and his fists were clenched. Jackson trotted in behind him, a purple bandanna tied around his neck.

"What are you doing in here?" he asked.

"This is my room," I said. "Where'd Jackson get the bandanna?"

"Silver gave it to him." Russell sat down on the edge of the bed, bounced on it twice.

"She did?"

"Yup. She said her horse has one, too."

I shuddered at the mention of the horse. "Did she take you to see him yet?"

"I don't want to see him," Russell said. "I don't like horses."

"Why not?"

"Because they're crazy. And they have big teeth."

I grinned and put my arm around my little brother. That was one of the reasons I was afraid of horses, too.

Big teeth, hooves that could stomp you to pieces, and the ability to move at breathtaking speeds. A bad combination, no matter which way you looked at it. "Listen, how're you doing? You feeling okay? Do you want to talk about anything?"

"I feel hungry," Russell said, shrugging my arm off. "When's dinner? Does that lady know I like pancakes?"

"She's our aunt, Russell, not some lady."

"Does she know I like pancakes?" he persisted.

"I don't know, but if she doesn't have them, you have to promise you won't make a fuss."

"What do you mean, if she doesn't have them?" Russell frowned. "This is America! Everyone has pancakes!"

I sighed. "We'll have to wait and see."

Russell bounced up and down again on the side of the bed. "Is this where we're sleeping?"

"This is where *I'm* sleeping." I stood up and took his hand. "Come on, I'll show you your room. It's right next . . ."

"Uh-uh." Russell hung back. "No way."

I pulled a little on his hand, already knowing it was no use. Jackson pricked his ears as I tried again. "Russell, it's right next to . . ."

Russell dug his heels into the floor. "No way, Ho-say. I'm not staying here unless I can sleep with you."

I let go of his hand, stared at him for a minute. The only thing Russell knew for sure right now was that

Jackson and I were still here with him. Everything else was up in the air, with no real promise that when things came back down again, they would be the same as before.

"Okay, buddy," I said. "Don't worry. You can sleep in here with me."

Downstairs, Aunt Marianne had rolled up her sleeves, tied an apron around her waist, and was in the process of setting out several dishes filled with food on the kitchen table. I looked around nervously as Russell and I stood there watching her, but there was still no sign of Silver.

"What're you doing?" Russell asked.

"Making dinner." Aunt Marianne nodded at the dishes. "These are called Make-It-Yourself Kabobs. Silver and I eat them a lot, and I think you might like them. After you pick what kinds of things you want on your kabobs, you can skewer them and I'll go out back and grill them up. Go ahead and help yourself."

I surveyed the table. Inside the little dishes were all sorts of different things—cubed pieces of chicken, chunks of steak, mushrooms, cherry tomatoes, yellow and orange peppers, and purple onions. I couldn't remember the last time Momma had made anything with vegetables. She usually whipped up a quick batch of pasta along with a jar of sauce, or we ordered pizza. Sometimes we even had pancakes and scrambled eggs. In the last month, of course, she hadn't made anything. Dad had brought home takeout most nights.

Russell frowned. "We don't eat vegetables. I need pancakes."

"Pancakes?" Aunt Marianne dumped a pile of mushroom chunks into a bowl. "I have pancakes. Wren, do you want pancakes, too?"

I shook my head, a little in awe of Aunt Marianne's unflappability. It didn't seem like anything fazed her. Maybe I'd been too quick about judging her before. "I'll be fine with the kabobs," I said. "But thanks."

"There's another episode of *Captain Commando* on now," Russell said. "I have to watch him or else I go insane."

"Go right ahead," Aunt Marianne said. "I'll call you when your pancakes are ready."

"Come on, Jackson!" Russell ran out of the kitchen and plopped down on the rug in front of the TV. Jackson trotted obediently after him, the edges of his purple bandanna fluttering around his neck, and settled in a pile at Russell's feet.

The sound of feet pummeled the steps. I held my breath and clutched the edge of the counter as Silver bounded across the living room and into the kitchen. She had changed out of her school outfit into gray sweatpants, a beat-up T-shirt with a faded picture of Strawberry Shortcake on the front, and pink fuzzy socks. Her long hair hung down her back like a column of rippling light. I felt nauseated standing there next to her, as if I were an unwanted intruder she was about to discover in her very own kitchen.

"Hey," she said, glancing quickly at me.

"Hi."

"Mmmm, kabobs," Silver said, leaning over the table and popping a yellow pepper chunk into her mouth. "I want extra veggies on mine, Mom."

"We don't eat any vegetables!" Russell called from the living room. "I'm having pancakes."

Silver stopped chewing as she turned and looked at Russell. I closed my eyes, praying for the floor to open up beneath me and swallow me whole. "You don't eat vegetables?" Silver asked. "*Ever?*"

Russell watched Silver carefully, his eyes flicking back and forth between her and the TV screen. I could tell he thought she was pretty. Russell liked pretty things. "Just corn," he said. "With butter and salt. Nothing else. *Definitely* nothing green."

Silver held up an orange pepper. "This isn't green." She held up a yellow pepper chunk. "And neither is this." She did the same thing for the purple onion, the mushroom, and the cherry tomatoes. "You gonna try 'em?" she asked. "They're not green."

Russell scowled. "I want pancakes."

"Okay." Silver shrugged and popped another pepper into her mouth. "But if you don't at least try it, you'll never know what you're missing."

I watched Russell out of the corner of my eye as Silver kept chewing. He scowled again and looked back at the TV. But I could tell by the way he kept sneaking glances her way that she'd had an effect on him.

Maybe even a good one.

Chapter 10

"So how was school today?" Aunt Marianne asked, surveying the three of us as we began to eat. Along with the kabobs and Russell's pancakes, she had set out a bowl of buttered noodles and a small wicker basket filled with rolls. There was lemonade in big blue glasses with slices of lemon floating on top, and cloth napkins, too. I wondered if Aunt Marianne was just trying to impress us, since we were her guests. It was hard to imagine anyone eating like this every night.

"It was good for me," Silver said. "Not so good for Mr. Tunlaw, our history teacher." She looked over at me. "Right, Wren?"

It felt weird to hear her call me by my name. Technically, up until this point, I wasn't even sure she remembered my name. Plus, with everything else going on, I'd almost forgotten about poor Mr. Tunlaw. "Yeah." I nodded.

"What happened?" Aunt Marianne asked.

"He got stung by a bunch of wasps," Silver said. "Like

six or seven times. They had to take him to the hospital. Mr. Pringle said he was allergic."

"Oh my goodness." Aunt Marianne put the serving spoon back and stared at Silver. "That's terrible! Is he all right?"

Silver shrugged. "No one really knows. Mr. Pringle said he would tell us, but we hadn't heard anything by the end of the day."

"Where did the wasps come from?" Aunt Marianne asked.

"There was a nest behind the board," Silver answered. "I guess he must've bumped against it or something by accident . . ."

Aunt Marianne shook her head. "It can be very dangerous to get stung like that. Especially if you're allergic. I hope he's all right."

"Is he gonna die?" Russell crammed a huge piece of pancake into his mouth. A thin stream of syrup dribbled down his chin.

"No, Russell. They have medicine at the hospital. He'll be okay." I mimed wiping my chin, hoping he would copy me. Instead, Russell opened his mouth so I could get a good look at all the disgusting, chewed-up food inside. I shook my head and looked away.

Aunt Marianne sighed. "I'm sure you're right, Wren. They'll take good care of him in the hospital." She spooned a pile of noodles onto her plate. "What's Mr. Tunlaw teaching you in history, anyway?"

"Oh!" Silver straightened up a bit in her chair. Her face brightened. "He actually gave us this really cool assignment today."

"Oh?" Aunt Marianne raised one eyebrow. "What about?"

"He said we have to do a project about Pennsylvania. Anything at all, as long as it has to do with the history of our state." Silver leaned forward. "And I know exactly what I'm going to do mine on. It's gonna be awesome!"

I'd almost forgotten about Silver's conversation in history class, but now it came back to me like a slap in the face. Maybe there was a chance she'd changed her mind, though, especially after everyone's negative reaction to it. If she had any sense, she'd have thought of something else by now.

"Well . . ." Aunt Marianne coaxed. "Are you going to tell me about it or not?"

"I'm going to do a paper about Witch Weatherly!" Silver grinned.

Just hearing Witch Weatherly's name out loud again made the tiny hairs on my arms stand up.

Russell dropped his fork. It made a dull clattering sound against the floor. "Witch Weatherly?" he repeated.

Silver nodded. "Yup."

Aunt Marianne stopped chewing. "What in the world would possess you to do a history report on her?"

Silver's eyes went wide. "Because she sounds so amazing! *You're* the one who told me about her, Mom!"

"Well, I know," Aunt Marianne said. "But . . ."

Silver cut her off. "Just the fact that she's one hundred and eight years old is enough of a reason to want to meet her. She's like a legend! She's probably seen or heard about everything that's ever happened in Sudbury! And I mean, how much more historical can you get than that?"

Aunt Marianne blotted her mouth with her napkin. "All that may be true, honey, but she's a very old woman, and from what I've heard, she's extremely private. I really don't think she would take kindly to a young girl going up there, pestering her about her personal life."

"I won't pester her," Silver argued. "I'll be very polite. And think about how amazing my paper would turn out! Can you imagine how cool it would be if I went up there and came back with an actual person-to-person interview?"

Had Silver been listening at *all* to any of the things said in class about Witch Weatherly? Had she really missed the parts about the red raven and the pits with the pointed sticks? And what about the hornet-head snakes? Or Shining Falls?

Somehow, I found my voice in the back of my throat. "There's a reason people won't set foot near her place, you know."

"Yeah!" Russell shouted. "She's a witch!"

"Oh, I know people *say* that." Silver looked at her mother. "What do you think, Mom?"

"We already talked about this, honey." Aunt Marianne speared a piece of chicken. "I really don't think there's any such thing as witches."

Silver turned to me. "Wren, you don't believe she's a witch, do you?"

I stared at Silver, hoping that my eyes conveyed just how much I did believe such a thing without actually having to say it.

"Of course she's a witch, you idiot!" Russell looked horrified.

"Russell!" I hissed. "No blankety-blanks!"

"Well, she is an idiot," Russell mumbled. "That lady's name is *Witch* Weatherly. So of course she's a witch."

"People aren't always what other people say they are." Silver was watching Russell with steady eyes. It was hard to know if her feelings were hurt or not; the expression on her face hadn't changed. She got up suddenly and went over to the window. "See that smoke coming out between those trees over there? All the way at the top?" I stared straight ahead as Russell scrambled out of his chair and ran to the window. "Ever since we moved here, that smoke has been coming out of someone's chimney. Now if what people around here say is true, and Witch Weatherly is the only person who lives on Creeper Mountain, that smoke has got to be coming out of her house. Which means that she lives only a mile or so behind us."

I reached down and hung on to the sides of my chair so I would not fall off. She could see the smoke from here? A *mile or so*? Were we really that close to Witch Weatherly?

"Silver." The pleading tone in Aunt Marianne's voice was gone. She was all business now. "I appreciate you wanting to do a good job on your history paper, but I do *not* want you going anywhere near Creeper Mountain or bothering Ms. Weatherly. Now, I mean it, honey. Aside from it being completely impossible for you to even get up that mountain since it is so overgrown and dangerous, Witch—" Aunt Marianne caught herself and then cleared her throat. "*Ms.* Weatherly is very old, and very private, and very—" Aunt Marianne stopped again and stared down at the tablecloth. "Well, *odd*, I guess, is the word I'm looking for here. She's odd, Silver. She's been living alone for years and years. She's not used to having people around. If you just showed up, it could—it would—make things very uncomfortable." Silver opened her mouth, but Aunt Marianne lifted her hand. The silver bracelet around her wrist tinkled. "*No.* Not another word. You are not to go and that's final. I'm sorry, but you're just going to have to find another topic to do your history report on."

Silver glowered at her mother. "What happened to living out loud?" she asked. "What happened to doing things our way?"

"This has nothing to do with living out loud," Aunt Marianne said, casting a sidelong glance in my direction. "This has to do with respecting someone's privacy. It's as simple as that. And that is the end of the *discussion*, Silver." She raised an eyebrow. "I mean it."

"Fine." Silver slid back into her chair and toyed with a chunk of yellow pepper at the end of her fork. "Whatever."

"Your momma's smart," Russell said. " 'Cause there's poisonous snakes on that mountain, and that old lady has a gigantic red bird that likes to eat eyeballs." He ripped off a chunk of pancake and stared at Silver. "You have pretty eyes," he said. "You should really try to keep them."

I snuck a glance in Silver's direction. Usually, Russell's final assessment of a situation, which he always blurted out whether someone wanted him to or not, infuriated me. Silver, however, didn't seem to mind.

In fact, I wondered if she had even heard him at all.

Chapter 11

Dear Momma,

I wrote in my notebook that night after Russell had fallen asleep in bed next to me.

I miss you. I don't understand why no one can tell me what's going on yet, but Dad said that he would explain everything later. Aunt Marianne and Silver's place is nice. They're nice, too. I thought it was going to be weird because Silver is so popular at school and we really don't know each other, but it's actually turning out to be weird in a whole other way. I don't know if I can explain it right now, but I will try later. Things were a little hard for Russell at first, but Jackson is here, and Aunt Marianne lets him watch Captain Commando, and she made him pancakes for dinner, so I think he is okay now.

I stopped writing and looked over at Russell, who was dressed in his Captain Commando T-shirt and a pair of Incredible Hulk underwear. He snored loudly next to me. Russell doesn't like to wear pajamas. He says they make him too hot—even in the middle of winter. A piece of his brown hair hung over his eyes, and his hand flopped down off the side of the mattress, inches away from Jackson, who was curled up on the floor next to the bed. He actually looked sweet, lying there sleeping. But that was probably because his mouth was shut and he wasn't moving. I reached over and smoothed his hair along the front of his forehead. He mumbled something and rolled over. I went back to Momma's letter.

I hope you are feeling all right. Our teacher, Mr. Tunlaw, got stung today by wasps, and is in the hospital, too. No one knows yet if he is going to be okay, either, but we are all trying to think positive. Please write back to me soon and tell me how you are. And don't worry about anything; I will make sure Russell brushes his teeth every day and takes his medicine at night.

I love you.

Wren

I put my head down on top of the letter, and took a deep breath. It hurt, missing Momma like this. It hurt even worse not knowing how she was feeling, or what she was thinking. I think sometimes Momma and I are cut from the same cloth. Except for the fact that she is a lot older, we have a lot in common. We both love pizza, for instance, although she's not as crazy about pepperoni as I am. We both like to sleep in late on the weekends, and neither of us ever go anywhere without a sweater, because we always get cold. We worry about a lot of the same things, too. If Dad is later getting home some nights than he usually is, the two of us will pace up and down in front of the curtains in the living room until the head-lights of his truck finally appear through the dark. And if Russell's been too quiet for a while (which is almost never), Momma and I will bump into each other as we rush into his room to check on him. It's almost as if we think the same things, feel the same way. And when I know she isn't okay—like right now—I don't feel like I'm okay, either.

After a while, I lifted my head again. I folded the let-ter into threes, stuffed it inside an envelope, and put it on my dresser. I shoved my underwear into the waist-band of my pajama bottoms and went into the bathroom. Besides washing out my underwear, I also had to floss and brush my teeth, but I planned on being quick. I didn't want to hold anyone up—especially Silver. She probably had a whole nightly beauty routine that took hours.

I finished my teeth and gargled twice. Then I pulled out my underwear. The little orange soap dispenser next to the sink was the only type of cleaning liquid I could find, but it would have to do. I poured a little of it into my palm, worked up a sudsy lather, and began to scrub. The soap smelled good, like peaches and vanilla. I rinsed it off, wrung my underwear out, and hid them back inside my pajamas. Then I tiptoed back into my room. I shut the door tight, hung the underpants over the knob of the closet door, and slipped into bed next to Russell. He made a grunting sound as he turned over again and smacked his lips.

Outside the window, I could hear the slow, steady sound of raindrops hitting the glass. I closed my eyes and counted to ten. Rain didn't scare me, but storms did. I could hear the big oak trees in the yard swishing in the wind. Slowly, the rain picked up. More wind blew. The sky outside lit up with a slash of white lightning. I held my breath—one, two, three—and then a rumble of thunder sounded in the distance. I whimpered and squeezed my eyes shut, burrowing in closer to Russell.

Listening to the storm howl outside made me think of another thunderstorm that had happened just a few weeks ago. It had been a big one, with booming thunder, and fingers of electricity that snaked down from the sky. The power had gone out after a sudden clap of thunder and, outside the house, the wind rattled the shingles on the roof. Terrified, I ran into Momma and Dad's room.

Dad already had one arm wrapped around Momma, who was dressed in his bathrobe again, and he let me slip in under the other one. Rain pelted their bedroom windows with such force that it sounded as if great handfuls of marbles were being thrown against the glass. Every time the thunder bellowed, I screamed and buried my face into Dad's side.

But Dad just laughed at me, and tickled my ribs. "It's okay, butterbean," he said. "You're in here with me and Momma. You're safe."

I lifted my head slowly, just as another sheet of lightning cracked across the black sky. For a split second, the room lit up, as if someone had turned on the lights, and it was then that I saw Momma, still hunched under Dad's other arm. She looked as if she was in some kind of trance. Her eyes were wide as quarters, the pupils so dilated they looked almost hollow. She was whispering something—a single word—over and over again. *Great? Grit?* Her voice was so faint, it was hard to hear.

Dad must have seen Momma's face, too, because he stopped laughing, and grabbed her with his other arm. "Greta," he said gently. "Greta, honey. I'm here. I'm right here."

Now, I rolled over and buried my face into the pillow. I could feel the jagged side of Momma's bird necklace pushing against the soft part of my throat. The pillow-case smelled clean and powdery, but strangely unfamiliar, too. My pillowcases at home smelled like Momma—a mix of rose petals and cut grass.

Behind my lids, my eyes welled with tears that leaked out in a slow stream down the curve of my cheek.

I just wanted to go home.

Chapter 12

We piled into Old Betsy the next morning: Russell up front with Aunt Marianne, Silver and I squeezed into the small, cab-like compartment behind them. I was already exhausted. Russell had thrown a fit at breakfast, screaming that he didn't want to ride the strange bus with weird kids he didn't know. Nothing I said or did could calm him down, until Aunt Marianne came downstairs and said, calm as anything, that he didn't have to take the bus. She would drive us to school.

"You mean forever?" Russell asked.

"Well, you won't be here forever, Russell," Aunt Marianne answered, ruffling his hair. "But I'll drive you for as long as you are."

I held my breath, waiting for Russell to dart out from under Aunt Marianne's hand or even strike out at her for touching his hair, but he didn't move. He only nodded and sat back down to finish his breakfast. I watched Aunt Marianne as she moved throughout the kitchen, buttering a bagel, pouring herself a cup of coffee. She didn't seem annoyed or upset by Russell's outburst; in fact, she was whistling a little through her teeth. I wondered how much longer her patience was going to hold out.

Silver was eating a piece of peanut butter toast, except that she had rolled it up like a taco and was taking bites from both ends. I kept my eyes on Russell in the front seat, who was saying something to Aunt Marianne. The small window that separated us prevented me from hearing what it was, but I could tell by the way his muscles around his mouth were beginning to tighten that something was definitely wrong. Without warning, he kicked the dashboard, hard. I leaned forward quickly and knocked on the glass.

Aunt Marianne slid the window open a little with one hand, and then waved. "Everything's okay, Wren. We were just talking about Jackson, and how's he going to feel being alone at the house all day. It's all right now though, right, Russell?"

Russell glared out the window.

"Russell," I said. He ignored me. Or maybe he couldn't hear me through the window. I sat forward a little and tapped on the glass behind his head. "Russell," I said, a little louder.

"I'm o*kay*, Wren," Russell said without turning around. "Stop being so annoying. I really hate you."

I sat back, stung. A knot formed in the back of my throat, and I swallowed hard, forcing myself not to cry. I know Russell's different. And I know he doesn't really mean the things he says. But sometimes it hurts anyway. I reached up and felt for Momma's necklace.

Next to me, Silver opened a blue notebook and began to write something across the top. I tried not to watch, but it was impossible, given the tight quarters of our seating arrangement.

WITCH WEATHERLY PROJECT appeared on the page, spelled out in capital letters. Finished, Silver sat back, and then looked at me.

My fingers stopped fiddling as I turned and stared at her with disbelief. "You're doing it?" I whispered.

She nodded, underlining the words, as if to emphasize her decision. "You won't tell my mom, will you?"

I swallowed again. It didn't seem fair that she'd decided to burden me with her secret. It was a big one and terrifying to boot. She had to be crazy. There was no doubt about it. Anyone who knew all there was to know about Creeper Mountain and Witch Weatherly, and was going to go there anyway, had to be completely out of their mind. But there was another part of me that felt just the tiniest bit thrilled that she had let me in on her plans. It was as if she already trusted me, or wanted to, at least.

"Wren?" She elbowed me, her wide eyes searching mine.

"No," I whispered. "I won't tell."

"Thanks." Silver's eyes dropped to my fingers. "That's a cool necklace. Where'd you get it?"

"It's my mom's."

"Does someone have the other half?"

"No. It broke when she was younger and fell off her bike. She never found the other piece."

"It's so different looking." Silver leaned in closer. "I like the little bird and the leaves. And what do those letters mean?"

"I think it's part of her name. You know, for Greta."

"It's nice she let you have it."

"Yeah." I shrugged and tucked the medallion back inside my shirt.

I turned away from her then and looked out the window. I didn't want to talk about Momma anymore.

Not now.

Maybe not ever.

It could have been the fact that Aunt Marianne didn't let Old Betsy's speedometer fall under sixty for the whole ride, or the three yellow lights she sped through, but somehow she got all of us to school with two whole minutes to spare. She let Russell out at the elementary school across the street and pulled the truck into the middle school parking lot.

The usual throng of sixth and seventh-grade kids was hanging around out front, Dylan, Jeremy, and Nathan among them. They were sitting on the front steps the way they usually did, watching and commenting on everyone who came in, but they stood up when they spotted Silver in the window of Old Betsy. I scooched farther down in my seat, trying to ignore the dampness that was starting to collect under my arms, and the floppy feeling inside my belly.

Silver pushed her way out of the truck and paused, waiting for me. Behind her, the three boys had already started to approach. They eyed Old Betsy cautiously, as if not quite sure what to make of her.

"Is that your car?" Jeremy looked confused.

Silver shut the truck door. "Yup."

Aunt Marianne leaned across the front seat, catching Silver's eye. "Do you have cheerleading today, honey?"

"No," Silver said. "Tomorrow, Friday, and Saturday."

"All right." Aunt Marianne looked over at me. "I'll pick Russell up at 3:00 and then you guys at 3:15, okay?"

"Okay, Mom." Silver waved. "Bye."

"Bye, honey." Aunt Marianne grinned. "See you, Wren."

I tried to smile but it came out more like a grimace. I stared down at the pavement as the truck roared off, and bit my lip.

"You coming, Wren?" Silver stepped around the throng of boys. I moved behind her on wooden legs.

"Wait, why didn't you just take the bus?" Dylan asked. "Like you always do?"

"We didn't feel like it," Silver answered.

Jeremy looked as if he was about to ask another question, but then his eyes fell on me. "What's *she* doing riding with you?"

"She needed a ride," Silver answered.

I closed my eyes, hoping against hope I would discover that I was in the middle of a dream. Or even a nightmare. At the very least, I would wake up and find out none of this was real.

"But she doesn't even live near you," Jeremy pressed. "Doesn't she live all the way over on the west side?"

I wondered briefly if Jeremy thought I didn't have ears.

"Actually, she's staying with me for a while." Silver headed for the front door, talking over her shoulder. "And if you want to know why, ask her. It's none of my business."

I had to actually think about moving my legs, so that I wouldn't stand there in total shock. Had Silver Jones just told Jeremy Winters that the reason I was staying with her was none of *her* business? Who said things like that? About me?

And to the cutest boy in sixth grade?

Chapter 13

Nora and Cassie clobbered me as soon as I got to our third-period math class.

"Is it true?" Nora shrieked. "Holy cow, tell me it's true!"

I dumped my backpack on the floor and slid into my seat. "Tell you what's true?"

"That you're staying at the Joneses'!" Cassie swatted me playfully. "Don't even try to keep secrets from us, Wren!" Bits of pink and blue Lucky Charms stuck out from her braces.

"Ow." I rubbed my arm.

"Wren! Talk to us!" Nora put her hand on her hip. "I mean, the whole school knows by now that you're staying with Silver Jones. How come? What's going on?"

I rubbed my palms over my face. There was no way I could go into the real story with them. I didn't want to. Neither of them had ever even met Momma. Besides, it wasn't any of their business.

I took a deep breath. "She's my cousin, actually."

The two girls drew back as if I had just spit at them. "*You're* related to Silver Jones," Nora said. It was a statement, not a question.

"Yeah." I began to unzip my bag and take out my books. "Why do you even care? Just yesterday, you were saying what an idiot she was."

Cassie and Nora exchanged a glance and then rolled their eyes. "That was just because of the wasp thing," Cassie said. "Wait, what kind of cousins are you? Like real cousins, or second cousins forty times removed?"

"Her mom and my mom are sisters," I said. "We're first cousins."

"You are?" Nora jumped up and down a little. "That is *so* cool! So why are you staying with them? Did your parents go on vacation?"

"Yeah." I took out my pencil and began to spin it along my knuckles. "They did, actually." I was relieved that she had provided me with an explanation, even if it was mostly untrue.

"What's her house like?" Nora asked. "Did you see her room? They're, like, totally super rich, right? Does she have boys over all the time? Do they have an indoor pool?"

I shook my head. "No. Actually, it's nothing like that. At all."

"I heard Jeremy tell Mandy that some lady with pig-tails drove you and Silver to school this morning in a beat-up old truck," Cassie said, fiddling with one of the tiny rubber bands inside her mouth. "Was that their maid?"

"No." I stifled a laugh. "That was my Aunt Marianne. Silver's mom. They don't have maids."

"That was Silver's *mother*?" Nora cocked her head and raised her eyebrow. "You're lying."

"I am not," I protested. "It's just . . ." I struggled for words I didn't even want to say, as I tried to figure out what it was they wanted to hear. "I don't know. Silver's just normal, I guess. You know, regular, like everyone else."

Now Cassie tilted her head. "*Regular?*" she repeated.

"Yeah." I shrugged and put my pencil away. "She is. I mean, I've only been there for one night, but from what I can tell, her life is pretty normal. I don't know what else to tell you."

"I think I know what's happening here." Nora swept the top of the desk lightly with her palm, brushing invisible crumbs out of the way.

"You do?" Cassie asked.

Nora nodded without taking her eyes off me. "Wren's ditching us."

"Ditching you?" I repeated. "What do you mean?"

"For Silver," Nora went on. "You don't want to tell us what she's really like because you're protecting her. You're keeping everything you know about her a secret because she's your cousin, and now it's more important to you to be her friend than ours. Even after we asked

97

you to be part of our secret club last summer and everything."

I stared up at her, aghast. "That's not true at all!"

"Oh, please." Nora stood up and put her hand on her hip. "Real friends don't keep things from each other."

"Yeah," Cassie echoed. "My mother always says, *you never know who your true friends are until someone bigger comes along.*"

"Exactly." Nora's face darkened. "And then, anything can happen."

Chapter 14

Miss Crumb's daily blackboard question in English class was another interesting one:

What three superpowers would you most like to have? Why?

I wrote quickly, without thinking:

1. I would like to be able to automatically transport myself, so that I could go visit Momma today after school and be back in time for bed.

2. I would like to be able to have X-ray vision, so that even when visiting hours were over at the hospital, I could still see Momma through the walls.

3. I would like to be telepathic, because then I could understand what it is that really makes Momma sad, and be able to fix it. Also, I would be

able to change all my scaredy-cat feelings into strong ones, and then maybe get up the nerve to tell Cassie and Nora to go shove it.

~~~~~~~~

We had a substitute teacher for Mr. Tunlaw's class, which was not a surprise, since Mr. Pringle had made an announcement that morning that Mr. Tunlaw would be out for the next few days until he felt better. The substitute's name was Miss Coin. She was a short woman with a square, mannish-looking face. When she turned to the side, she looked a little like George Washington, except with curly blonde hair.

"Okay, people," she said, clapping her hands. "Let's discuss the topics you're thinking about for your history project. Oh, and before I forget, Mr. Tunlaw has asked me to tell you that you may work in pairs on this project if you would like."

I looked out the window, searching for squirrels. I still hadn't given a single thought yet to what I was going to do for the history project. Truthfully, I wasn't even sure I would do it at all. After what had happened with Momma, everything else seemed so trivial. So unimportant. But one thing was for sure: If I was going to do it, there was no way I was going to work with anyone. I worked much better alone.

A small square of paper flew across the top of my desk, startling me out of my thoughts. I clapped my hand over it before it fell to the floor, and glanced around.

Who was throwing things at me? Then my eyes fell on Silver. She nodded and flicked her eyes at the note, indicating that I should read it. I unfolded the tiny piece of paper and stared at the message inside.

Do you want to be my partner for the history project?

Maybe she thought she was in over her head. Or maybe she was starting to chicken out a little, now that she'd had some time to think over all the things we'd told her about Witch Weatherly. Whatever it was, she couldn't pay me five million bucks to be her partner. I felt a sharp stab of fear, just thinking about it. There was no way I'd ever set foot on that mountain, much less go anywhere near Witch Weatherly. Project or no project.

Silver was still staring at me, waiting for a response.

No, thanks, I mouthed silently.

For a brief second, she looked crushed. Her shoulders sagged and her whole face seemed to cave in with disappointment.

Then she shrugged, took out a tube of pineapple lip-gloss, and rolled it across her lips.

I looked back out the window.

Somehow, disappointing her felt almost as bad as thinking about Creeper Mountain.

Cassie and Nora were already sitting at the lunch table on the patio when I came over. They gave each other a sidelong glance as I sat down. Nora moved over so that there was an empty seat between us.

I looked at her. "You don't want me to sit with you anymore?"

She sniffed and looked away.

"Sit wherever you want," Cassie said. She was picking through a bag of Chex Mix, taking out the pretzels, which she didn't like, and stacking them in a little pile next to her tray. "It's a free country."

I sat down and stared at the tray of food in front of me: a chicken patty on a bun, ten or twelve tater tots, a small pile of shriveled peas, and a mound of diced pears. Aunt Marianne had offered to pack everyone's lunch this morning, but Silver hadn't wanted her to. "I keep telling you, Mom," she'd said. "It's not like Florida. Everyone here buys their lunches. Every day." For a moment, I wondered what lunch had been like in Florida. Did the kids there bring their lunches in picnic baskets? Eat outside under wide palm trees?

I picked up my chicken sandwich and took a bite. The bun was dry and mealy. The chicken tasted like sawdust.

"So, like I was saying," Nora spoke directly to Cassie. "*Bone Chillers* comes out tonight. My mom can drop us off at seven thirty, and we can go to the eight o'clock show. Then afterward we can go to the Hot Spot for pizza, and you can sleep over at my house."

"Awesome!" Cassie grinned and clapped her hands. "I can't wait!"

"I can't believe *Bone Chillers* is finally here." I maneuvered the words around the wad of chicken in my mouth. "It feels like we've been waiting forever to see that movie."

Nora looked at me with feigned surprise. "Oh, are you going? I thought you hated horror movies."

I put my sandwich down.

"Is Aunt Marianne gonna bring you?" Cassie chimed in. "Or maybe you *and* Silver?"

I shook my head. "Why are you acting like this?"

"Like what?" Nora asked innocently.

"Like you hate me all of a sudden. It's not like I can help what's going on, you know."

"We wouldn't know," Nora replied. "Because you won't tell us anything about her."

I stood up. "I wasn't talking about Silver. I was talking about me."

And with that, I took my tray, dumped it into the garbage can by the door, and wandered over to the little sapling by the chain link fence. I leaned against the wires as I took out my pencil.

I could feel Nora's and Cassie's eyes on me, but neither of them got up.

And the longer I sat there, the more I realized that I didn't want them to.

Chapter 15

Aunt Marianne made something called beef fajitas for dinner two nights later. They were pieces of grilled steak that she mixed with the leftover peppers, onions, and mushrooms, all wrapped up in a tortilla. I ate two of them, surprised at how good they were. Silver unrolled her tortilla and sprinkled grated cheese and sour cream on top. Then she rolled it back up and dipped the ends in salsa. Russell refused to try them at all, so Aunt Marianne made him another batch of pancakes. He gave the leftovers to Jackson when Aunt Marianne wasn't watching, and then wiped his fingers on the front of his shirt. I was just about to remind him to use his napkin when he looked at Aunt Marianne.

"You and Momma are sisters, right?"

"Yes." Aunt Marianne nodded. "We are."

"Are you bigger or smaller?"

Aunt Marianne smiled. "I'm three years older than your mom."

Russell nodded, deliberating this, and then looked

over at me. "Are you a good big sister?" he asked. "Or annoying, like Wren?"

"Russell!" I kicked him lightly under the table. He kicked me back.

"From what I've seen, Wren is a very good sister to you, Russell." Aunt Marianne spoke quietly, her eyes moving between us. "In fact, I think she's a lot better at it than I ever was."

"What do you mean?" asked Russell. "You didn't like having Momma as a sister?"

"Of course I liked her, Russell." Aunt Marianne chewed more slowly and then swallowed. "I loved her. I still love her. When we were really little, we even had a secret hiding place."

"A secret hiding place?" Russell sat up straighter.

Aunt Marianne nodded. "There used to be a gigantic oak tree in our backyard. It was so big you could barely see the top of it. And it had these enormous branches that spread out on either side like really thick arms. You could climb all the way out on one of those branches and see as far as the river. That's how big they were. And in the summertime, the leaves were so thick that we could hide on one of those branches all day and our parents wouldn't have the faintest idea where we were." Aunt Marianne smiled. "Your mother called it the *We Tree*."

" 'The We Tree,' " Russell repeated softly. "So what happened to it?"

"Well, a few years later, our parents got divorced, and I had to move to California with Grandma Ruthie, while your mom stayed here with Grandpa William. They moved to another house, too, and we never saw the We Tree again."

"That's sad," Russell said.

"We didn't get to see each other very much, either." Aunt Marianne lowered her eyes. "And even after I got older, I wasn't very good about staying in touch."

I sat very still. Momma had never said anything to me about being separated from her sister. But then, she had never said much of anything when it came to Aunt Marianne. Why hadn't this information ever come up? What didn't she want me to know?

"Is that why Momma hardly ever talks to you?" Russell asked. "Because you were mean to her before?"

"Oh, Russell," I groaned, closing my eyes. It was no use trying to explain to him the benefits of good manners or why certain topics were better not brought up at the dinner table—or even ever. You could try, of course. But it wouldn't stop him from doing it again.

"Oh, we talk," Aunt Marianne said encouragingly. "We do. Especially since Silver and I have moved back here. Your mom's just not interested in talking very much to anyone right now. But she will again. Don't worry."

"Can we talk about something else?" I blurted out. "Please?"

"It's okay, Wren." Aunt Marianne began chewing her food again. "If Russell wants to know some—"

"Then you can talk about it with him," I interrupted. "Alone."

"You're not the boss of me." Russell glared in my direction. "*Or* Aunt Marianne."

"How about the horses?" Silver said suddenly. "Would you guys like to see our horses?"

Russell and I continued glaring at each other.

"That's a great idea!" Aunt Marianne said. "Russell? Wren? How about it?"

"I don't like horses," Russell said, without dropping eye contact.

"Why not?" Silver sounded disappointed.

"Their teeth are too big," Russell said.

Aunt Marianne and Silver looked at each other and laughed. I struggled not to let my irritation show. Why were they laughing? Horses' teeth *were* too big. And everyone knew what had happened to the guy who played Superman in those movies. He fell off a horse, and ended up in a *wheelchair* for the rest of his life, just like Ray Bradstreet. There was certainly nothing funny about that.

"Don't worry," Aunt Marianne said. "Horses do have big teeth, but Manchester and Roo haven't bitten anyone in their whole lives. They won't bite you."

Russell broke my gaze, turning to Aunt Marianne. "You swear to God?" He looked suspicious.

Aunt Marianne held up her right hand. "I swear."

"To *God in Heaven*?" Russell pressed.

"To God in Heaven." Aunt Marianne held up a flat palm.

"Okay." Russell hopped out of his chair. "C'mon, Jackson. Let's go!"

~~~~~~~

I trudged behind the three of them and concentrated on taking deep breaths, which sometimes helped when I felt really nervous. Running in the opposite direction worked wonders, too, but that wasn't going to happen now. I didn't need Silver telling the whole sixth grade that I was afraid of her horse.

At times like this, I wondered if it would be easier to have a brain like Russell's. I wasn't sure if it was because his worked a little faster than others, but sometimes it didn't take much to convince him to do something he wasn't too sure of. Why couldn't I do the same thing? What was it about my brain that wouldn't let me believe people were telling the truth?

The barn, which looked more like a gigantic shed, was small and cramped. There was a hole in the roof, and the inside smelled like a combination of soupy cereal and poop. Two large stalls, one across from the other, took up most of the room, while the walls were covered with long strips of leather and metal bits. A pitchfork and a shovel were propped up next to a black bucket, and the floor was nearly obscured with clumps of hay. Flies buzzed and zoomed through the air. The sound of neighing emerged from the stall on our right as we walked in, but the stall on the left stayed silent.

"Manchester!" Silver walked toward an enormous horse standing in the stall on the right. "Hi, big guy! How are you?"

Manchester obviously knew Silver. His long, sleek head bobbed up and down as she came toward him, and when she slipped her hands around his neck, he nuzzled the back of her head. I took a step back. His teeth were almost as big as my own fingers. And they were inches from Silver's neck.

"That's Manchester," Aunt Marianne said, as if we hadn't heard Silver. "He's a thoroughbred. Actually, he used to be a racehorse when he was younger. Now, though, he's just . . ."

"Shhhh . . ." Silver interrupted. "He can *hear* you, Mom."

"I know, I know," Aunt Marianne said. "I forgot." She looked at me, and raised an eyebrow. "Silver doesn't like it when I talk about Manchester's glory days—or his getting-old days—in front of him. He's a sensitive horse."

"They're all sensitive," Silver said softly. She smoothed the fine hairs along Manchester's neck. "Aren't you Manchester? Aren't you, sweet guy?"

"Where's the other one?" Russell inquired.

"Right over here," Aunt Marianne said. We followed her over to the stall on the left. Inside, a short, wide horse was crammed into a corner. Its rear end pointed directly at us as it lowered its head into a feed bucket and chewed.

"She's not little at all!" Russell said. "She's huge! And she has a really fat butt!"

"Russell!" Silver's eyebrows narrowed. "Please don't say things like that in front of her. She can hear you." It was the first time I'd heard her sound cross with Russell. Maybe these horses meant more to her than I realized.

"It's a horse," Russell said flatly.

"I know it's a horse," Silver retorted. "But she still has ears. And feelings."

"Horses can't have feelings," Russell said. "They're animals."

"Don't you think Jackson has feelings?" Silver raised an eyebrow.

"No," Russell said stubbornly. "Because animals don't *have* feelings. They have instincts."

"Actually, I think you're both right," Aunt Marianne said, cutting in between the two of them. "And Russell is also accurate when he says that Roo is overweight. Now that she's older, Roo isn't that keen on getting her workouts. Taking her out can be a real exercise in patience. I think she'd much rather hang out on a couch all day and eat bonbons." She grinned at me.

"Couch?" Russell asked, peering into the stall. "What couch? I don't see a couch."

"There's no couch, Russell," I said, pulling him away from the stall. "That's just a saying."

"Oh." Russell paused. "What's a saying?"

"It's when someone tries to explain something by using a silly example," Silver said.

"Oh." Russell squinted his eyes. "I don't get it."

I rolled my eyes. "Don't worry about it, Russell."

"I'm not *worried* about it," Russell retorted. "I said I don't *get* it."

I looked away.

"*You're* the one who worries about everything," Russell added.

I gave him a look.

"It's true," he said. "And you know it."

I tried to pretend that I hadn't seen the look Silver and Aunt Marianne exchanged with each other just then, but it was hard not to. It was one of those moments where I wished I could just shrink down into nothing, or disappear altogether. Instead, I looked down at the floor and drew the toe of my sneaker through a pool of straw. But I looked up again, quickly, as Silver began to lead Manchester out of his stall.

"He really wants to run, Mom," she said. "Can I take him out?"

"Of course," Aunt Marianne said. "Would you like to go with her, Wren? You're more than welcome to ride Roo."

"Oh, no." I took a step back. And then another one, just to be on the safe side. "I mean, no, but thanks."

"She won't run," Aunt Marianne said helpfully. "You'll be lucky to get her to walk, to be honest with you."

I shook my head. "Thanks, but I'd rather not."

"Okay." Aunt Marianne reached in and gave Roo a pat on the rear end. "Some other time, Roo-Roo."

"See?" Russell whispered as we followed Silver and Manchester out of the barn. "You *are* afraid of everything. Even dumb, fat horses with huge butts." He stuck his tongue out at me.

I elbowed him in the ribs.

He elbowed me back.

Hard.

"You're in for a real treat," Aunt Marianne said, as Russell and I followed her to the edge of the pasture. "One of my favorite things in the world is watching Silver ride. She's a natural. It's like she was born on top of a horse."

"How can you be born on top of a horse?" Russell asked.

I rolled my eyes again.

Aunt Marianne laughed. "It's just another saying, Russell," she said. "It means she's really, really good at it." She held up a hand to shield her eyes as Silver and Manchester trotted into the field ahead. A slip of sun hovered in the distance and the light was starting to drain from the sky. Pale purple clouds stretched out across the horizon like gauze, and the tips of the grass looked as if they'd been brushed with gold. "Okay, she'll start off slow," Aunt Marianne said. "And then she'll drop the reins and let him go. Watch, now."

I followed her gaze as Manchester carried Silver deeper into the pasture. Silver sat as straight as a ruler, her hands loose and relaxed in front of her. But slowly, as Manchester's lopsided gait began to gather speed, she hunched forward. It looked as if she were talking to him as she held on to both sides of his neck, whispering into his ear, letting him in on a secret that only the two of them would ever know. Manchester's front legs began to move in tandem with his back ones, as if he had suddenly remembered how to run—and how to do it well. It was such a smooth, clean movement that it almost didn't look real. For a moment, the only noise was the steady thud of the horse's hooves pounding across the field like a single drumbeat, over and over again, in a steady, perfect rhythm.

For as frightened as I was—*what if Manchester tripped, and Silver went flying? What if she broke her neck like the guy from Superman?*—it was also impossible to look away. Silver's knees were pressed tight against the saddle, both hands clutching tufts of the horse's mane along with the reins. Her legs seemed to move with the horse, up and down, up and down, as if the two of them were connected by an innate force all their own. Manchester's neck strained forward, and foam had begun to collect at the corners of his mouth. Gusts of hair streamed behind Silver, a gold curtain flapping in the wind. And then, suddenly, a sound burst out across the sky—a *"hooooo-wah!"*—as she lifted her arms, and threw back her head.

"Was that the horse?" Russell asked in alarm. "Or did Silver make that noise?"

"That was Silver!" Aunt Marianne's eyes were shining; both hands were clasped tight against her mouth. "Look at her go!"

On they went, horse and girl flat against the purple sky, fluid as a dream. For a moment, it looked as though they might never stop, as if they might merge with the sky itself and then keep going, riding among the clouds. But as they neared the other side of the pasture, they slowed again. I watched with relief as Silver turned Manchester around and trotted back toward us. Not only was she still in one piece, but her mouth was split in an enormous grin as she waved from the saddle.

She didn't look frightened in the least.

In fact, I realized with amazement, as she came closer and closer, she looked somehow as if she was lit from within.

Chapter 16

That night, after Russell fell asleep and I heard Silver's door shut, I crept into the bathroom and got to work again on my underwear. I had just soaped them up into a good lather when I heard a creak behind me. I froze and nearly fell over as the door flew open behind me.

"Oh!" Silver said. "I'm sorry! I didn't know anyone was in here!" She glanced down at my wet underpants, still dripping in my hands.

I nodded, biting down hard on my lower lip, and waited. My face was so hot I thought it might burst into flames. Silver was still staring at my underwear. "I'll . . . be right out," I managed to squeak.

She looked back up at me. "Right. Um . . . sorry." She shut the bathroom door with a soft click.

I stood there for at least five minutes, trying to comprehend what had just happened. Had she seen the underwear? Of course she'd seen the underwear. She'd stared right at it. Did she know what I was doing? And if she did, why hadn't she said anything? Would she say anything on Monday? To Jeremy or Dylan?

After a while, I realized I was still standing in the bathroom Silver needed to use. Quickly, I squeezed the rest of the water out, shoved the underwear inside the waistband of my pajamas again, and hurried back to my room. Hanging the wet underwear on the closet doorknob, I climbed into bed next to Russell and lay down. My face was still warm, and a sour taste pooled in the back of my throat. I squeezed my eyes shut and tried to go to sleep.

~~~~~~~~~~

Russell poked me awake the next morning, holding something I did not recognize in his hand. "Jackson was chewing on this," he said, tossing it on the bed. "You gotta keep your stuff off the floor, Wren. Otherwise, he thinks its food."

I sat up and rubbed my eyes. There on the quilt in front of me was a brand-new package of girls' underwear. Eight pairs of them, light blue with white trim around the edges. On top of the package was a bright purple sticky note, slightly damp from Jackson's chewing.

"*Keep these*," the note said. "*Mom always buys me extra. Silver.*"

~~~~~~~~~~

I came downstairs cautiously, looking over my shoulder, and peeked around the corner, but the only one downstairs was Russell. It was Saturday. Aunt Marianne and Silver could be anywhere.

"Hey, Russell," I said. "Where is everyone?"

He shrugged, not taking his eyes off the TV.

"Russell!" I leaned against the doorjamb. "Are they here?"

"Don't yell at me." He raised his arm and pointed behind me. "Aunt Marianne left you a note."

The note was tucked under a pan of half-eaten cinnamon buns. They were still warm, and the pan left a damp stain on the top half of the paper as I slid it out to read:

Dear Wren:

I didn't want to wake you, so I left this note. Russell has eaten breakfast and is watching TV in the living room. I had to take Silver to cheerleading practice, which will only take an hour. She will get a ride home after. I have to help a friend with some painting at her house, so I won't be home until 3:00. You have my cell phone number. Please call me right away if you need anything.

Love, Aunt Marianne

P.S. I made monkey bread this morning. Enjoy!

I glanced over at the pan of cinnamon buns again. Was that the monkey bread? I'd never heard of such a thing. I fished one out of the pan and took a bite. It was warm, buttery, and sweet, all at the same time. I ate another piece, drank a glass of milk, and then brought my homework downstairs and spread it out on the couch behind Russell. I might as well be productive while I had the time.

Russell was lying on the floor with his head against Jackson's ribs. Every few minutes, he laughed out loud at some stupid thing Captain Commando said. Besides being a superhero, Captain Commando also had a good sense of humor. Or at least Russell thought he did. Jackson must have thought so, too. Every time Russell laughed, Jackson leaned over and licked Russell's ear.

I had two pages in my math textbook to do, and twenty words to look up for spelling. Plus, I still hadn't come up with my history project topic. The substitute had said that Mr. Tunlaw was going to be back on Monday, and that we had to give him our final topic then. No exceptions. But I didn't even want to start thinking about it now. The whole deal was starting to give me a headache.

The phone rang, startling me out of my thoughts.

"I'll get it!" Russell screamed, barreling into the kitchen.

"Russell, no! It's not our . . ." My words trailed off as Russell snatched the receiver off the hook and pressed it to his ear.

"Hello?" he demanded. There was a pause, and then his eyes widened. "Dad!"

I flew from my spot on the couch. "Let me talk to him, Russell. Give me the phone."

"When are you coming home?" Russell turned away. He clutched the cordless receiver and stalked into the living room. I followed. "Are you bringing Momma?" Another pause. "Well, can I talk to her? Right now?" He furrowed his eyebrows. "But what's wrong? Doesn't she love me anymore?"

I put my hand on Russell's shoulder. He shrugged it off and scurried away from me. I followed him, worried that he might throw the phone.

"Okay. Tell Momma I love her. Okay. I have to give the phone to Wren now. She keeps on touching me." He turned, handing me the phone, and then punched me hard in the upper thigh.

"Ow!" I yelled, pressing the receiver against my chest. Russell settled himself in front of the TV, resting his head along Jackson's hip. I headed for the kitchen and pressed the phone against my ear. "Dad?"

"You all right?" Dad's voice sounded like home.

"Yeah." I cleared my throat. "Russell just punched me."

"Oh, Wren. I'm sorry. It's the only way he—"

"I know," I interrupted. "It's all right." I pushed open the screen door and stepped out into the backyard. The air was light and cool against my face; the sky the color of a pearl. "How's Momma?"

"She's doing . . . better."

119

"Did they figure out what's wrong?"

"Well . . ." Dad sounded cautious, which made me nervous. "They're right in the middle of trying to do that. It's going to take a little more time."

"How much time?"

"I'm still not sure, honey. But I promise we'll know more every day. Try not to worry, okay?"

I took a pencil out of my back pocket and started spinning it along the top of my hand. "It's hard," I said. "I don't like not knowing."

"I know," Dad said. "I feel the same way."

"When can we see her?"

"Not for a little while, honey. Probably not till she comes home."

"When's that gonna be?"

"At least another few weeks."

"What's a few?"

"Two," he said. "Maybe three."

"Dad, that's so long!"

"I'm going to drive up next Friday to see Russell and you. We'll all go out to the Hot Spot and have dinner and talk. Just the three of us, okay? And then before you know it, Wren, it'll be the four of us again. Just like always."

The pencil moved faster and faster across my fingers until it was just one long blur.

"How is it at Aunt Marianne's?" Dad asked. "Do you like it there?"

"It's okay. They painted the house purple."

120

"I noticed that." Dad chuckled. "Aunt Marianne is a really nice lady, isn't she? It was great of her to offer to take care of you while . . ." He paused. "While we're going through this."

"Yeah." I stood up and poked at a forlorn-looking weed with the toe of my sneaker, then stared out into the distance. Something clutched at the back of my throat. There, in between two pine trees, I could make out the faint trail of smoke again. It slithered up into the sky, winding its way in and among the clouds. So Silver had been right. And I hadn't imagined it that day during the fire drill. It was right there. Right in front of my eyes. Again.

"Wren?" Dad asked. "What's the matter, honey?"

"Witch Weatherly lives right behind the house. Like only a mile or two away. We can see the smoke coming out of her chimney."

"Really?" Dad didn't sound as freaked out as I hoped he would. Then again, he was originally from Maine. He had heard the stories about Witch Weatherly, but like Silver, who hadn't grown up in Sudbury, he didn't really believe all of them, either. "You're not worried about it or anything, are you?"

"Well . . ." I didn't want to add any more stress to Dad's life right now. "Do you think we're safe?"

"Of course you're safe, honey." Dad's voice was soft. "Nothing's going to happen, Wren."

"You don't think she ever comes down the mountain, do you?"

"Nah," Dad said. "From what I've heard, she's a pretty private person."

"Yeah." I put the pencil back in my pocket. "I guess you're right."

"Okay," Dad said. "Listen, honey, I hate to cut this short, but I have to go. I'm meeting with Momma's doctors in about ten minutes, and I still have to go back to the motel and shave so that I don't look like a grizzly bear."

"Doctors?" I repeated. "Momma has more than one?"

Dad paused. "Well, yes. But it's no reason to get alarmed. It just means that she's getting more help. Okay?"

I had a sinking feeling Dad was purposely leaving things out so I wouldn't get scared. It made me mad. But there was another side of me that didn't want to know, either. *That* made me mad, too. "Yeah," I said. "Okay."

"I love you, Wren," Dad said. "Please try not to worry. I'll be there on Friday and the first thing we'll do is make a family sandwich."

"No," I whispered.

"No?" Dad repeated.

"Not without Momma."

Dad was quiet. "No," he said finally. "You're right. We'll wait for Momma."

Chapter 17

Silver came home a little while later, throwing her blue and silver pom-poms on the kitchen counter. Russell sat up straight as she came into the living room, and looked her over before turning his attention back to the TV. She was dressed in old sweatpants and a T-shirt, and her hair had been pulled up into a ponytail. It swished back and forth behind her head like a very clean, very blonde mop.

"Hey," she said, plopping down on the couch next to me. "What's up?"

"Not much." I was still in my pajamas. After the conversation with Dad about Momma, I'd gone into the living room and sat down on the couch. I hadn't gotten back up. Now, I tucked my bare feet under my legs, praying that Silver wouldn't bring up the underwear issue. But maybe she was waiting for me to thank her. Or to tell her if they fit.

"Your mom went to paint?" I asked instead.

"Oh, yeah," Silver said, leaning her head against the back of the couch. "She's doing a mural or something for a friend's wall. She loves to paint."

"What kind of painting does she do?" Russell asked, without taking his eyes off the TV. He's a bugger, my brother. You can never be sure if he's concentrating on his show, or eavesdropping on one of your conversations.

"Watercolors, mostly. Although she'll do just about anything." Silver pointed to a picture that hung on one of the walls across the room. The reflection of a crescent moon shimmered along a stretch of dark ocean water. Tiny waves curled at the tips with white foam, and if you looked very carefully, you could make out a porpoise fin in the far right-hand corner. "She did that one last year. Down in Florida."

"It's pretty," I said, although I didn't think it was pretty at all. I thought it was spooky looking and a little bit creepy, too.

Russell got up to study the painting. "It's dark," he said after a minute. "How're you supposed to see anything in the dark?"

Silver shrugged. "I guess she saw it in her imagination. She says that's where all her ideas come from."

Russell scowled. Jackson lifted his head as my brother rearranged himself on the floor and then lay back down again.

Silver straightened her legs in front of her. They were as smooth and slender as a deer's. "I don't know if I'm going to stick with cheerleading. I'm not sure if I really like it." She turned and looked at me. "Have you ever been a cheerleader?"

"Me?" I pointed to my chest, trying not to laugh. "No. I'm not exactly the cheerleading type." It was out before I realized what I had said. "I mean . . ." I stammered. "I didn't mean for that to sound the way—"

"No," Silver said. "I think that's exactly what I don't like about it. Because it does make you a *type*. And I don't want to be a *type* of anything. You know?"

I nodded, a little dumbfounded. Didn't Silver know that her beauty and popularity already made her a type? And not just any type, but the highest, most prized type you could be in middle school?

"Although *not* wanting to be a type makes you a certain type anyway, doesn't it?" Silver sounded thoughtful. "Sort of an anti-type, I guess." She blinked. "Do you consider yourself any kind of type?"

I shrugged, reaching for Momma's bird necklace. "I never really thought about it."

"She's a dork type," Russell said, without moving.

I ignored him, zipping the medallion along the silver chain.

Silver giggled. "You're definitely not the dork type."

Really? She didn't think I was a dork? I wondered what type she did think I was.

"I think I'm an animal type," Silver said. "Especially when it comes to horses. I just love them. I think they're amazing."

I didn't say anything. Secretly, though, I thought she was right. Silver did have an uncanny way with animals. The run-in with the wasp in Mr. Tunlaw's room was a perfect example. And I'd never seen anyone ride a horse the way she had last night. It was almost magical.

She stood up and stretched, arching her perfect body into an impossible curve. "You know, the only way Mom could finally convince me that leaving Florida wouldn't be the end of the world was when she told me about Roo and Manchester. She understands how much I need to ride." She pulled a strand of hair between her fingers and studied the ends of it. "Well, I'm going upstairs to shower. And then I'm going to take Manchester out. Why don't you come with me this time? You and Russell can get on Roo together, so it's not so scary. I'm telling you, she's super sweet. Then when we get back, we can all eat that ziti casserole I saw on the counter. My mom makes killer ziti." She pulled the elastic from around her ponytail and shook out her hair. She sounded as if she was making plans to go to the beach.

"We don't really ride horses," I said. "Russell and me, I mean."

"You said that yesterday," Silver said. "But do you think you could just try it? I wouldn't lie to you, Wren. Roo is a total angel. Seriously. Manchester's a little wilder, but Roo is about as relaxed as they come. All she cares about is eating. She'll just walk real slow with you. Come on, it'll be fun!"

My brain started skipping around like crazy. A little part of me felt like I owed Silver because of the whole underwear situation. But the other—much bigger—part of my brain flashed like a red neon stop sign. *DON'T GO*, it blared in my head. *RUN!!!*

"Well," Silver said, grabbing the staircase railing. "Like I said, I'm going to take a quick shower. Just think about it."

I looked over at Russell as Silver disappeared up the stairs. He would be my out. All I had to do was tell Silver that he was afraid of horses again, and being outside in strange places . . .

"What do you think, Russell?" I said.

"Let's go!" Russell said, scrambling to his feet.

I stared at him, aghast.

"We can go on the old fat one!" Russell yelled. "She doesn't have any teeth!"

I groaned and slumped down on the couch. I'd just lost my only out. Now I had to go, or risk looking like a chicken in front of Silver.

"You're annoying," I said, poking Russell with my toe.

"And you're a butt," Russell replied.

I'll take being a butt, I thought, staring out the window. *It's better than being a chicken.*

At least for today.

Chapter 18

I stood on the opposite side of the barn as Silver led Manchester out of his stall. She spoke softly to him the whole time, cupping his pink nose into her palm. I wondered how she had learned to get animals to trust her like that. Had she ever been afraid of them? Or had she been the type of person that always loved them right from the start?

The top of Silver's head came just to the middle of Manchester's neck, and he stood motionless as Silver saddled him and pulled the belt taut around his waist. He really was a beautiful animal. His honey-gold coat gleamed against his shoulder blades, and the black tuft of hair between his ears looked as soft as butter. Thick muscles rippled in the span of chest above his legs, and his tail flicked back and forth like a switch. Silver slipped the harness over his head, and then moved over to the opposite stall, where Roo stood, munching on a wad of straw. Her head hung low between her front legs, and her salt-and-pepper coat was dull. Manchester's eyes were wild and glossy; Roo's had a rheumy quality that gave her an exhausted, worn-out appearance.

"We're gonna ride this one, right?" Russell asked, peering into Roo's stall.

"Yup," Silver said.

"She looks kinda sick today." Russell sounded worried.

I nodded silently in agreement.

Silver laughed and put her lips close to one of Roo's ears. "You hear that, girl? They think you look sick. How 'bout showing them a little bit of the Roo I know?"

At the sound of Silver's voice, Roo lifted her head. Silver stroked the side of her neck and continued talking softly to her. The horse's gray ears perked forward. She stomped one of her back legs, as if just awaking from a dream. And then she lifted her head toward Silver, and nuzzled her neck.

"See? All she needs is a little love," Silver said. "A little extra love and attention. Just like everyone else."

I watched in amazement as Silver moved through the barn, grabbing reins, another saddle, and a pair of stir-rups. *She could probably find her way around this place blindfolded*, I thought. When she was done prepping the horses, she snatched two riding helmets from a corner in the barn and held them out to us.

I took one skeptically. "I thought you said Roo was just going to walk. Why do we have to wear these if she's going to go slow?"

Silver shook her head. "Those are the rules, whether you're walking, running, or sitting. If you're up on a horse, you have to wear a helmet."

Russell pulled his on and snapped the elastic strap around his chin. "Awesome!" He stuck both thumbs up in the air. "I look like *Captain Commando*!"

"You do not," I said, already irritated. "Captain Commando wears a mask, not a riding helmet."

"It's the same thing," Russell said, jabbing me hard in the ribs. "Besides, who asked you?"

Aside from the fact that Russell sometimes made me want to pull my hair out, I was glad to be riding with him. His body might have been small and crammed tightly into the saddle in front of me, but it made me feel less frightened. I tried to keep my eyes looking out in front of us, because every time I looked down at the ground, I thought I might throw up. I gripped the reins between my fingers the way Silver showed me, kept my knees squeezed against both sides of Roo's belly, and concentrated on keeping Russell's hair, which was sticking out like a cactus plant, away from my mouth.

"Now, just follow me." Silver turned all the way around in her saddle, resting her hand on Manchester's haunches as she spoke. She looked so relaxed, so free up there, that for a moment, I almost forgot I was sitting on top of a horse as we started to amble out into the field. Then Roo stumbled. It was a small, jerking movement, probably her foot just tripping over a stone, but it jostled Russell and me in the saddle.

"Whoaahh!" Russell shouted, as I clutched the reins. The horse neighed, startled by the loudness of his voice, and picked up her walking pace.

"Okay now, Russell." Silver waved her hand in his direction. "Remember what I said about making loud noises. Roo gets scared, just like you would if someone shouted in your ear. You have to try not to yell, all right?"

Russell nodded. He was taking this seriously. He had the same expression on his face he got when a brand-new episode of *Captain Commando* came on.

"And Wren?" Silver went on. I looked up, my mouth set in a tight line. "You can let go of those reins a little. Roo's not going to be able to breathe if you pull back like that."

I let go of the reins an inch or so.

"Good," Silver said. "You can rest them in your lap, too, you know. You don't have to hold them all the way up against your chest."

I lowered the reins another inch.

Silver grinned. "Okay." She turned back around in her saddle. "Looks like we're all set." She sat up straighter and made a clicking sound with her mouth. Manchester threw his head up in the air and began to trot.

The high yellow grass in the pasture came up past the horse's legs and brushed the soles of our sneakers. Above us, the sky was pale blue, dotted with cobblestone clouds. The hot sun hung heavy as a pendulum and the air was still as church. This made taking deep breaths a little harder, but I did it anyway. In. Out. In. Out.

"You're breathing on my neck!" Russell said, twisting to glare at me.

I clutched again at the reins. "Russell. Don't turn around in the seat like that. You'll fall."

"Well, quit breathing on me!" Russell said. "It feels like a dragon back there."

We plodded on, making it about halfway through the pasture without anything terrible happening. Every few minutes or so, Roo would give an irritated, exhausted-sounding snort beneath us, but she didn't try to run. She probably didn't have the energy. In front of us, Manchester pranced gaily along, as Silver lifted herself neatly in the saddle. Every so often, as Manchester picked up the pace, Roo's haunches would quiver, almost as if she remembered doing such a thing a long time ago. But then she would drop her head, reaching out to nibble a passing stalk of grass, and meander forward once more.

Silver turned around for the third time to check our progress. "You guys are doing great!" she said. "Are you having fun?"

"No," Russell said flatly. "This is boring."

I poked him in the back when he said that, but secretly I agreed. Now that Roo had proven she was no runner, moving along at a snail's pace was barely more interesting than watching grass grow.

"You can ask her to go a little faster, if you want." Silver raised her eyebrows. "Just squeeze her around the belly with your legs and make a clicking sound with your mouth."

"No, Russell." I spoke in a low voice behind him. "No way."

"Wren says no!" Russell shouted. "She's afraid!"

It took all my energy not to dig my finger into his back.

"It's okay," Silver said. "It's your first time out. It's probably better if you just keep things nice and slow." I could feel her eyes on me. I stared at the back of Russell's head.

Ten more minutes passed. I eyed Silver nervously as we approached the opposite side of the pasture. Not thirty feet ahead of us was the beginning of a trail that led up the west side of Creeper Mountain. Witch Weatherly's side of Creeper Mountain. It was so clotted with dead branches at the front that it was nearly impossible to imagine what lay beyond it, but I could see it perfectly in my mind's eye. A dark, pitted road, edged with claw-sized thorns. Overhead, a carpet made of thickly strung leaves and vines probably blocked even the smallest thread of sunlight. The faint rustle of dry leaves as hornet-head snakes glided beneath them. A raven's shriek in the distance. I shut my eyes to block it out.

"Man!" Silver sounded downright disappointed as she surveyed the bottom of the trail.

"What man?" Russell asked.

"No, I mean, look at that trail." Silver pointed, and shook her head. "I betcha that's the one that leads right up to Witch Weatherly's house. But look at all those branches and thorns! It'd take a weed whacker to get through all that stuff. Maybe even two."

"You're not *s'posed* to go up to Witch Weatherly's house," Russell said. "I even heard your mom say that."

"We shouldn't be this close to the mountain." I hoped Silver couldn't hear the fear in my voice. But really, what was she doing? If she was comfortable going against her mother's rules and heading up to visit Witch Weatherly, that was her problem. But it was another thing entirely for her to drag Russell and me into it. Especially when we were both stuck on top of a horse.

"Oh, I know." Silver sounded distracted. "We won't stay long. I just want to see something." She threw one leg over Manchester and slid off him.

"What're you doing?" My fear was being replaced with anger. Had this been Silver's whole purpose of taking us out here to begin with? Had she staged the whole horse ride just so she could poke around out here? See where it was she needed to go to interview Witch Weatherly? "Silver, come on," I urged. "We should go."

"Wait, I thought I saw something." Silver held up one hand as she moved toward the trail. "Hold on."

Russell glanced back at me and then turned around again. "Don't go in there, Silver! It's bad!"

"Silver," I pleaded. "Please."

"Shhh . . ." She put her fingers to her lips. "I thought I heard . . ."

I held my breath as she moved closer toward the mouth of the trail. Beneath us, Roo chewed noisily, but there was another sound, too . . . Rustling. Something— or someone—was shifting against the leaves. I could smell something like a match being lit and hear the sound of a twig snapping. Suddenly, out of the corner of my eye, I saw a wide red shape flit through the pine trees. It fluttered once, and then disappeared.

"It's the red raven!" I screamed, yanking on Roo's reins. "We have to get out of here! It's going to claw our eyes out!"

Russell popped up in the saddle, nearly falling off. "Where?" he yelled. "I don't see any red raven! Where is it?"

The red shape appeared behind the leaves again, but closer this time, as if moving in for the kill. Slowly, it began to rise, the sharp beak first, followed by the sound of steady flapping. Russell threw his head back and bellowed. I screamed so loud that something in my ear popped and I kicked Roo as hard as I could. The horse reared up wildly and, before either of us had a moment to breathe, took off in a dead run.

Chapter 19

Roo streaked across the pasture, as if someone had taken a branding iron and pressed it against her wide haunches. Her ears were pressed down flat, and her speed seemed to increase the closer she moved toward the barn. Beneath me, I could feel her front and back legs moving in a fluid sort of tandem, just as Manchester's had last night, and I prayed that she wouldn't trip. Silver and Manchester were galloping behind me; I could hear Silver screaming, "Whoa, Roo! Whoa, girl!" and the sound of Manchester's powerful hooves as they got closer and closer.

But Roo paid no attention. She ran as if her life depended on it. She galloped so hard and so fast that the trees on either side of us blurred and the grass beneath our feet disappeared. I forgot about the reins and clutched Russell with both arms, holding on to him for dear life. Russell himself lay nearly flat against Roo's neck, gripping tufts of the horse's mane with a deathlike vise. I shut my eyes and prayed that we would not fall off.

"Whoo-hooo!" I heard suddenly. I opened my eyes. It was Russell. He was still hanging on to Roo's neck, but he had opened his eyes, and the smile across his face was huge. "Look, Wren! We're flying! Just like Captain Commando!" He shut his eyes tight and took a deep breath. "Whoo-*hooooo!*" he screamed.

I grabbed at him with both hands, pulling hard on the waistband of his pants, as if he had tried to stand up on the horse. "Russell! Stop it! We'll fall!"

Almost as if she had heard the warning, Roo stumbled, tripping over the reins that were by now dangling alongside her feet. Before I knew it, Russell and I went flying over her head. For a split second, I saw the blue of the sky, wide and smooth as a robin's egg as it curved over me, and then I fell face first in the grass.

Plunk!

A sharp pain shot through the side of my head.

A split second later, Russell landed next to me. He clambered back up and dusted himself off, then stared as Roo raced on toward the barn. "That was awesome!" he yelled. "Now I really *am* Captain Commando!"

"Would you *stop* it with the stupid Captain Commando?" I shouted, struggling back up to my feet. I was near tears by now, and so frightened that I thought I might faint. The pain along my forehead had turned sharp and it stung as the breeze blew against it. I couldn't even imagine what kind of damage had been done. Brain injuries were the worst.

Manchester flew toward me until Silver pulled on the reins to slow him to a halt. Her face was white. "Are you guys okay?" she asked, swinging down from her saddle.

"Roo's running away!" Russell yelled, pointing.

"She's okay." Silver glanced in the direction of the barn. "She knows how to get back to the barn. She'll just hang out there till we get back." She took a step closer to me. "Wren, did you get hurt? Are you okay?"

I reached up and touched my forehead where the pain still smarted. Something wet and warm brushed against my fingertips. Blood. I was bleeding. I stared at the red smear on my fingers and tried not to throw up. "No, I'm not okay. I'm *bleeding*. I want to go back. *Now*." I glared at Silver with as much dignity as I could muster. "Right now, Silver."

"Can I just see?" she asked softly, stepping closer without waiting for me to answer. I lowered my fingers so that she could look and stared at Manchester's heaving, sweating chest as Silver peered at my forehead. "It's not too bad," she said, wincing. "The blood's actually slowing down. I don't think it's deep." She reached out and fingered Momma's bird necklace.

I lurched back, swatting at her arm. "What are you doing? Don't touch that!"

Silver looked stricken. "It was caught. Around your shirt. I . . . I was just trying to straighten it for you."

I looked down. The necklace was in a crazy knot around the edges of my collar; the tiny bird medallion flung along the side of my neck. I fiddled with it for a minute, and then stuffed it back inside my shirt.

"I'm so sorry about this, Wren," Silver said. "That has never, ever happened before. Roo must've gotten spooked when you guys screamed. Come on. We'll go back and fix you up. It'll be all right."

I shrugged her arm off my shoulder and headed toward the barn. It would *not* be all right. Nothing was all right. And I didn't know if it ever would be again.

~~~~~~

Silver walked Manchester across the rest of the pasture in silence. Russell walked next to her, but I strode ahead, staying at a good distance. The sun was still high overhead, and the shards of sky peeking through the clouds were a watery blue. How could Silver have been so dumb? What was she thinking, bringing us so close to the mountain? My hands trembled at the thought of almost running into Witch Weatherly's red raven. We could have had our eyes pecked out! Been clawed to shreds! Maybe now Silver would start believing everything we'd been telling her. Maybe this would make her stop pooh-poohing all the "stories" about Witch Weatherly.

It wasn't until we were inside the barn that Silver finally spoke again. Her long hair had gotten tangled from the wind and her cheeks were flushed pink. "Listen, guys. Can I ask you not to say anything about this to my mom? I mean, about going near the mountain? She's going to be upset with me enough that you fell off Roo, and I just . . . I don't want her to get all freaked out about the rest. She gets a little nuts when she finds out I've done stuff that she tells me not to."

"Our momma gets freaked out by lots of stuff, too," Russell said.

"Russell." My shoulders sagged. I almost didn't care right now that he was talking about Momma.

"Well, she does!" He glared at me. "She's scared of everything, just like you!"

Silver looked at me with an expression I could not read, almost as if she felt sorry for me. I looked away, furious all over again. "Just drop it, Russell, okay?"

"I can't drop it," Russell said. "I'm not even holding it."

I closed my eyes.

"Anyway," Silver said, hanging a pair of reins on a nail in the wall. "Would you guys mind not saying anything? I mean, could this just sort of be our secret?"

"Secrets are bad," Russell said. "My teacher said."

"Yeah, I know." Silver looked tired all of a sudden. "I just don't want to get into trouble."

"I'll have to think about it," Russell said.

"All right," Silver said. "I guess that's fair."

"Okay, I thought about it," Russell said. "I won't tell. *This* time."

Silver turned to me then, waiting expectantly.

But I turned around, and walked out of the barn without a word.

Chapter 20

Dear Momma,

I wrote later that night after Russell had fallen asleep.

How are you doing? What is the hospital like? Dad said that you have two doctors. I think that is a good thing. Now you will get better twice as fast. Russell and I are doing fine. Russell and Jackson watch Captain Commando every afternoon, and Jackson sleeps right next to his bed at night. I am making sure Russell takes his medicine at night and brushes his teeth, so don't worry.

Aunt Marianne and Silver have two horses named Manchester and Roo. Russell and I got to ride Roo today.

I spun my pencil for a few moments, wondering if I should write about being thrown off. I decided not to. Momma already had enough to worry about.

Aunt Marianne told us that you and she grew up far away from each other. I think that is sad. How come you never told me that before?

I glanced up as a soft knock sounded on my door, and shoved the notebook under my covers. "Yeah?" I whispered.

The door opened a crack. Silver poked her head through. "Can I come in?"

I glanced over at Russell. It was too late to throw the blanket over his head to hide him from view. Besides, he was snoring so loudly that Witch Weatherly could probably hear him. "Okay," I said.

Silver was wearing little shortie pajamas in yellow with white trim. Her bare legs stuck out of them like string beans, and her toenails were painted purple. If she thought it was weird that Russell was in bed with me, she didn't let on. Instead, she just sat down on the floor and hugged her knees to her chest.

"I just wanted to apologize again for everything that happened today." She fiddled with her toes while she spoke. "I mean, I know the whole thing kind of freaked you out and I guess I just feel responsible. You know, since I sort of pushed you to come with me and everything."

"It's okay." I waved my hand casually, as if I was totally over it. Which, in a weird sort of way, was almost the truth. I wasn't talking about the red raven, of course, and the cut on my head still stung a little, but that afternoon, after I had stormed out of the barn and lay down on my bed, I realized that I had actually ridden a horse. I had ridden a *running* horse. And yes, I had been thrown off, but I had also lived. I was not in a wheelchair. I had not broken a bone. It was kind of amazing, when I stopped to think about it. And sort of cool, too.

"Thanks for not saying anything to my mom, either," Silver said. "I mean, about going near the mountain."

I'd surprised myself when Aunt Marianne had pushed for information after seeing the Band-Aid on my forehead. Why had Roo started running in the first place? And how had she been able to run so far? Where had we been? I let Silver do most of the talking, nodding in agreement as she explained that Roo had been startled by a squirrel and then bolted. Being near the mountain hadn't come up at all. After the conversation was over, and Aunt Marianne was sure I was okay, the whole thing was dropped. It hadn't seemed important.

Silver ran a hand through her bangs and then let them fall against her forehead. "I still can't believe Roo took off like that. I didn't even know she had it in her to run that fast. You guys really spooked her."

I looked at her, dumbfounded that she really didn't get what had happened. "It wasn't the yelling," I said. "She got spooked by the red raven. Didn't you see it coming out of the bushes?"

"I saw *something* red," Silver said. "It moved, but when I tried to get closer, that's when Roo went nuts."

"She's not nuts," I said. "She's smart." *Smarter than you*, I thought. *At least she had the sense to run away when she sensed danger.*

"Do you really think it was the red raven?" Silver asked.

"Of course it was. Other people have seen it, Silver. Lots of times. I know you don't think that a lot of the things you've heard about Witch Weatherly are real, but I'm telling you, they are. The red raven definitely is."

Silver studied me for a moment, as if trying to figure out whether or not to believe me. "Okay," she said finally. "So maybe the red raven is real. But how much of all the rest of it is true? I mean, Dylan and Jeremy made it sound like Witch Weatherly doesn't even have a face!"

"I believe all of it," I whispered. "It's a legend, Silver, that goes way, way back. Legends are real."

"Not all the time." She folded her knees back up. "I mean, when stories are passed down like that, don't you think some people forget some of the details? Or exaggerate?"

"Not when it comes to Witch Weatherly." I shook my head. "She's one hundred percent for real, Silver. I'm telling you. People around here know."

"Well." Silver tilted her head to one side. "Maybe you're right." I knew she still didn't believe me. But I didn't care. Besides, it didn't matter what I thought. I wasn't the one about to throw all common sense out the front door and run up Creeper Mountain to meet Witch Weatherly. She was.

"I wish it was already summer vacation," she said suddenly. "School is so boring."

I looked at her curiously. "What was school like in Florida? Did you like it there?"

She shrugged. "It was all right."

"Were you popular?"

"Popular?" She smiled a little bit. "No, I wouldn't say popular."

"Not like here, huh?"

"What do you mean?"

"Silver." I shook my head, amazed and irritated at the same time. "Don't you know how popular you are at our school? And pretty?"

She sighed. I waited for her to say something totally airheaded like, *Do you really think I'm pretty?*

Instead, Silver Jones said, "I don't think I know anything anymore."

"What do you mean?"

She shrugged, picking at a scab on her knee. "I don't

know. A lot of things feel kind of messed up right now. I'm just trying to figure it all out."

"What kinds of things?" I asked.

She bit the inside of her cheek as her fingernail caught the underside of the scab shell on her knee. A tiny drop of blood emerged from underneath it. She winced, closed one eye, and yanked. "Like why my dad doesn't call me anymore," she said, exhaling. We both stared at the thin rivulet of blood dripping down the front of her leg. I leaned over, grabbed a tissue off the little nightstand next to the bed, and held it out to her. She pressed it hard against the wound.

I thought fast. "Maybe he just doesn't have your number up here yet."

"We've been here for more than two months," Silver said. "He has it. He's called my mom a few times about money." She shrugged. "I just . . . I don't know what I did to make him not want to call me."

"Why do you think *you* did anything?"

She stared down at the tissue. A large red dot was beginning to seep through the other side. "It's gotta be something. There's a reason he's not calling."

"When's the last time you talked to him?"

"The day we left Florida," she whispered.

I struggled not to let my mouth drop open. I hadn't talked to Momma in four days and already it felt like a lifetime. I couldn't imagine not talking to her for two whole months. I'd probably lose my mind. "Wow," I whispered. "That is a long time." A moment passed as I gathered my courage. "Why don't you call *him*?"

"I did, once." Silver's face looked so sad that I almost reached out for her hand. "I just got his voice mail. I tried to leave a message . . ." She stopped, letting the thought drift off between us. "But after I said the word *Dad*, I didn't know what else to say. So I hung up."

"Maybe he didn't get the message. You know, because it was so short. Maybe you hung up too quick."

Silver gave me a look that said, *Please stop saying dumb things just to make me feel better.* My cheeks felt hot. It was a stupid thing to say. But I didn't know what else to tell her.

"Aren't adults the ones that are supposed to have everything together?" Silver shook her head. "I mean, they've had their whole *lives* to figure things out. It's not fair that they still get to act like jerks sometimes. Especially when it comes to us." Her face darkened. "The whole thing just sucks."

Our situations weren't the same, but for a moment, I thought I might understand what Silver meant. I knew what it was like to want a parent to be there. To *really* be there, instead of drifting in and out of the shadows the way Momma did all the time. Even before Grandpa William died, it was as if she was living half her life with us and the other half somewhere else. Maybe it felt that way for Silver, too. Most of her life was spent with Aunt Marianne. But there was another part of it—a big part—

that wanted the other half there, too. The dad half. She deserved to have both, just as I did.

"Yeah," I said softly. "I know."

The shadows from Russell's night-light flickered against the wall, and I could hear a rustling sound as the wind blew the leaves outside. Silver lifted the bloody tissue off her knee one last time, and peered at the raw, pink skin beneath. The bleeding had stopped. She tossed the tissue into the trash and then looked at me. "You know, Wren, if things ever get too hard with your mom being away right now . . ." She hesitated, and looked back down at her knee. "I mean, you can come hang out with me if you want. You know, in my room."

"Thanks."

"You're welcome." She stood up. Her eyes traveled over Russell's small, lumpy shape, and her face softened. "You're a really good sister."

I blinked, feeling a little stunned. "Thanks," I said again.

"Okay, well, good night."

"Good night."

I stared at the door for a long time after Silver left. Then I took my notebook back out from under the covers. But instead of finishing the letter to Momma, I held the notebook against my chest and lay back down again, staring up at the ceiling.

Dad had told me once that I should never judge a book by its cover, but I don't think I really understood what he meant until just that moment. It was strange how people could turn out to be so much different from what you first thought of them. Stranger, too, how those differences could also be so much like yours.

My eyes grew heavy and then closed, and I fell asleep like that, still holding Momma's letter against my heart.

Chapter 21

Aunt Marianne, Silver, and Russell were already sitting around the kitchen table when I came down the next morning. "Hey there." Silver put her glass of orange juice down and grinned. "Perfect timing. We were just about to start talking about what we wanted to do today." She scooted over a little on the bench she was sitting on. "Here, have a seat."

I sat down next to her, hoping I didn't have morning breath. Aunt Marianne was preoccupied at the stove, stirring something in a frying pan. A pair of reading glasses were perched atop her head, and she was wearing an apron dotted with pink owls.

"Hey, Wren, it's Windy Sunday!" Russell wiped his mouth with the back of his hand, and then rapped on the table to get Silver's and Aunt Marianne's attention. "What's Windy Sunday again, you guys?"

"Windy Sunday means that one of us gets to pick whatever we want to do today," Silver said, "no matter how crazy it seems. Sort of like letting the wind take us in whatever direction it wants to blow. Mom and I do it every week." She looked over at Aunt Marianne. "Right, Mom?"

Aunt Marianne turned around from the stove, one hand on her hip. "Yes, that's right," she said. "Who would like to pick what we do today?"

Russell's hand shot up. "Me!"

"Of course." I sighed.

Russell scowled. "What's wrong with me?"

Aunt Marianne laughed. "Nothing's wrong with you, Russell. In fact, I was going to ask you if you would like to be the one to pick. Maybe Wren can do it next Sunday."

Silver looked over at me and raised an eyebrow.

"Sure," I said, although I couldn't possibly imagine what I would pick.

"Okay, Russell," Silver said. "It's all you. What would you like to do today?"

"I want to go skydiving!" Russell shouted.

Aunt Marianne and Silver looked at each other.

"It has to be reasonable, Russell," I said. "We don't know how to skydive."

"Silver said *any*thing." Russell glowered at me. "And that's what I want to do."

Aunt Marianne bit her lower lip. "Your sister's right, sweetheart. It can be anything that we already know how to do." Her eyes skittered around the top of the table, the way Momma's sometimes did when she was thinking fast. "Last Sunday, for example, Silver wanted to eat breakfast in the tree outside. So we made really big egg-and-cheese biscuits and poured our orange juice into a thermos, and we climbed the tree outside and ate our meal up in the branches! Would you like to do something like that?"

"No," Russell said. "That's stupid."

"Russell!" I yanked his pajama sleeve. "Mind your manners! No blankety-blanks."

But Aunt Marianne and Silver just laughed. "That's exactly it, Russell," Silver said. "It can be stupid or dumb or silly, just like you said. The point is that *you* get to pick. And no matter what anyone else says or thinks, we all have to do it." There was a pause. "Except for things that we don't know how to do. Like skydiving."

Russell made growling sounds for a few moments. He kicked the underside of the kitchen table and fiddled with his Captain Commando figurine. I could feel the back of my neck start to get hot as everyone waited.

"I want to go in a plane," he said finally. "Just to sit."

My heart fell as I began to anticipate the next scene Russell would throw. Sitting in a plane was just as impossible as skydiving. Sudbury didn't even have an airport.

Aunt Marianne opened her mouth to say something and then shut it again. Without warning, her eyes lit up and she clapped her hands. "That's a great idea, Russell!" she said. "And I know just the place we can go!"

"Where?" Silver asked.

Something was cutting off the air in the back of my throat. She wasn't serious, was she?

"Come on!" Aunt Marianne stood up. "I'll show you!"

Who knew Sudbury had an airport? It wasn't a real airport, of course, or at least not like the ones I'd seen on TV, with the gigantic jet planes and endless runways. This airport was in the middle of a huge field. A slightly weedy runway cut down the middle of it, and off to one side, in a very small hangar, were four airplanes. Actually, even the word *airplane* was debatable, in my opinion. None of the pieces of junk inside looked like they could get to the end of the runway, let alone lift up into the sky.

"This is a glider airport," Aunt Marianne explained as she parked Old Betsy. "It's the only one in four counties. Before Grandma Ruthie and I moved to California, we used to come here all the time with Grandpa William. He was a glider pilot."

She waved at someone as we got closer to the hangar. An older man dressed in a denim jumpsuit and a baseball cap ambled toward us, wiping his hands on an oil-stained rag. "I know that's not little Marianne Woodbine," he said. His voice was low and gravelly.

"Pete Moses!" Aunt Marianne beamed. "It's me, all right! And look at you! Exactly the same, right down to your Red Sox cap!" Mr. Moses wrapped his arms around Aunt Marianne, laughing and smacking her hard on the back. I snuck a look over at Silver. She didn't seem embarrassed at all. In fact, she was grinning.

"We're here for the planes," Russell demanded. "Where are they?"

"Just gliders here, little man," Mr. Moses said, still holding Aunt Marianne around the waist. "No airplanes."

Russell's eyebrows narrowed. "But I said I wanted to go in a *plane*. Not a glider."

"Oh, a glider is very much a plane, Russell," Aunt Marianne said. "It just doesn't have a motor."

"How does it get up in the sky then?" Russell asked.

"A little plane has to pull it up into the sky with a big cable," Aunt Marianne said. "And then once they're both up high enough, and the wind is just right, it lets it go."

"And then it just hangs there?" I looked at Aunt Marianne incredulously. "How can it do that? What if it falls?"

Aunt Marianne smiled and looked at Mr. Moses. "Gliders depend on two things," he said, holding up his first and second fingers. "Its wings, which are shaped especially for flying, and the air."

"So it has magic wings?" Russell's eyes were huge.

"No, not quite magic," Mr. Moses said. "I've got one over here that's just about to go out. Come on and look." The four of us traipsed inside the hangar after Mr. Moses. He had heavy work boots on that reminded me of Dad, and his eyebrows were thick and bristly.

Inside the building, an enormous glider was parked off to one side. With its long, narrow body, and sleek wingspan, it looked like a plane, except more modest. There was no row of windows, no fancy tail wings or lights. In fact, it was almost like someone had started to build a plane—and then stopped.

Mr. Moses pointed to the wings. "See how these babies are curved a little at the tip?" he asked. "That's because gliders need to catch as much air as possible once they're up there. The more air the glider catches, and the better the air itself is, the longer it can stay up. Completely on its own."

"Wow," Russell breathed. "Just like Captain Commando!"

"Can they sit inside, Pete?" Aunt Marianne clasped her hands together in front of her, almost as if she was about to beg. "Just for a little bit?"

"I'll do you one better," Mr. Moses said. "I've got a guy coming over in about ten minutes to take this one out. He can only fit one passenger in at a time, but I bet he'd be happy to take them up for a few practice runs."

"Really?" Silver sounded awestruck and overjoyed at the same time.

"Yesssss!" Russell's fist shot up into the air. "I've *always* wanted to go into a real plane!"

Somehow, I managed to retrieve my voice, which had plummeted down around my belly button. "Russell, no," I said. "You should really just do something like that with Dad. And I don't even know if he would . . ."

"Dad's not here," Russell interrupted. "And this guy said I could. And he's in charge of the whole *airport*."

"Russell." I put both hands on his shoulders and leaned in close. He had to understand the seriousness of this. This wasn't a game. It wasn't even riding a horse. This was serious. Ten-thousand-feet-in-the-air serious. Momma had told me countless times how dangerous planes were. Especially after 9-11. It was why she never took them, why she'd spend three days traveling across the country in a train to get to Arizona. People died in planes every day. Every. Single. Day. It was just too risky. "Listen, you can't, okay?" I said. "You just can't. Not today."

"You're not the boss of me." Russell looked over at Aunt Marianne. "Is she?"

Aunt Marianne cleared her throat. She looked over at Silver, as if hoping she might give her some advice, but Silver didn't say a word. "Russell, honey. The plan was just to *sit* in the plane. Why don't we keep it at that?"

"We got some passengers today?" a voice boomed out behind us.

We turned around and saw a man striding toward us holding a pilot's cap. He was much younger than Mr. Moses and had a head of bright red hair.

"Me!" Russell hopped up and down as the man got closer. "I'm a passenger! I'm going with you!"

"Russell," I tried again, pulling him to one side, and lowering my voice. "You *cannot* go up there by yourself. What if you get scared? What if you start to feel frustrated? You can't kick anything in that plane like you do

156

down here. If you get freaked out, there's nowhere for you to go. Do you understand me?"

"But I *won't*." Russell was pleading with me now. "Come on, Wren. Stop being such a poop-head."

"If you want to go with him, you can." I looked over nervously, hoping the man was addressing someone else, but he was speaking directly to me. "The seat back there only holds one, but you're about as wide as a beanpole. I bet we could fit both of you into it, and still have some room to spare."

My heart missed a beat. The only thing scarier than the thought of Russell going up there alone was me going up there with him.

I wasn't ready for that.

Not now, or ever.

"Go ahead, Wren." Aunt Marianne was looking at me encouragingly. "You'll love it. I flew in the glider a hundred times as a kid. It'll be one of the best experiences of your life."

"Try it, Wren!" Silver nodded her head behind her mother. "And then when they're done, can I go?" she asked.

"Absolutely," said the pilot.

And just like that, things started moving. I didn't have time to protest, and even if I did, I doubt anyone would have heard me. Russell and I were helped into a space the size of a shoebox, directly behind the pilot's chair. We sat side by side on the glider's single passenger seat, which left about a quarter of an inch of room, and even less than that for my knees. Russell plastered himself against the tiny window, and began to smack it with his hands. "Yeehawwww!" he screamed. "I'm going flying! For real!"

I snatched at his hands, stricken. "Russell! Stop it! You're going to break the window!" My voice was trembling. I was hot. Nauseated, too. What if—after the glider crashed, and Russell and I were killed—I threw up in front of everyone? What then?

Russell paused then and looked at me. "You're sweating." He pointed to my forehead, and then jabbed at my upper lip. "There, and there. You're sweating. What's wrong?"

Where could I start? I looked away, blinking back tears.

Russell put his arm around me as the plane began to pull our small aircraft out of the hangar. I craned my neck, trying to get a glimpse of the cord attached to the plane, but it was too far out front. Russell patted me lightly on the back, and kept patting me, over and over. Like a hundred times. "I'm right here, Wren," he said. "It's me. So don't worry, okay? It's just a little glider plane, Wren. That's all it is. We're going to be perfectly okay."

I kept my eyes closed as our pilot began to talk. "We'll be up in the air in about thirty seconds. Pete just needs to get the plane in front of us to pick up a little more speed."

Beneath us, I could feel the single wheel beneath the

belly of the glider moving faster. The sides of the glider began to tremble. "Russell," I whispered.

"Move over more," Russell ordered. "You're stepping on my foot."

I lifted my foot without opening my eyes, and pushed my face into the soft leather seat.

"Okay!" the pilot said up front. "Here we go!"

Russell's arm was still around me. I could feel his fingers squeeze my shoulder, his nails digging into my skin. I almost screamed as the glider tipped up, pushing Russell and me farther back into the seat.

"One thousand feet," the pilot said into a small headset.

"One thousand's nothing," Russell muttered. "I want to go to a million feet. A *zillion*."

"Russell, don't talk." I was holding my breath now, squeezing his other hand so tight that I was sure he was going to hit me at any second.

Instead, my brother said, "Why're you squeezing your eyes, Wren? Don't close your eyes! You're missing all of it!"

I ignored him, aware only of the lightness in my head, the whooshing sound in my ears, and the odd, hollow sensation in my belly. My breathing began to come in short gasps, and the hair on my scalp prickled.

"Holy cow!" Russell sounded genuinely awestruck. "Holy Captain Commando!"

"Two thousand feet," the pilot said. "Take a look, you two. It's not every day you get to see the world from up here."

Russell poked me right in the cheek. "You gotta look, Wren. You *gotta* look."

Slowly, I peeled one eye open. Then the other. I forced an eyeball to the left, just barely peeking out of the window. My head turned a quarter of an inch. Then a half inch. I leaned forward just a little so that I could bring my eyes into focus.

It was hard to pinpoint exactly when my breathing started to slow, or when I stopped sweating. Actually, I might not have stopped sweating at all. But something did pause and then settle just the tiniest bit when I looked out at the view below, a patchwork of green-and-yellow fields punctuated every so often by a red or white silo. Blue swimming pools the size of dominoes gleamed up at us, and ribbons of highway, smooth as silk, meandered in and out of the lush countryside. It was so quiet up here. So quiet and beautiful.

"It's like what birds see," Russell sounded mesmerized. "Right, Wren? Birds?"

"Uh-huh." For a single, ridiculous second, I wondered if birds ever felt afraid when it came to flying. Was there ever some little runt who just didn't have it in him the way his brothers and sisters did, who hovered fearfully at the lip of the nest, staring down at the enormous expanse below? And if there was, what did it do? How did it learn to let go one day and fly?

"Look over this way, Wren!" Russell said.

I peeked over the top of Russell's head. There was the mall, or at least what I thought was the mall, with its huge conglomeration of tan buildings shoved in tightly together and enormous expanse of empty parking lots. And there, on the other side of the highway, was the Susquehanna River, no wider now than a Tootsie Roll, its sludgy blue water the color of mud. Farther ahead was someone's cornfield, the edges of it cut sharply like a square, and to the left of it, a gigantic mountaintop, which rose up into the sky in a sea of trees.

My heart lurched as I looked at it again. Was that Creeper Mountain? It was hard to know from all the way up here. I stared at it again, waiting, perhaps, for Witch Weatherly to appear all of a sudden at the very tip-top, her red raven perched on her shoulder, shaking her fist at us. But there was nothing to see except a slew of tall pines, which bent and swayed in the wind like feathers. And then suddenly I caught sight of it: the ever-present thread of white smoke, which twined its way up through the trees and then disappeared into the air above them. My fingers trembled against Russell's as we passed over the top of it, and then moved on, erasing it from view.

"Man, oh man," Russell breathed. "Windy Sundays are one of the best things ever." He squeezed my hand again. "Don't you think so, Wren?"

I didn't answer, still clutching the edge of my little brother's shirt as the glider tilted to one side and then turned around, leading us back home again. All I could think about was getting back down to the airport in one piece and putting my feet down on solid ground. But another little part of me was still wondering about those baby birds. Was the answer really as simple as I guessed it might be? Could it be that the only way they learned to fly was to tiptoe up to the very edge of the nest?

And then jump?

Chapter 22

"Mr. Tunlaw's supposed to be back today," Silver said, climbing into the back of Old Betsy the next morning. "Did you pick your history topic yet?"

It was Monday. Only four more days and then Dad would be back to take Russell and me to the Hot Spot so that he could tell us what was really going on with Momma and how she was doing. Russell and Aunt Marianne sat up front, deeply immersed in conversation. I took a bite of my breakfast: a banana smeared with peanut butter.

"I was thinking I might do it on the Liberty Bell," I said. This was an outright lie. I still had no idea what my history project was going to be on, nor had I given it a passing thought since Friday. Come to think of it, I hadn't even finished my math homework last night. I was still trying to recover from the weekend, first with the phone call from Dad, then the accident with Roo, and finally the plane ride on Windy Sunday. I was lucky I was still upright.

"Huh." Silver's voice sounded forced. "The Liberty Bell. That should be interesting." She looked past me for a split second, and then leveled her eyes with mine. "What're your friends doing their projects on?"

"My friends?"

"You know, those two girls you always sit with at lunch? What are they doing their history projects on?"

She was talking about Nora and Cassie, I realized. She thought they were my friends. Which they were, I guessed. Maybe. "I don't know what they're doing," I said, looking out the window.

"You haven't asked them?" Silver pressed.

"No, not yet."

She took a bite of her granola bar and chewed thoughtfully. "Are you working with either of them on it?"

"No," I said. "I don't think Mr. Tunlaw would let me work with someone from another class. Besides, I don't really like working with anyone. I'd rather do my own thing."

Silver nodded, as if she understood such a thing perfectly and didn't say any more.

Miss Crumb's blackboard question in English made me scowl:

If you could take back anything you've ever said to anyone, what would it be?

It wasn't that it wasn't a good question. It was a very good question. It was just that it made me think about something that I would have much rather not ever thought of again, something that created an actual physical pain in my stomach whenever I was reminded of it.

For Momma's birthday last year, Dad threw her a surprise party. Because of work, he'd missed her birthday the year before, and he wanted to make it up to her in a big way. Four of Momma's friends were coming, and some of them were bringing their husbands, too. Dad had invited a few of his own friends just to round things out, and Grandma was supposed to arrive early that morning. Russell and I helped Dad for weeks before the big day, going with him to Party City to pick out balloons and fancy decorations, and helping him order all of Momma's favorite dishes from Vincenzo's, which was her favorite Italian restaurant in town. Dad put me in charge of the cake, which he was going to get from the bakery. He said I could decorate it with Momma's favorite colored sprinkles and put all the candles on.

Each night, for two weeks before the party, Dad would ask Russell and me if we wanted to go for a walk with him after dinner. Just in case Momma was watching, Dad and I would meander slowly down our street, acting casual and disinterested as Russell gunned on ahead on his black Hot Wheels bike. But as soon as we turned the corner, Dad would pull his hands out of his pockets and start waving them around. His eyes lit up as he talked about who else was coming to the party, or what kind of cake he'd decided to order. I skipped along next to him, trying to keep up, while Russell pedaled furiously around the corner. But the faster Dad talked, the faster he walked. I'd never seen him so excited about anything in my whole life.

On the morning of the party, he came in to my bedroom and kissed me awake. "Tonight's the big night." His eyes were shining in the dark. "Everything's all set, right? You can't think of anything we missed?"

I shook my head. "She's gonna love it, Dad. You've worked so hard."

"*We've* worked so hard." He squeezed my hand. "I couldn't have done it without you, butterbean."

I nodded, my heart bursting.

"I'll see you tonight, all right? You know what to do. Don't be late!"

"I won't," I said. "Bye, Dad. I love you."

My job was to take Momma out for a walk that night and then bring her back to the house where everyone would be waiting to surprise her. I was worried about the time, so I led her to the park at the end of our street where we sat on the swings. It was dusk. The light was soft and silvery, almost as if you could put your hand inside it and pull out a little piece of cloud. Momma sat on one of the swings and drifted back and forth. She had a dreamy expression on her face, not quite sad, but not quite happy, either. Well, I thought to myself, that was about to change. By the time I led Momma back to the house, my heart was banging so loudly inside my chest it felt like someone was playing kick the can in there.

Momma didn't seem to notice the unusual number of cars parked out on the sidewalk, or the fact that the blinds had been drawn across the front bay window. I held on to the back of her shirt as she turned the doorknob, and was so excited by this point that I thought I might fall over.

"SURPRISE!"

Dad stood in the middle of everyone, holding Momma's cake, a beautiful three-tiered double chocolate cake with buttercream frosting. There were roses on top, big as lemons, and small lattice designs on the sides. And, of course, Momma's favorite sprinkles, a combination of blue and pink sugar stars. Dad's face beamed over the glow of all the candles, but Momma's face turned white. Her mouth formed a little O shape and something like a scream came out of it. Still clinging to the doorknob, she sank to the floor and pressed her hand against her chest. At first I thought she was crying tears of joy. But as a few seconds went by and her cries turned to sobs, I realized that something was terribly wrong.

Dad put the cake down and ran over, gathering her in his arms. Everything got quiet as he held Momma and rocked her back and forth. She was shaking all over. "It's okay," he kept saying over and over again. "It was a surprise. I'm sorry, I didn't realize . . . Everything's all right. Everything's fine now."

Russell tiptoed over and stood a little ways from her. "Get up now, Momma!" he demanded. "Come on! We have cake! And food from Vinny's!"

Momma's skin was too pale, and her fingertips trembled, but she got up. I watched as she dried her eyes and blew her nose and laughed with everyone about having been so frightened. Silly her. She didn't know what had gotten into her, carrying on in such a way. Those nerves of hers! She hugged me tightly, and told me how sorry she was that she had made such a fuss. The party went on. Momma's friends brought her beautiful presents, and everyone sang "Happy Birthday" when Dad served the cake.

But as the night wore on, after the excitement died down, things shifted again. I could tell Dad noticed it, too. He served the food from Vincenzo's with a big smile on his face, and ladled Grandma's ice-cream punch from her enormous crystal bowl into each of the matching crystal cups. He even led a conga line around the dining room table after Russell turned the stereo on. But Dad's eyes kept skittering over to Momma who kept fiddling with a loose strand of her long hair, and rubbing her blemished hands. Her face, even with all the beaming people around, would suddenly revert again into another sad, glossed-over stare, as if she was thinking about something else completely. Dad looked heartbroken.

Later, much later, after everyone had gone home, and Momma and Dad were sitting on the couch eating another piece of cake, Momma stretched out her arms as I walked by. "Come here, sweetie, and give me one more birthday kiss."

"No." I kept walking.

Her arms dropped. I could feel her eyes on me, but I didn't slow down.

"Wren?" Dad asked.

"You ruined it," I said, turning around suddenly and looking straight at her. "You ruined the whole party."

Momma's blue eyes widened. "How? Because I got scared when everyone yelled?"

"Scared?" I turned on her. "You weren't scared. You *freaked*! Crying and acting like a crazy person!" My voice was starting to rise, but I didn't care.

Dad stood up. "Wren Baker," he said sternly.

"No!" I yelled. "It's not fair! You have no idea how much work Dad did for your party! Weeks and weeks of work! Just to make you happy! And you went and ruined it because of your stupid nerves! Why are you even like that? What's *wrong* with you?"

Momma sat there speechless, as I turned and ran from the room.

We never spoke of that conversation again. But now, in Miss Crumb's class, as I thought about that day, I realized I would give anything to be able to take my words back.

Every single one of them.

Chapter 23

Except for a slightly pale face, on his first day back, Mr. Tunlaw looked pretty much like he always did. Short sleeves, an orange-and-green striped tie, his blue cowboy boots. A fresh box of Twinkies, already opened, lay on his desk next to a wilting plant, and a discarded wrapper sat next to it.

"Hey, gang!" he said as we all got in our seats. "It's good to see you! Good to be back!"

Everyone just stared at him. I wondered if he remembered that he had taken off his pants in front of all of us and danced around the room like a maniac. Maybe getting stung by wasps caused amnesia in some people.

Jeremy raised his hand.

"Yes, Jeremy?"

"Did you get stung on your butt?"

Silver shot him a disgusted look as the rest of the class laughed, but Mr. Tunlaw just nodded and smiled. "Actually," he said, "I got stung five times on my rear and eight times on my chest."

"Thirteen stings!" Dylan said. "Mr. Pringle said you'd only been stung six times!"

"Those were just the ones they were able to see," Mr. Tunlaw said. "It wasn't until I stopped breathing that they realized there had been a lot more."

The class fell silent. It was obvious that Mr. Tunlaw had been through a terrible ordeal. Jeremy looked down at his desk. Dylan coughed once and let out a nervous laugh.

"It's all right, though." Mr. Tunlaw began to walk around the room. "Everything worked out, and I'm good as new. Now let's get back to work. I'm very excited to hear what your history projects are all about."

I began to spin my pencil as Mr. Tunlaw went around the room, calling on students by row. Dylan and Jeremy were going to work together on a project about the history of coal mining. Sarah Byrnes and Mandy Dunkin were teaming up on a project about the Amish people. With each topic, Mr. Tunlaw nodded and wrote something down in a notebook on top of his desk.

"How about you, Silver?" he asked.

"I've definitely decided to do mine on Witch Weatherly," Silver said, sidling a glance in my direction.

Heads began to shake around the room.

"Have you talked to your parents about this?" Mr. Tunlaw asked.

"Oh yeah." Silver shot me a guilty look. "My mom's fine with it."

Mr. Tunlaw regarded Silver with an odd expression, as if deliberating whether or not to argue with her. Finally, he shrugged. "I don't know how safe it is, Silver, but if your mother's given you permission, I'll let you give it a shot. If you can get up there, and find some interesting historical facts about Sudbury from Ms. Weatherly, then you've got a deal. But if it's too difficult to climb the mountain, or she refuses to talk to you, you're going to have to change your topic. Deal?"

"Deal," Silver said. "Thanks, Mr. Tunlaw."

Deal? He was just going to let Silver try to claw her way up Creeper Mountain? Even if she got through the ridiculously thorny underbrush, there were still the pits filled with sharpened sticks and the abundance of hornet-head snakes to worry about. And what about the red raven? None of this sounded anything like a deal to me.

"That just leaves you, Wren." Mr. Tunlaw nodded at me.

"Oh." I stopped spinning my pencil and thought fast. "I was, um . . . I thought maybe I'd do it on the Liberty Bell."

"Perfect." Mr. Tunlaw wrote it down. "All right, that's everyone." He closed his notebook and stood up. "Papers are due on Friday. Now let's talk about the sources I'd like you to use, and what kinds of information you can get from the Internet."

I didn't know anything about the Liberty Bell.

And I couldn't imagine wanting to, either.

Standing in the middle of the lunchroom holding my tray, I tried desperately to look like I knew where I was going. Which, of course, I didn't. Everywhere I turned, the lunch tables were full. There was one in the corner, right under the poster of LeBron James drinking a carton of milk, that looked as if it might have a few empty seats, but the band kids took up half of it. I didn't really want to sit at the band table, especially since last week three of them had gotten into a food fight, hurling spoonfuls of mashed potatoes across the cafeteria. Silver's table was completely filled with boys. And I couldn't sit with Nora and Cassie. After walking away from them on Friday, I was almost one hundred percent sure we weren't friends. I didn't really want to sit with them anyway. They were spiteful and rude, and—

"Wren!" Cassie was standing up at our table, waving to me. "Come sit with us!"

I hurried over, thankful not to keep standing there like an idiot, and doubly relieved that I was not going to be seen eating alone at the other end of the band table.

"Hey!" Nora had a bright smile plastered across her face. Blue-and-green beaded earrings cascaded from her earlobes. "How are you, Wren?"

"I'm okay." I picked up my chicken soft taco and took

a bite. Maybe they'd forgotten about everything. Maybe things were okay after all. "How're you guys?"

"We're good!" Nora said. "You seriously should've come with us to that movie, though. It was amazing."

"Yeah," Cassie agreed. "*So scary.*" She looked at me curiously. "You look different."

"I do?"

"Yeah," Cassie said. "You do. I can't figure it out, though."

"Oh wait, I know," Nora said. "It's that Band-Aid on her head." She leaned in closer to me. "What happened? Did you get into a fight with your new best friend?"

My jaw froze in the middle of a chew. We weren't still friends at all. They just wanted to make fun of me. To dig the knife in a little deeper.

"No," I said, getting up out of my seat. "But you and I might, if you don't stop being so mean."

Wait, had *I* just said that? And if I had, where had it come from?

Nora jumped out of her own seat. "Are you threatening me?"

I walked away. Fast. It was already bad enough that I'd said what I did, but the last thing I wanted was to get into a fight in front of the whole school.

"We don't want you sitting here anymore!" Cassie called after me. "Like, ever!"

"Don't worry." I turned around. "I was thinking the same thing."

I almost laughed at the expression that came over Nora's face. But I turned back around instead and dumped my tray into the garbage. *Even Roo would turn up her nose at those chicken tacos*, I thought, making my way toward the cafeteria door. So I didn't have a table to sit at during lunch anymore. I'd just go hang out in the bathroom until the bell rang.

Silver's table was right near the doors. She grinned when she saw me approaching, and then stood up as I kept going. "Wren, wait!"

I paused, shifting my backpack on my shoulder as Silver hurried over to me. She was still holding a piece of chicken taco. "I was just going to come over to your table. Can you meet me in the library after the final bell? I want to show you something."

"What is it?" I asked, trying to ignore Jeremy's stare across the table.

"I don't want to say here," Silver lowered her voice. "Can you come?"

"Don't you have cheerleading?"

"I'm skipping," Silver whispered. "Don't tell." She looked down, and then tossed the last of her chicken taco into the garbage can by the door. "This food stinks," she said, grimacing. "Do you like it?"

"I hate it."

"I'm going to ask my mom to start packing us lunches. That okay with you?"

"Yeah." I tried not to smile. "That's fine with me."

"Three o'clock." Silver pointed at me as she walked backward. "Library. Okay?"

"Okay," I said. "See you then."

I could see Nora and Cassie staring at us from across the cafeteria.

Good. Let them look.

Chapter 24

I walked slowly down the hall after the final bell rang. I didn't use the school library very often, and I wasn't all that anxious to get there. Miss Snow, the librarian, gave me the willies. She had about a million rules, and she screamed if you broke any of them. I heard her rip into a little sixth grader once for chewing gum, and the poor girl started crying. I don't need that kind of stress.

Silver sat near the back in front of a computer at one of the library's round wooden tables. She'd fastened her hair up in one of her plastic clips, and her lips were shiny with gloss. The air around her smelled like watermelon.

"Hey," I said softly.

"Oh, hi." She nodded at the seat next to her, her fingers still moving across the computer keyboard. "Can you sit down for a minute?"

"Sure." I felt uneasy for some reason, like I was in trouble. Which I wasn't. At least not that I knew of.

"Okay." Silver lifted her hands off the keyboard. She moved the computer toward me, adjusting it an angle so that I could see the screen. "Take a look and tell me who you think that is."

A picture of a woman stared out at me. She was pretty, with curly dark hair and blue eyes. A square neckline emphasized her pale skin, and a row of cloth-covered buttons ran down the front of her dress. I squinted and leaned in, examining the picture more closely. There was a pale brown mark of some kind, shaped like a butterfly, above the woman's right eye.

"Any guesses?" Silver asked.

"Uh-uh."

"*That* is Bedelia Weatherly." There was an edge of triumph to Silver's voice, as if she had just won a game I hadn't known we were playing.

"Bedelia Weatherly?"

"Otherwise known as Witch Weatherly."

"No *way*." I looked back at the picture. "Are you sure?"

"Totally." Silver pressed a few keys. "Look. I googled the names *Weatherly* and *Sudbury* and all this stuff came up." She sat back in her seat and pushed a few more keys. "There was only one picture, taken at her college graduation. It says here that she went to the University of New Hampshire and graduated with a degree in botany." Silver glanced from the screen to me. I was speechless. She laughed out loud. "I bet no one in this whole town would recognize her. Or even remember that she used to be a real person once." She paused. "And a pretty one, too."

"The botany stuff," I said. "That's plants, right?"

"Right," Silver said.

"I remember hearing something about her being really good with plants even before she went up to the mountain. Like, she'd use them to create her magic potions. That must've been where she got the information."

"Hmmmm . . ." Silver said.

"Is there anything in there about her house?" I asked. "That got burned down?

"That's the other thing I wanted to show you." Silver's fingers zipped across the keys until the image of a charred house came into view. The entire structure was gutted, every visible corner dark with soot. Only the chimney remained, standing like a proud, dirty soldier among the ruins. "It says here that Bedelia Weatherly came home from work on May 23, to find her house in flames." She sat back, her mouth over her hand, and continued reading: "*Despite violent protests from emergency personnel, Ms. Weatherly rushed into the building and disappeared from view. Two firemen ran after her and, moments later, emerged with her burned, unconscious body in their arms. Ms. Weatherly was taken to the hospital, and then transferred to a special burn unit for treatment.*"

Silver shook her head. "Can you imagine? Running into a burning building? Why would she do something like that?"

"She was probably trying to get her stuff," I said. "You know, all her magic books and things."

"Maybe." Silver looked thoughtful. "I doubt she was able to save anything, from the looks of this."

Overhead, the bell rang, signaling the start of bus lineup.

"Darn it," Silver said, clicking off the computer. "I wanted to print out the picture."

"Do it real quick," I said. "I'll wait."

~~~~~~~~~~

"I don't know why my mom's late." Silver put a hand over her eyes, and looked across the street at the elementary school. "Wait, is that her over there? Who's she talking to?"

I looked in the direction Silver was indicating. Russell's teacher, Mrs. Tyrone, a tall, willowy woman with short brown hair, was talking to Aunt Marianne. Mrs. Tyrone looked exhausted—and majorly aggravated. Russell was standing a few feet away from them, swinging his backpack from side to side and scowling.

Great.

Mrs. Tyrone never came out of the building to talk to a parent unless one of the kids had given her a hard time. It figured that Russell would pick today to act up in class. Without bothering to answer Silver, I stalked toward them. If anyone should be getting briefed by Mrs. Tyrone about Russell right now, it was me. Momma and Dad were AWOL. And for as good as Aunt Marianne could be with Russell, she still didn't know anything about him. Not really.

"Oh, hello, Wren." Mrs. Tyrone had a large brown mole on her upper lip, which I never seemed to be able to look away from when I talked to her. "How are you, honey?"

"Fine, thank you. What happened with Russell?"

Mrs. Tyrone and Aunt Marianne exchanged a glance. For a moment, I thought neither of them was going to say anything.

"I burped in class," Russell volunteered. "And farted, too. Real loud. I'm not s'posed to do those things."

Mrs. Tyrone fluttered her eyes and took a step toward me. "Wren, your father has made me aware of your family circumstances. And I know it's been very hard on both of you. May I ask you to encourage Russell to open up a little about things? Just between the two of you? I've tried, but he's not interested in talking to me about it, which is perfectly understandable, considering that it's such a personal matter. But I think part of the reason he might be acting up in class is because things are starting to build a little inside him. He needs to vent—in a positive, constructive way. He really does."

Talk with Russell? In a positive, constructive way? Was she serious? How was I going to talk about what was going on with Momma with someone whose primary concerns revolved around Captain Commando and pancakes? And even if Russell could sit through a conversation like that, what would I tell him? *I* still wasn't even sure what was going on.

"I'll try," I said to Mrs. Tyrone's mole. "He doesn't like to talk about a lot of heavy stuff, though."

"I do, too," Russell said. "The heavier, the better." He dropped his backpack and flexed his muscles. "People have no idea how strong I am."

Mrs. Tyrone took a step back and draped an arm over Russell's shoulders. She bent over so that she was at eye-level with him and tried to smile. "We'll have a better day tomorrow, Russell, won't we?"

"Depends." Russell scowled again.

"On what?" asked Mrs. Tyrone.

"On what kind of day it is," Russell said.

Aunt Marianne and Mrs. Tyrone exchanged the kind of look that Momma and Dad sometimes did whenever Russell said something that left them speechless.

I grabbed Russell's hand. "Yeah, let's go, Russell. Come on."

Ten minutes into the ride home, though, after Aunt Marianne announced she was out of pancake mix, Russell went ballistic. I watched with horror as he nailed Aunt Marianne in the side of the leg with his fist, causing her to swerve dangerously to one side of the road. Then he kicked the dashboard with both feet until something fell out of it. By the time we got him back to the house and into the living room, Russell was crying and screaming like a crazy person. Even Jackson, who tried to lick his face, couldn't calm him down. Russell pushed the dog away with two hands, and then, when Jackson came back, whacked him in the face. A high, piteous sound came out of the dog as he slunk away, his tail between his legs.

I grabbed Russell hard then, the way I'd seen Dad do, and shoved him on the couch. "Enough!" I yelled. Poor Jackson was whimpering in the corner. Silver and Aunt Marianne were behind us, trying not to watch, but I didn't care. "That is *enough*, Russell! You either tell me what's bothering you, or I will keep Jackson away from you for the rest of the day!"

He leapt to his feet and glowered at me. His little face was red and squished up, and tears were sliding out of his eyes. "I want my momma!" he yelled. "I want her back! I'll be good, damn it! I promise! I'll be good this time!"

I rushed toward him as he sank back down on the couch. He leaned over and buried his head against his knees, sobbing with great big gulping noises, as if he couldn't get air in fast enough. I put my arm around his back, hoping he could hear me. "She didn't leave because you were bad, Russellator," I whispered. "She left because she's sick, and she has to get better. It's not your fault, buddy. It has nothing at all to do with you. I promise. It's not your fault in any way."

Even as I said the words, I wished I believed them. But it didn't matter what I believed right now. Russell needed to hear good, positive things about Momma.

To my amazement, Russell didn't pull away. Instead, he sat still, listening to me. For a moment, the wet slurp of his breathing was the only sound in the room. And then he leaned into me and let me hold him. His hair smelled like blueberry pie for some reason, and his left sneaker had a hole in it. After another minute, he reached down, grabbed the edge of my T-shirt, and blew his nose into it.

"I used a blankety-blank," he said in a stuffy voice.

"I know."

"I'm sorry."

"It's okay." I stroked his hair.

"Can we call her?" he asked. "Just to say hi?"

"Of course you can call her!" Aunt Marianne started up, as if someone had lit a match beneath her bottom, and began rummaging around in the kitchen. "In fact, your father called me today at work, and left me the new number to her room. Let's give it a try right now."

She brought the phone over to the couch and sat down a little ways from Russell. He propped himself up on his knees and leaned in eagerly as she began punching the numbers.

I looked up, but Silver had disappeared.

"Dad?" Russell began to cry as soon as Aunt Marianne put the phone to his ear. "Dad, it's me. It's Russell. I was a pest to Momma and that's why she went away. I was driving her crazy. Can I tell her I'm sorry?"

My nose prickled with tears as I stroked the back of Russell's neck. He was such a pain in the butt, but I loved him so much. Sometimes I wondered how much he picked up about the truth of our family. How much of what was really going on did he know?

How much did I?

"Why not?" Russell rubbed one eye with a dirty fist. "She's still not feeling good? I thought you said there was doctors! Giving her medicine!" He stamped his foot. "I don't *want* to wait anymore! I want to talk to her! Now!" His lower lip jutted out as he listened for a moment. "No," he said. "I don't understand at all. And I think you're both stupid."

He pulled the phone away from his ear and threw it across the room. Then he raced toward the kitchen door.

"Russell!" I shouted.

Aunt Marianne rushed after him. "Let me take care of him," she said over her shoulder. "I'll get Jackson, too. You talk to your father."

I picked up the phone, watching as Aunt Marianne ran after Russell, chasing him through the backyard. Jackson raced after both of them. "Dad? What happened? Did something happen to Momma?"

"She just had a little bit of a setback today, Wren. That's all. She's fine. She's sleeping and can't come to the phone right now."

"What do you mean, a setback?" I asked.

"She just wasn't feeling as great today as she was yesterday."

"Like how?"

"She just . . . Oh, honey. I can't get into it all right now. I'm sorry. I promise I will when I come up on Friday though, all right? I'll tell you everything. You've got to trust me that everything's okay right now, all right?"

I felt like telling Dad that he was stupid, too. Stupid for thinking that we didn't know anything. Stupid for trying to make us believe that everything was fine, when in fact, just the opposite was true. "No," I said instead. "It's not all right. I'm not a little kid anymore, Dad. I'm twelve now, okay? And you need to tell me what's really going on with Momma."

"I will, honey. I promise. As soon as I come up on—"

"No, Dad. *Now*. I need to know right now. Russell and I have been having a really hard time, but the hardest part is thinking that you're keeping all the bad stuff a secret from us. That we might not know any of it until it's too late. And that's not fair. It's just not. You have to tell us, Dad. You have to tell me."

There was another long pause. I was clutching the phone receiver so hard that my fingers were turning white. *Please just tell me the truth. Pleasepleaseplease.*

"Wow," Dad said finally. "I had no idea you'd gotten so grown-up, Wren."

"I'm old enough to know the truth about Momma."

"All right." His voice sounded as if he were trying to pull it through cement. "The truth is that, well, Momma had a bit of a breakdown."

"What do you mean, a breakdown?" My heart was already speeding up. "I thought you said this had to do with something in her head."

"It does," Dad said. "Momma's been anxious and depressed for a very long time. It sort of grew and grew over the years, and then when she went to Grandpa's

186

funeral, it all came to a head. She just sort of crumbled and shut down. But she's with the most amazing doctors, Wren. They're helping her so much. And she's really doing great."

I could hear a noise that sounded like a man talking over the loudspeaker in the background.

Dad sighed. "Visiting hours are almost over. I have to go and check on Momma before I leave. Listen to me. We will talk more about this. I promise. I have to go right now. But I don't want you to worry, okay? I'll be there in a few days, and then we can talk some more. Be a good girl, honey. I love you."

"Dad!" There were a million other things I wanted to ask, a billion other things I needed to know.

"Sweetie, please. I'll call you later. I promise."

And with a click and a hum, he was gone.

Chapter 25

I hung up the phone and walked back outside. It was my favorite time of day, when the light filtered down through the clouds like lacy curtains, and the air was soft as cotton. Amazingly, Aunt Marianne and Russell were on the other side of the yard, playing catch with a small rubber ball. It was as if the terrible phone call between Dad and Russell hadn't even happened. Jackson raced in between them, leaping and begging for a turn. Silver was nowhere in sight. I settled into a nook in one of the pear trees and rested my head on my knees.

So Momma was more than sad. She was depressed. So depressed that she'd had a breakdown. It was weird thinking that those kinds of things could happen to adults, weirder still to think that it had actually happened to Momma. Dad said she was making progress in the hospital, but he'd also said that she'd had a setback this morning. Was she crying? Staring out the window again? Did it mean that it would take longer for her to get better? To come back to us? And was that something she still wanted to do?

"You mind if I sit with you for a little bit?" I looked up as Silver appeared. For some reason, she was holding the picture of Witch Weatherly she'd found earlier on the computer. Without waiting for an answer, she took a seat. "Everything go okay with your dad?"

"Yeah. He finally told me the truth about my mom." It came out before I realized I had opened my mouth.

Silver watched me, fiddling with the edge of the picture.

"She's been depressed for a long time, and I guess she kind of fell apart a little, which is why she had to go into a hospital." Was I really saying these things? Out loud? What was wrong with me? I kept my eyes on the ground, the skin on my face hot as a flame.

Off to the side, Russell shouted and Aunt Marianne laughed. Jackson barked twice, and bolted across the field again. His yellow fur glinted under the sun, and his tongue lolled out of the side of his mouth.

"It's so brave of her to go get help," Silver said. "Now she'll get better."

I lifted my head and peeked out at her from under my bangs. Suddenly, I knew exactly why I had told her. "I hope so."

"She will," Silver said. "Plus, she's got you and Russell and your dad to help her. And me and my mom, too, if she wants us."

"I hope you're right," I said softly.

Russell careened over to us then, his eyes wide with excitement. Jackson bounded behind him, followed by Aunt Marianne, pink-cheeked and breathless.

"Hey, Russell," I said. "You doing okay?"

He ignored the question. "Wren, guess what? Aunt Marianne said I could go with her on Saturday to help her paint! And that she'll help me paint a whole entire portrait of Captain Commando in my room at home!"

I glanced at Aunt Marianne. She was standing a few feet away, holding the little rubber ball. She had a smile on her face. "Wow, that's great, buddy," I said. "Did you say thank you?"

Russell turned around and cupped his hands around his mouth. "Thank you!" he hollered.

Aunt Marianne laughed and walked over. "You're more than welcome." She squatted down between Silver and Russell. "Why don't we go in the house now Russell, and let the girls fin—" She broke off mid-sentence as her eyes fell on the picture of Witch Weatherly. "Honey? Where did you get that?"

"I printed it off the computer," Silver said. "And don't worry, Mom, I'm not . . ." Her own voice trailed off as her mother took the picture out of her hand.

"But . . . why do you have it?" Aunt Marianne asked, studying the image with a puzzled expression. "How do you know her?"

"I don't know her," Silver said. "It's Witch Weatherly."

"Witch Weatherly?" Aunt Marianne blinked. "What do you mean? This isn't Witch Weatherly."

"Mom." Silver took the picture back, exasperated. "It's an old picture of her, obviously, before she went to live on the mountain and *became* Witch Weatherly. I got it off the Internet. It's no big deal."

"But I know that lady." Aunt Marianne shook her head, reaching for the picture a second time. She studied it again, the lines in her forehead growing deeper. "I *remember* her," she said, tapping the picture. "I do. When we came back to visit Greta that time for her birthday. She was in the apartment."

My blood ran cold. *Momma* had known Witch Weatherly? It couldn't be.

"Are you sure it was her?" I heard myself ask. "That was a pretty long time ago. It could have been anyone."

"No, no, I'm positive." Aunt Marianne pointed to Witch Weatherly's forehead. "I remember this strange little birthmark above her eye. It was so unusual that I just kept staring at it. It looks like a little moth or something, doesn't it? Oh yes, that's her. That's definitely her."

A shiver ran up and down the sides of my arms. Was it possible that Momma and Witch Weatherly had lived in the same building just a few feet away from one another?

"Was she in Momma's apartment?" I asked. "I mean, the day you saw her?"

Aunt Marianne frowned, deliberating this. "No," she said finally. "She was sitting on the front porch, reading a book. You know, the apartment building they lived in was really just an enormous house that had been sectioned off into different units. I believe Ms. Weatherly owned it. Your mom was sitting on the porch steps with her when we arrived, and Greta introduced us."

"And then what?" I pressed.

"She shook our hands." Aunt Marianne smiled. "And I stared at her birthmark a little, and that was the end of it. I didn't see her again until we left."

"What happened when you left?"

"Nothing happened. She was still on the porch, reading her book, and she put it down when we came out, and waved good-bye. I do remember the book for some reason. It had a very interesting cover, with pictures all over. I think it was called *The Secret Power of Plants*."

"*The Secret Power of Plants*?" The tiny hairs on my arms prickled.

"Yes." Aunt Marianne shrugged. "I think that was it." She handed the picture back to Silver. "That is just so weird. Sheesh, it's a small world, isn't it?"

"Yeah." Silver was watching me. "I guess."

"Why do you have this picture anyway?" Aunt Marianne said. "You know I told you I don't want you going—"

"I'm not going anywhere." Silver cut her off. "But I'm still doing a report on her for my history project. Just off the Internet."

"Okay." Aunt Marianne stood up and held out her hand. "Well, come on, Russell, let's go back in. I think it's almost time for *Captain Commando*."

Silver crossed her legs and twirled a piece of hair around her index finger as her mother and Russell walked off. "Wren?" She poked the front of my knee. "You okay?"

Her voice sounded far away. I felt dazed. My arms and legs felt separate from me, as if they belonged to someone else.

"Wren?"

"Yeah?"

"That's really weird, don'tcha think?"

"What is?"

"Your mom knowing Witch Weatherly all those years ago?"

"Yeah." I blinked, hoping the horror didn't show on my face. "It kind of is."

There was a pause.

"So I've decided when I'm going," Silver lowered her voice.

"Going where?"

"Up the mountain."

I looked at her fearfully. "When?"

"Saturday."

"*This* Saturday?" My eyes widened.

"Yup. My mom'll be busy painting again." Silver raised her eyebrows. "Looks like Russell's going with her, too."

"What about cheerleading?" I asked, sidestepping the Russell comment. "Don't you have practice on Saturdays?"

"I quit cheerleading." She shrugged. "Coach was mad, but I had to do it. Now I'll have more time to ride

Manchester." She paused, looking back at the mountain. "And to do this."

I swallowed. I couldn't believe she was actually going. That she had a real date set and everything. "Holy cow, Silver, are you really going to do it? All by yourself?"

"I'm really going to do it," she said. "All by myself."

There was no reason to doubt her.

I knew Silver Jones well enough by now to know that when she wanted to do something, she found a way to do it.

No matter what.

Chapter 26

Russell planted himself in Aunt Marianne's windowsill as soon as we got home from school on Friday and stayed there until Dad's car finally appeared around the bend, kicking up clouds of dust as it rolled down the long driveway.

"He's here!" he screamed, leaping from the ledge. "Wren, Dad's here! He's here!"

I was upstairs in my room, fixing my hair for the fourth time. I couldn't decide if I wanted to wear it pushed back with a headband, or down straight the way I always did. Dad wasn't the sort of person who'd ever been interested in things like clothes or hair when it came to me. And yet, for some reason today, it felt important that he notice. He'd finally told me the truth about Momma. He'd trusted me. And I wanted to make sure that he didn't feel he'd made a mistake. That he could trust me again—with anything—if he wanted.

I decided to go with the headband. My face looked

okay with my bangs pushed off my face. Maybe even a little bit older.

Dad was already holding Russell in a bear hug when I came downstairs, but he put him down when he caught sight of me. "Butterbean," he said softly. "Look at you."

I walked to him quickly, not wanting Silver or Aunt Marianne, who were sitting there in the kitchen, to notice my eyes getting wet. He pulled me into him, and kissed the top of my head. He smelled different than he usually did, like chlorine and cough drops, and I wondered if Momma's hospital had a pool.

"Oh, I've missed you," Dad said.

"Hey!" Russell poked Dad in the arm. "You didn't say you missed me!"

Dad laughed. "I missed you both. Who's ready for pizza?"

We went to the Hot Spot and got a booth in the back, near the arcade. Dad ordered an extra-large pizza with pepperoni for us, and cheese fries for Russell, who, for some reason, decided that he didn't like pepperoni today. Russell had flooded Dad with about a zillion questions about Momma on the way over, and now that he was satisfied she was all right, demanded a handful of quarters so he could go play in the arcade. Dad obliged, and Russell disappeared around the corner.

"So she really is okay?" I asked when I was sure Russell was out of sight.

"She really is. Getting better every day." Dad reached out and touched the side of my hair. "I like your hair like this, honey. You look so grown-up."

"Thanks." I blushed, pleased that he'd noticed. "But what about the setback you told me she had? You said you'd tell me."

He nodded, tracing an invisible line on the table with the edge of his thumb, and pressed his lips together.

"I know about Witch Weatherly," I blurted out.

His thumb stopped moving. "What do you mean?"

"You know, that she lived in the same house as Momma when she was little."

Dad's eyes crinkled at the corners.

"Aunt Marianne told us."

"Aunt Marianne wasn't there." Dad's crinkles got even deeper. "How'd she know?"

"She saw a picture Silver found on the Internet from a long time ago." Dad stared at me blankly, so I went back and told him about the history project and Silver picking Witch Weatherly as her topic. "She found Witch Weatherly's college graduation picture and printed it out for her report. And Aunt Marianne saw it and kind of wigged out because she said she knew her. That she remembered her from when she came to visit Momma one summer."

"Did Aunt Marianne say anything else?" Dad asked.

"Like what?"

"Anything."

"Well, she said she knew it was Witch Weatherly because of some birthmark on her face."

Dad nodded.

"And that she seemed quiet. She was reading some book about the power of plants on the porch when they got there."

"Anything else?"

I thought back, but nothing else came.

"Nothing about the fire?" Dad's voice was so soft that I could barely hear him.

I sat forward. "The what?"

"The fire." Dad cleared his throat. "The fire in the house that burned everything down. Did Aunt Marianne say anything about that?"

I shook my head, an uneasy feeling beginning to wind its way through the middle of my chest. "No. Why?"

Dad winced, as if something inside his stomach hurt. He brought a glass of soda to his lips and swallowed. I watched his Adam's apple move up and then down along the inside of his throat, like a tiny walnut. He put the glass back down and wiped his mouth with the back of his hand.

"That's what Momma's setback was about, honey," he said quietly. "She told us what happened. She was just a little girl. She didn't know any better. But she was alone one day, and she started playing with matches . . ." He stopped talking, looking at me desperately.

I didn't understand. Setback? Just a little girl? Playing with matches? Then a shudder ran through me. The people of Sudbury hadn't burned Witch Weatherly's house down.

Momma had.

Chapter 27

I lay in bed for a long time that night, staring at the ceiling after Russell started snoring, and trying not to think about everything that had happened in the past ninety-six hours. But it was impossible, like trying to stop sand from pouring out of a paper bag after you'd cut the bottom out. Russell's freak-out had exhausted me. And finding out how depressed Momma really was, followed by Aunt Marianne's recognition of the picture of Witch Weatherly, made my head spin. But the most frightening of all had been discovering that Momma had been responsible for setting the fire at Witch Weatherly's house all those years ago. No wonder she'd been so terrified of lightning storms. And now I understood why she had collapsed at the sight of her birthday cake with all those burning candles.

"It was an accident, Wren." Dad's voice echoed in my ears. "She didn't mean to do it. But she never told anyone, and she's carried the guilt of it for years. *I* didn't even know about it until four days ago. But it explains everything, when you think about it. The sadness all these years, her shutting down like she did after Grandpa died, maybe even her hair turning gray."

I didn't think it explained any of that.

In fact, the more I thought about it, the more I realized that things were starting to add up in a completely different direction. Momma's gray hair, her breakdown, the blotches all over her hands, which appeared every single spring without fail, at the exact same time of year as the fire; they were all part of Witch Weatherly's revenge. The people of Sudbury said that Witch Weatherly had gone and haunted Creeper Mountain as payback for losing her house. She'd had a score to settle, vengeance to take. But no one except Witch Weatherly knew the truth about Momma. Which meant that Witch Weatherly hadn't just haunted Creeper Mountain.

She'd haunted Momma, too.

I got out of bed as quickly as possible without disturbing Russell and headed for the bathroom. I sat down on the floor, drawing my legs up against my chest. The wall was cold against my back, the tiles cool under my bare feet. I stared through the little space between my knees. The familiar buzzing sound began in my head, the kind that started when things started to get too crazy, too hard to sort out.

Maybe I was jumping to conclusions. Making a mountain out of a molehill, the way Dad always liked to say. But what if I wasn't? What if I was right, and Momma was stuck inside one of Witch Weatherly's spells?

No. It couldn't be. That was ridiculous.

I got up again and began to pace back and forth along the bathroom floor, trying to shake the anxious feeling inside my chest, which had settled there like some kind of rock. It felt as if my whole body was shaking from the inside out, as if something was trying to push its way through to the other side. My eye fell on a water glass sitting on one of the bathroom shelves. It was filled with Aunt Marianne's eyeliner pencils and makeup brushes. I took out a bright blue pencil and positioned it between my fingers. Over, over, in, under. Over, over, in, under. Again. And again. And again.

My breathing started to slow. The shakiness began to lift. For a single moment, staring at the spinning pencil, all my thoughts about Momma and Witch Weatherly moved somewhere deep in the back of my head.

Suddenly, the pencil slipped. I watched as it dropped between my fingers and fell to the floor. I made no move to pick it up. Instead, a ticker tape of thoughts moved steadily through my head, like a train on a track: Only one person in the world could lift the spell that Witch Weatherly had put on Momma. But it could only happen if that someone went up that mountain and convinced Witch Weatherly to do it.

A sudden wave of nausea forced me to my knees. I leaned forward and pressed my head against the floor. But a sour taste pooled along the back of my tongue, and I crawled on all fours, holding on to the side of the toilet as I retched once and then again, gasping for breath.

There is no way, I told myself. *There is just no way.*

A knock sounded on the door. I closed my eyes and put my head down on the edge of the seat.

Silver opened it a crack and peeked in. "Hey, you okay?"

"Uh-huh."

"What happened?" She leaned in a little farther. "Oh my gosh, did you get sick?"

I lifted my head and stared past her, waiting for the room to stop swimming. *There is just no way. It's completely, one hundred percent, absolutely impossible.*

Isn't it?

It occurred to me again that I had just ridden a horse. A galloping horse, at that. I'd been thrown from it, too, and lived. I'd also ridden in a plane—without an engine! I'd been six thousand feet up in the air, and I'd come back down without a scratch. I'd even told off Cassie and Nora—and come away in one piece. In a little more than a week, I'd done three things I'd previously thought were impossible. At least for me. Which meant . . .

"Wren?"

"I want to go with you tomorrow," I whispered.

Silver stepped inside quickly and shut the door. "Are you sure?"

No, I was not sure. Maybe, in fact, I had just gone temporarily insane. But if I didn't try to help Momma, who would?

As I looked up at Silver, I realized there was something else, too. Over the past weeks, somehow she'd become my friend. And I cared—a lot—about her safety.

Which meant that I didn't want anything to happen to her on that mountain tomorrow.

"I'm sure," I said. "I don't want you to go by yourself. I think it's better if you have someone with you."

"It's going to be steep," Silver said.

"I know."

"We'll have to use hatchets. To cut the brush."

"I know."

"We might run into hornet-head snakes."

"I know." I shuddered. "And we have to keep an eye out for the hidden pits."

"Oh, Wren!" Silver threw her arms around me. "Thank you!"

I held her tightly, a tiny part of me feeling glad to have made her so happy after all she'd done for me.

But another, much larger part of me could only pray that we would get back down the mountain alive.

Chapter 28

"Do you think your mom suspected anything before she left?" I struggled to keep up with Silver as we started out across the pasture the next morning. Her natural gait was nearly twice as fast as mine, and even with my long legs, I had to trot to keep up. "I mean, our backpacks are pretty full for a little picnic."

"Nah." Silver strode on ahead. "She was too busy getting all her painting stuff into the car. Don't worry. We're fine."

I bit my lip, thinking of our cover story, which had involved a lame explanation about cloud-watching, sunbathing, and picnicking out in the field. Aunt Marianne had even offered to take Russell to dinner since we seemed so intent on having the whole day to ourselves, and so our curfew had been inadvertently extended until six o'clock.

In reality, our backpacks were close to bursting. We had two rusty hatchets we'd found in the barn for cutting back the brush and thorns, bug spray, sunscreen, and two cans of Mace, which Silver said would kill—or at least slow down—any hornet-head snake that crossed our path. I'd managed to sneak a large white sheet inside my backpack to throw over the red raven—just in case—and we each had a pen and paper, two peanut butter sandwiches, four granola bars, six sticks of string cheese, and three bottles of water. Silver had her cell phone, too, of course, in case of emergency, and she had packed a small tin of Aunt Marianne's caramel fudge brownies as a housewarming gift for Witch Weatherly. It was the least she could do, she said, since the old woman was going to give us some of her time.

I hoped that was all she was going to give us.

The weather, at least, was on our side. It was a warm, sunny day. An azure expanse of sky hung over us like an upside-down bowl, and a light breeze brushed the tops of our arms. Silver didn't seem to mind that I was lagging behind. She chatted easily, glancing at me over her shoulder every so often, as if we were just heading out to pick flowers.

"I can't wait to see what Russell brings back from the art studio," she said, laughing. "A full-size Captain Commando for his room? I mean, that's something I *gotta* see!"

"Yeah, it should be cool," I answered softly, hoping she didn't detect the breathlessness in my voice. I felt guilty about leaving Russell, even if he was going to do something fun. What if we were late getting back, and he panicked? Or what if something terrible happened and this morning was the last time I would ever see him? I tried to remind myself for the millionth time that I was going up there to help Momma, but it wasn't working quite as well as it had before. Now I was just struggling not to hyperventilate.

"I didn't really sleep last night," Silver went on. "I was too excited. But I don't even feel tired." She glanced at me. "How about you?"

"I slept a little."

I was being generous. In fact, I had lain awake for most of the night, fingering Momma's tiny bird necklace, as if it might impart some kind of luck through my skin, and trying not to throw up again.

"It'll catch up to us later, probably," Silver said. "Like when we get to the top. But right now, I feel like I could climb this mountain two or three times!"

"Do you have all your interview questions?" I asked.

"Yup." Silver tapped her backpack. "Right here in the front pocket. When we take a break, I'll go over them with you. You can tell me if you think they sound all right."

"Okay." I still hadn't told Silver about my plan to confront Witch Weatherly with the spell she'd cast on Momma. I wasn't too sure what she'd have to say about something like that. As far as she knew, I was just going with her to keep her company. Which was fine with me.

"Hoo-boy!" For once, Silver looked daunted. We had reached the thickly weeded entrance to the path up the mountain. "We're going to have to start somewhere," she said. "Let's just hope we can find our way to Witch Weatherly's place. You got your hatchet?"

I dislodged it from the belt loop of my jeans and held it up. My hand was shaking.

"Perfect. Let's go." Silver took a swing with her hatchet, slicing through a clotted mess of brambles. Then she did it again. And again. I was surprised at how strong her blows were, how cleanly the blade cut through the tangles. A few more swipes, and most of the vines had been hacked away. She stepped through the newly formed opening. "Oooo, wow!" Her voice drifted out from inside. "Come look!"

I squeezed through the bramble hole, holding my breath. There in front of us was something that looked like it had once been a path. Much of it was obscured by dense foliage, and rotting tree branches littered the edges. But there was no getting around the fact that in the middle of everything was a very narrow, very deliberate walking trail.

"You ready to do this?" Silver's pretty face was already shiny with perspiration.

Not in a million years. I nodded and took a deep breath. "Let's go."

We climbed for over an hour, making our ascent slowly, inch by inch, foot by foot. The air was thick with the scent of sun and wet dirt. Every so often, a sudden scurrying sound to the right or the left of us made my heart fall into my stomach. It could be anything, I told myself—maybe even a cute little mouse running for cover. It didn't have to be a squirrel. And it wasn't necessarily a hornet-head snake, either.

Silver moved at a relentless pace, her arms swinging from side to side like some kind of machine. I struggled to keep up, but it was hard work pushing through the thick underbrush with a five or six-pound backpack strapped between my shoulders. A blister popped out on the bottom of my thumb, and sweat began to trickle down the front of my shirt. Over and over, we stopped to swing our hatchets at low-lying branches, or to clear blocked passages in the middle of the trail with our hands and feet. Five or six times, we paused to draw big red circles on the trees we passed, so that we could find them again on our way back down. By the time the sun had shifted position, Silver's cell phone said it was 10:30, and I was so tired I thought my arms might literally fall from their sockets. I sat down on a rotted tree stump and wiped my face with the back of my sleeve.

Silver turned around. "You okay?"

I nodded, too tired to justify my actions. "Just want to sit for a minute."

"Thank goodness." She plopped down next to me. "I was afraid you were never going to stop."

"*Me?* You're the one gunning through this place! I can hardly keep up with you!"

"No way." She leaned her elbows back against the top of the stump and raised her face to the sky. Trickles of sweat gleamed against her throat. "I've just been waiting for you to take a breather. This trip was my idea. I don't want you to think I'm flaking out or anything by complaining."

I looked at her for a moment. Was this girl ever going to stop surprising me?

"Hey," I said. "Can I tell you something?"

Silver lifted her bangs out from her forehead, and blew a stream of air up through her lips. "Sure."

"It's kind of weird."

"I like weird."

"Okay." I hesitated, wondering if I was really going to say this out loud. It wasn't like me to get so personal. Especially with people I still wasn't one hundred percent sure of. Then I remembered what I had already told her about Momma. And how nice she'd been about it. "You know I have English with Miss Crumb, right?"

"She's the one with the squeaky voice and all the cool rings?"

I nodded.

"You're lucky," Silver said. "I have Miss Randall. She's so old. And cranky. She makes all of us use the hand sanitizer outside of her room before we go in, and then when we leave again!" She rolled her eyes. "Anyway, sorry. Go ahead."

"Well, every day at the beginning of class, Miss Crumb has us write in our notebooks. We have to answer a question she puts on the board. And a couple of weeks ago, one of the questions was *if you could have any two wishes granted, what would they be?*"

Silver was quiet, watching me in that thoughtful way of hers.

"So my first wish was that I could be a little braver." I picked at the end of my shoelace, feeling self-conscious again. "You know, in general. I'm kind of afraid of a lot of things. If you haven't already noticed."

"That was a good wish then," Silver said.

I looked up quickly, but there was no trace of sarcasm in her voice, no hidden sneer behind the soft look on her face.

"I couldn't think of another one," I went on. "At least, not right then. But then I went to our history class with Mr. Tunlaw. It was the day that everything happened, with him getting stung by the wasps and running out of the room." My face was getting hot, a light heat spreading from the bottom of my neck up along the sides of my throat. I pressed the backs of my hands against my cheeks, as if I could stop it. Silver was looking at me curiously, waiting. I cleared my throat. "I know this is going to sound weird, but when I saw you do that thing with the wasp, I kind of thought of my second wish."

"Which was what?" Silver asked.

"Get to know you," I said. "I thought maybe if I did, some of the brave stuff you had might rub off on me."

"I'm not really that brave." Silver smiled.

"I think you are." I shrugged. "Braver than me, anyway."

"Maybe about some things."

I thought about this for a minute and decided Silver was just being nice. There was absolutely nothing I could think of that frightened her. She was brave all the way through, from beginning to end.

"Well," I said. "Anyway. It's kind of weird how things have ended up. You know, with Russell and me having to stay with you and Aunt Marianne. I actually think some of your bravery *has* rubbed off on me a little bit."

"Like how?" Silver pursed her lips.

"Well, riding the horses," I said. "I'm not in *love* with them or anything now, but I'm not nearly as freaked out by them anymore, either. And then the plane ride. Silver, I've been terrified of planes since I could walk. I never thought I'd be inside one, much less go up in one! And now this." I looked up, staring through the latticework of leaves overhead. Bits of white and blue sky peeked through, like pieces of a checkerboard. It was actually pretty up here. Maybe even beautiful. "This whole trip. I'm still scared to death, but I'm here. I'm doing it. And I'm pretty sure I wouldn't have even *thought* about doing it if it hadn't been for you wanting to go first."

"Wow," Silver said softly. "That might be the nicest thing anyone's ever said to me."

"Well, it's true."

Silver stared at me for so long that I started to get nervous.

"What?" I said. "Why're you looking at me like that?"

"Don't get mad when I say this," she said slowly, "but sometimes I wonder if you're really afraid of all the things you think you are."

I sat up a little straighter. "What do you mean?"

"It seems to me you're afraid of things because someone else was afraid of it first. Like the horses. Were you really afraid of horses? Or did you start to think you were because your brother said they had big teeth?"

I opened my mouth, and then closed it. In fact, it was Momma who had been the one to mention that horses had big teeth. She'd argued with Dad the day he took me to Mr. Rawlins's horse farm, the day I'd cried when I sat on top of Traveler. "No horses," she said. "They could turn around and bite her with those gigantic teeth of theirs. Don't let her get near them."

"And the day we went flying," Silver went on. "You told me you'd never gone flying. Not ever. How can you be afraid of something you've never even done? Did someone tell you planes were scary?"

Momma again. She'd decided to take an eighteen-hour train ride out to Grandpa William's funeral rather than get inside one of those *tin cans people call planes*.

Now, I shrugged. "Maybe. I never really thought about it before."

"It doesn't really matter," Silver said. "I just think you're a lot braver than you think you are."

I bit my lip, considering this. If such a thing were possible, it would mean both of my wishes had just come true. Which, sitting on a mountain with a witch nearby, might have been a very good thing after all.

Chapter 29

Overhead, the wind stirred and leaves rustled. A shadow skittered across the path, and I glanced around quickly, scanning the ground for snakes, then tipped my head back, looking for the raven. So far, there had been no sign of either. But we still had a long way to go.

"Are you hungry?" Silver asked.

"Starving." I smiled.

We each devoured a peanut butter sandwich, two granola bars, and three cheese sticks, and drank a bottle of water. Then we got up and started along the trail once more. The air was much warmer than it had been, and I was getting another blister—this one on my left heel. I took a deep breath, trying to detect the wayward scent of smoke in the air. Maybe we were on the wrong trail. Or maybe the way to Witch Weatherly's house didn't involve a trail at all.

After another hour, I stopped again, leaning against the trunk of a strange tree planted directly in the middle of the path. Unlike most of the other trees up here, this one did not have red or gold leaves. Its branches, thick with silvery blue needles, draped over us like an umbrella, and the trunk was gnarled and twisted. It leaned heavily to one side, as if trying to press an ear to the ground. I wiped my forehead with the back of my hand, then checked my watch. It was almost 12:30. "How much longer do you think we have to go?"

"Not sure." Silver slid down along the base of the tree and squinted up through the branches. "I hope not too much farther, though. I'm really . . ." She stopped, her eyes roving over the expanse of forest in the distance. "Wait, did you hear that?"

I strained my ears, but the only thing I could hear was the wind moving through the leaves. It rustled lightly, like sheets snapping in the breeze.

"A whooshing sound?" Silver rose slowly to her feet. "Like *sssshhhhh*?"

My heart clenched inside my chest. I turned my head to the left, and then to the right, praying Silver was wrong. And then I heard it. A noise ahead—something that sounded like a muted roar. The inside of my head felt light. Maybe Witch Weatherly had another animal besides the red raven that guarded her place. Something with big teeth and sharp claws. Something that roared when it knew people were approaching.

"It's coming from over there." Silver turned sharply to the right and took off. "Come on!"

My head spun as I struggled to keep up. Why did she have to *race* after everything? Why couldn't she just stop

216

and think first, for once? What if we were running right into one of Witch Weatherly's traps? What if . . .

"Holy cow!" Silver shouted, pointing at something ahead. "Look, Wren!"

"Shining Falls," I whispered, as the great waterfall slowly materialized in front of us. "It's Shining Falls!" We stared down at the vast wall of rushing water spilling over the lip to a churning pool below us. Frothy gobs of foam tumbled across the surface of the pool. Farther out, the water settled into a tranquil circle, blue and cold, with a nearly opaque surface.

"This is the one that people say Witch Weatherly poisoned, right?" Silver asked.

"That's the story," I said. "Ray Bradstreet said there's some kind of weird light that shoots up from the bottom. If you try to swim here, it paralyzes your arms and legs."

"So you'd drown if you didn't get out quick enough," Silver said softly. She stared down into the pool. I crept up next to her and looked down, too. The water itself was a liquid sapphire color, and so dark that it was impossible to see anything deeper than a few feet. Still, it seemed lighter to me at its deepest point, almost as if something was glowing faintly down there.

"Over there!" Silver said, pointing. "Look!"

I turned to the right just in time to see a flash shoot up from the bottom of the pool. It looked like a watery lightning bolt, but thicker around the middle.

"And there!" I shrieked, pointing to where another bolt had surfaced. I clung to Silver's arm. "Ray was right. It is haunted."

"Maybe." Silver looked puzzled. "But it doesn't really make sense. I mean, think about it. *Light* can't paralyze a person. So how could . . ." She stopped talking, letting the rest of her sentence trail off in front of her. "Oh wow," she whispered after a moment. "Oh *man*."

I froze. "What?"

She stepped to one side and pointed. "Over there. Right between those two trees. Can you see it?"

I looked in the direction Silver was pointing.

It was a house, right across from Shining Falls. A real one, with a pointed roof, and a chimney, and a black front door. Something unmistakably red loomed atop the chimney, and a bulky form peered out from behind the front window. Maybe the stories about the lights at the bottom of Shining Falls were puzzling, but this was not. This was one hundred percent real. Someone was in there, and she was looking right at me. Through me.

My heart flip-flopped like a fish on a line.

Okay, Wren.

I took a step back.

You can do this.

Another step.

Think of Momma. Do it for Momma.

And then a third.

"Wren?" Silver was holding out her hand. "You okay?"

It was here. The moment we had been waiting for. My whole body flushed hot and then cold. And before I knew what had happened, I turned around and ran as fast as I could in the opposite direction.

Chapter 30

"Wren, wait!"

But I didn't stop. I ran as fast as my legs would carry me, harder than I had ever run in my life.

"I can't do it," I whispered, over and over again. "I just can't. I'm sorry, I can't." I leapt over fallen branches, stumbling and sliding down the path. I even tripped once and lurched toward a branch hanging overhead, just barely managing to avoid landing on my face. But I kept going.

"Wren, come on! Don't leave! *Wait!*"

Silver's voice behind me only made me run faster, panic building in the middle of my chest like a growing storm. I forgot about her bravery rubbing off on me, and her interview for the history project. I pushed the whole reason I'd thought coming up here was a good idea far back into a little corner inside my head. I must have been out of my mind. I must've been *insane*.

"Wren, *please*! Stop!"

I felt like someone was squeezing my lungs, siphoning off my breath an inch at a time. Bare branches, thin and sharp as whips, slapped at my face and arms, and thorns jabbed under my pant legs. No matter. I kept going. I had to get off this mountain, away from Shining Falls and that house, away from whatever was sitting *inside* and on *top* of that house.

The path veered sharply. Too sharply. Before my brain could register what was happening, I flew forward and landed in a heap of scrub pine. Tiny needles pricked my body all over, pushing into my soft skin like safety pins.

Silver rushed up as I struggled to extricate myself. She was panting heavily as she grabbed my wrist. "*Wren!*"

I tried to wrench my hand out of her grip, but she held on fast. "Let me go!" I screamed. "Please! Let go!"

"*Wait* a minute!" Silver released my wrist, but only to readjust her grasp farther up my arm. "At least let me help you out of there!" She pulled me up out of the pile of scrub pine and clutched both my shoulders with her hands. "Are you okay?" she panted. "Are you hurt?"

I shook my head and tried to twist myself from her grasp again. But she was stronger. "Let go of me!" I yelled. "I want to get out of here!"

"Okay." Silver was still panting, and the edges of her nostrils were white. "Okay. But just tell me why."

I looked at her like she was crazy. "*Why?*" I repeated. "Didn't you see the house?"

"Yes, but then what?"

"What do you mean, *then what?*"

"I mean, *then what?*" Silver repeated. "Nothing happened!" She squeezed my shoulders as if to emphasize her point. "You ran out of there like someone came charging out of the front door with a chainsaw, but nothing even happened!"

I stared at her, feeling my lungs unclench a fraction of an inch. She was right. Nothing had *happened*. But the house was enough. So was the musty front window Witch Weatherly most definitely lurked behind, and the horrifying red thing on the chimney. What if something happened once we got closer? What if . . .? At the thought of it, I fell against her, exhausted and overwhelmed. And then I began to cry great gulping sobs that overtook me like waves and shook my whole body.

Silver let me cry. And cry. My nose began to run and my head hurt.

"All right," she said finally. "C'mere and sit down for a minute." She led me over to a rotting stump where I sat down on shaky legs. "Just take a breather." She unzipped her backpack and took out a bottle of water. I tried to take a sip, but it wasn't easy. My lips felt like rubber. Water dribbled down my chin and onto the front of my shirt.

"Wren, listen to me for—" Silver started.

"*No.*" I wiped my chin with the back of my sleeve, not caring if I sounded rude. "Don't try to talk me into going back up there. You're not *from* here, Silver. You don't know all the things I know about Witch Weatherly. You don't know what she could do to us."

Silver studied me for a moment. "So you really just want to go, then?"

"*Yes.*"

"What about what you said last night?" she asked. "About not wanting me to go by myself?"

"I know." I shook my head, as if to dislodge the memory. "I'm sorry, Silver, but I wasn't thinking right. There's no way either of us should be going anywhere near that lady. She's crazy. I mean, she's been living all alone on top of this mountain for, like, eighty years! And I know you don't think so, but she totally haunted Shining Falls. You just saw it with your own eyes. And the raven's there, too! Right on top of her chimney! Did you see it?"

"I saw something red," Silver said.

"It was the raven!" I shuddered, pressing my palms against either side of my face. "I can't believe we were just standing there in front of Witch Weatherly's actual *house*! Did you see the window? The real big one, right in front? There was a huge blob on one side of it. I know it was her. She's gotta be behind it, just watching us!"

"Wren . . ." Silver started.

"Did you or did you not just see Witch Weatherly's house?" I demanded. "And her raven on top of it?"

"I saw a house," Silver said. "And I saw something red on the chimney." She took my hand. "But Wren, listen to me. Don't you think you got scared up there because of the things everyone *else* has said about this lady? And not because of what you think you saw?"

"I *know* what I saw, Silver. And all those other things are true! Look at the falls! The lights are totally there!"

"Okay." Silver still sounded calm. "I won't argue with you about the lights. I saw them, too. But how do you know what else is really true about Witch Weatherly and what isn't?"

"Because I just do," I answered stubbornly. "When people tell you certain things, you just have to believe them. That's how it works. That's how things go."

"Like why horses are scary?" Silver put a hand on her hip. "Or why planes are dangerous?"

I squinted at her, trying to tell if she was serious or not.

"Or why your mom had to go away to a hospital for a while?" she said softly.

"Hey!" I pointed at her, my lower lip trembling. "That's not fair! My dad was just trying to protect us!"

"And your mom has been trying to protect you," Silver said. "But it hasn't worked, Wren, has it? It's just made things worse."

I stared at her, too dumbfounded to answer. This girl was either really, really crazy, or really, really smart.

"You know," Silver went on. "The truth is that I was scared about coming up here, too. Until I realized that what I was scared of was all the things people were telling me about her. And not what I really knew."

"All you know is that she went to college." My voice sounded a little hollow in my ears.

"True." Silver nodded. "And that your mother knew her. And that her house burned down."

"What about the book your mom said she was reading? *The Secret Power of Plants?*"

Silver frowned. "What about it?"

"Don't you think that's weird? Plants don't have powers! It was probably a book of spells, or something about how to create some kind of power out of plants. Silver, I'm telling you . . ."

"Wren." She crouched down in front of me, and put both hands on my knees. "You're spending too much time in your head." She smiled. "It's like a bad neighborhood in there. You've got to get out of it." She squeezed my knees. "Come on. We've come all this way. And we've got one shot at this. After today, who knows when we'll get a whole day to ourselves again? Let's go back up there and knock on her door. Ask her for ourselves why she's been living on this mountain for so long."

I opened my mouth to respond, but nothing came out.

"Wren?"

I pointed behind Silver as the rustling noise sounded again.

Slowly, she turned around.

There, not two feet away from her, was a hornet-head snake, poised and ready to strike.

Chapter 31

I might not have noticed the snake at all if it hadn't lifted its head from inside the small pile of leaves it was hiding under to glare at us. It was small; much smaller than any of the stories had ever claimed it to be. From head to tail, it couldn't have been longer than eight inches. Its skin was a pale yellow, darker on top than on its underbelly, and black eyes glowered from its triangular head. Black dots, like freckles, were sprinkled up and down its back and two little horns jutted out atop its head.

"Don't. Move." Silver's voice was no more than a whisper. Her eyes were fixed on the snake, almost as if she was staring it down. The reptile began to sway its head from side to side, slowly at first, and then picking up speed, as if something had agitated it. "Don't do anything," Silver whispered again. "Just stay still."

My heart hammered in my ears as the snake rocked back and forth in front of us. Its black eyes glittered, and every few seconds, a forked tongue shot out silently from between a pair of long, curved fangs. Bands of heat pulsed along the sides of my neck, but my mouth was ice-cold. Slowly, carefully, I squeezed my hands together to stop them from shaking.

Abruptly, the snake stopped swaying. It moved its head back a few inches, and then, as if rethinking things altogether, dropped to its belly and slid away.

Silver turned around. Her face was flushed pink, her eyes as bright as stars. "Wasn't that amazing?" she whispered.

"*Amazing?*" I brought my hands up along either side of my face and pressed down hard. "Are you crazy? It was just about to bite us!"

"No, it wasn't." Silver paused. "Well, maybe it was *thinking* about biting us. But that's the thing about animals, Wren. They won't hurt you unless they think you're about to hurt them first. That snake totally scoped us out. He was watching us. Waiting. And when he figured out that we weren't going to do anything, he went on his way."

I thought about the wasp in Mr. Tunlaw's room again, how quiet Silver had been, despite the fact that everyone else in the room was running around screaming, and how softly she talked to Manchester when he seemed agitated. I didn't know how she did it.

"So, what do you think?" Silver asked. "You want to go up there again? See what happens?"

No, I did not. But maybe it would not be quite so scary with Silver around. "If you promise to stay really close," I said.

"Deal." Silver lifted her backpack along her shoulders again. "Let's go. We don't have much time left."

I kept my eyes fastened to the ground as we plodded back up the mountain, and held a can of Mace in one hand. No hornet-head snake was going to dart out and bite me. At least, not while I could help it. Silver, however, strode forward with big steps, her head raised, her gaze fixed ahead as if nothing had happened.

"Don't you get scared?" I asked. "I mean, with animals. Especially wild ones. You can't know for sure what they're going to do."

"True." Silver drew a hand across her sweaty forehead. "But I guess I'd rather think the best about them, instead of automatically thinking the worst. Maybe I'm wrong. I don't know. But it seems to work most of the time."

I wondered if she was talking about animals just then, or people. Maybe she was talking about both. "Are you afraid of *anything*?" I asked.

Silver looked at me funny, as if I had just asked her if she was a girl. "Of course I am."

"Like what?"

She shrugged, her eyes skittering over the forest floor, as if the answer might be hidden somewhere beneath the leaves. "I'm scared of calling my dad again," she said without lifting her eyes. "But you already know that."

I stayed quiet.

Silver pressed her lips together. "Do you remember when I said I didn't know why he wasn't calling me?" I nodded. "Well, that wasn't really true." She began to walk a little faster. "The truth is that I know exactly why he isn't calling me. And it's sort of all my fault."

"How?"

"We got into a big fight right before we left Florida. And I said some really, really mean things to him."

I pulled on my bottom lip.

"The real reason we left Florida was because he cheated on my mom," Silver blurted out. "Actually, it was worse than that. She found out he was living some of the time with this lady. Can you even believe that? They had a house and everything, all the way on the other side of town. Anyway, he and Mom had this huge blow-up, and he filed for divorce, and then she said she had to get out of Florida, that she didn't even want to live in the same state as him anymore." Silver kept her eyes fastened on a solitary spot on the ground as she spoke. "I didn't see him again until the day we left. He came to the house to say good-bye and . . ." She stopped suddenly, as if the memory had jerked her backward. "It was like nothing had even happened. He acted like we were just going on a trip, and that we'd be back later. He even helped my mom finish packing the U-Haul. It was so weird. And so confusing. I kept waiting for him to pull me aside, you know? To tell me that he was sorry. Or that he'd see me at Christmas. Or even tell me one of his goofy knock-knock jokes. I don't know. *Something.* But he didn't say anything. He just gave me a hug, and then I got in the passenger seat of the U-Haul, and my mom started driving away. I watched him in the rearview mirror as he waved good-bye, and I realized that that was really going to be it. We were driving halfway across the country to live somewhere else because of something *he* did, and that was just the way it was going to be."

She started walking again—long, angry strides. Her mouth was pinched tight, and I struggled to keep up.

"I told my mom to stop the truck. And then I got out and walked over to him. I told him I hated his guts, and that I was glad we were going so far away, because he was the biggest jerk in the entire world, and I hoped that stupid lady made him happy, because I never, ever wanted to see him again." She exhaled a long, shuddering sound, and leaned against a tree, covering her face with her hands. "I didn't mean it. At least, I don't think I did. I was just so . . . angry. I mean, he cheated on my mom! And it broke up our family."

I didn't move. I didn't blink. I wasn't even sure I was breathing. It was very hard to imagine Silver saying something like that to another person, especially her father. But it was even harder to see how much saying those words had hurt her. How much they still hurt her.

"I said something really mean to my mom once." My voice was soft, shaky around the edges.

Silver lowered her hands. "*That* mean?"

"Yeah. Kind of." I told Silver the story about the surprise party, and how frightened Momma had been when we all jumped out at her and she saw the flaming cake. I told her about watching Dad for the rest of the night, how hard he'd tried to appear happy when, deep down, I knew he was crushed that she'd been so scared. And I told her how I turned on Momma later that night, accusing her of ruining the surprise, blaming her crazy nerves on everything.

"Did you ever talk about it again?" Silver asked. "I mean, afterward?"

"No." I ran a thumb over the front of my jeans. "I don't think either of us really knew what to say."

"You didn't want to tell her you were sorry?"

"Part of me did. But another part of me didn't."

Silver nodded. "I know exactly what you mean."

Neither of us said anything for a moment. I wasn't sure if the warm feeling in the middle of my belly meant that I was happy—or that somehow, in some strange way, I felt safe.

"You know, I've never told anyone that before," Silver said. "Not even any of my friends in Florida."

"Me either." I gave her a little smile.

She stuck out her hand. "Thanks."

I took her hand and squeezed it tight.

"So before we get started again, you want to go over some of the interview questions?" Silver unzipped her backpack and took out a piece of paper. "I'll tell you what I have, and you can tell me what you think. Then you can add whatever else you want."

"Deal."

We went over the series of questions, ten in all, which ranged from the basic: "What year were you born?" to the not so basic: "What kinds of things did you learn getting your botany degree from the University of New Hampshire?"

"Those are really good," I said as we came to the end of the sheet. "I like them all."

"Anything you want to ask?" Silver said.

I had plenty of things I wanted to ask, but I wasn't going to tell Silver any of them. I thought about mentioning the plant book, but decided against it. Silver would probably say something else about the inside of my head being a bad neighborhood. "'Please don't eat me?'" I asked instead.

Silver laughed and stood back up. "Something might come to you later, when we're actually there."

She took a few steps forward and, without warning, plummeted through the ground, disappearing from sight.

Chapter 32

"Silver!" I stared down into a hole the size of two big trash cans. It was a roughly hewn pit of some sort—wide and very deep, disguised on top with heaps of vines and pine needles and leaves. It was one of Witch Weatherly's secret pits, just like everyone had said! I got down on my belly and leaned over the side of it until I could see just the top of Silver's head. It was slumped awkwardly to one side, resting against the dirt.

"Silver!" I screamed again. "Are you all right?"

She angled her head back in the tight space until she was looking up at me. Her face was white; her mouth contorted in pain. "I think I'm . . ." She brought her hand out from under her shirt, and cried out as she caught sight of her own blood. It dripped down the sides of her wrist and coated the tips of her fingers like red paint. ". . . bleeding," she finished. "Wren, help me!"

My heart caught in my throat. I was not good with blood. Just the sight of it made me nauseated, sometimes even to the point where I actually threw up. But Silver needed me. I leaned in farther against the lip of the pit and stretched out my arm. "Can you grab my hand?" I yelled. "I'll pull you up!" I strained and stretched, even feeling a muscle pull in my armpit, but it was no use. She was too far away.

"Can you find some kind of rope?" Silver asked hoarsely. I sprang to my feet and looked around. There were long, green vines everywhere that might work. I grabbed one, knotting it together with another, and lowered them into the hole. It broke on the way up, sending Silver plummeting back down, where she crashed against the sides of the pit. She cried out again as she fell, and I cried with her, desperate now to get her out. This time, I went back and doubled the vines, twisting them around one another until I had fashioned a thick cord. I lowered it back down.

"Hold on," Silver cried. "I'm going to wrap it around my wrist this time!"

I dug my heels into the ground and inched backward when she was ready, pulling with all my might. I held my breath, but the vines were strong—much stronger than I thought they would be—and they did not break this time as I dragged her out.

Silver whimpered as she came to the surface. The skin around her lips had turned blue, and a little bit of drool leaked out of the side of her mouth. I knelt down next to her, and tried not to scream as I saw the dark red blood on the front of her shirt. There was a lot of it. "What happened?" I asked frantically. "Was it a sharp stick?"

234

"I don't know," Silver gasped. "Something was sticking right out of one side of the pit. It was too dark down there to see what it was, but I must've fallen right on it."

I lifted the hem of her shirt as gently as I could, not wanting to see what was beneath. The wound itself was only as wide as my thumb, but it was so deep that I could see bits of fat and muscle sticking out from inside. A thin rivulet of blood dribbled from it steadily, as if a bottle inside of her had been uncorked and turned on its side. I drew back in horror, and pressed my fist against my mouth. "Oh, Silver. This is really bad."

She nodded. "We have to get something to tie around it, to stop the blood."

I rummaged through the backpacks looking for something, anything, to use as a bandage. But the only things we had left were a few granola bars, some cheese sticks, the bug spray, and Mace.

"The sheet," Silver said, clutching her side. "We can use that."

I grabbed the sheet out of my backpack and hacked at it with my hatchet until I had a long, straight piece. I folded it in thirds and wrapped the whole thing carefully around Silver's back like a bandage. She closed her eyes as I turned her to one side, and grunted when I tied a knot over the top of the wound. Already, I could see faint spots of blood staining the material underneath. "Is it too tight?"

"No," she panted. "That's good." She lifted her right arm, exposing the section of wrist where she had wrapped the vine. "Can you get this thing off? It feels like a razor cutting into my skin."

I clawed at the branch, but it didn't give easily. It was thin but wiry, almost like dental floss. "I can't get it," I said after a moment. "It's too tight."

"Get the hatchet," Silver said.

I sawed carefully at the vine with the blade until the tangle finally broke. The skin beneath it was ringed pink and tinged with blood in some spots. I rubbed it with my fingers to get the blood flowing again. By then, Silver was shuddering, trying not to cry. "I'm sorry," I said. "Am I hurting you?"

"It's my side." Tears leaked out of the corners of her eyes. "Oh, Wren, it feels like my guts are spilling out. Get my phone out of the backpack. We have to call my mom. I'm sorry. I know I ruined the whole trip. But I have to get to a hospital."

I was already dialing Aunt Marianne's cell number. I pressed the phone to my ear and waited. Nothing. I looked at the phone, but there were no bars in the upper right-hand corner. I shook it a minute.

"No service?" Silver asked weakly. "Are you sure?"

"I don't know." I dialed again, waiting for the phone to start ringing, for Aunt Marianne's voice to come singing through the other end of the line. But the only sound I heard was silence. My eyes began to water.

"Go up on that little hill over there, where there aren't so many trees," Silver said. "Maybe it'll help."

I took off running and scaled the small hill on the other side of the path, where I tried again.

Silver was watching me intently, still holding her side. "Anything?" she gasped.

I shook my head as I came back down toward her. "There aren't any bars up there, either. We must be too far up the mountain."

"Oh, Wren." Silver let her head fall against her shoulder.

I scanned the area around me desperately. But all I could see was miles and miles of trees and vines and rocks. The only one who could help Silver right now was me.

"I'll have to build a stretcher or something," I said, stuffing the phone back into the pack. "There's no way I'm going to be able to carry you back down the mountain."

"Back *down*?" Silver repeated. "Wren, do you know how far up we are? It would take us another three hours to get back down. And by then it'll be dark."

"Well, what are we going to do?" I asked. "I can't just leave you here."

"We have to go to Witch Weatherly's. If she can't help us, we can at least use her phone."

I stared at her, a ladybug of fear crawling inside the pit of my stomach.

"Wren," Silver said, as if anticipating my argument. "We were going there anyway. Besides, there's no other way. She's right up there. Behind Shining Falls. We saw her house. We can get up there in ten minutes."

I swallowed hard. Why was I still balking? Twenty minutes ago, I'd been trudging up this very trail for this very purpose. Was there some part of me that really believed we weren't actually going to go through with it, even though we'd gotten so close and come so far?

"Wren." Silver's tone was all business now. "You know how you said you wanted some of my brave stuff to rub off on you?"

I nodded, not wanting to hear what she was going to say next.

"Well, the only thing I know about being brave is that it includes being scared. You're scared and you do it anyway. That's what I do. Now, come on. Help me up. We have to go."

It occurred to me then that Silver might still be scared of Witch Weatherly, too. And that, despite her fear, she had no intention of turning back. If she could do it, then so could I.

I squatted down next to her and put my hand on her knee. "Are you sure you can walk if you lean on me?"

"Yes," Silver said grimly.

I helped her up, positioning her arm over my shoulders. She kept her free hand pressed tightly against her injury, as if something inside might fall out if she didn't. "We're going to have to go slow," she said. "I'm serious. It hurts like a you-know-what."

"What's a you-know-what?"

"The worst word you can think of," Silver said. "Like in the entire universe."

"Oh." I helped her take a step forward. "You mean like a blankety-blank?"

Silver giggled. But it came out weird, the pain still audible in her voice. "Exactly," she said. "A blankety-blank. Times one hundred."

Chapter 33

The sun looked like an electric tennis ball hovering midway in the sky. Shadows were beginning to lengthen, and the light was as pale as sand. Silver and I had been walking for over twenty minutes, but we'd only made it halfway to the falls. It was difficult to move, trying to manage the weight of her and both backpacks, without losing my balance. Still, it was obvious that Silver was having a harder time. Every ten steps or so, she would bend over, clutching my shoulder with her fingers and gasp. The muscles in her neck stood out like ropes, and sweat leaked down the bridge of her nose.

"Silver," I said as we stopped yet again so that she could catch her breath. "This is too hard for you. Sit here. I'll go by myself."

"No." Silver clutched at me. "Don't leave me here alone. I'm going with you. I can do it. Besides, we're almost there."

"Okay." I looked at her out of the corner of my cyc as we continued on. Since when did Silver not want to be left alone anywhere?

Inch by inch, we plowed ahead, Shining Falls roaring in the distance with each step. Another quarter mile, and we would be in front of Witch Weatherly's house.

"Tell me something about you that I don't know," Silver said.

"What?"

"Just to take my mind off things for a minute." She stopped again, closed her eyes, and inhaled. Her whole body trembled.

"I don't know."

"Anything," Silver said. "Like how about your friends?"

"My friends?"

"Yeah, you know. Those two girls you always sit with at lunch. Isn't one of them named Dora or something?"

"Nora," I corrected her.

"Yeah, Nora. And who's the other one?"

"Cassie."

Silver wiped her forehead with the back of her wrist. "Tell me about them."

"There's not really much to tell."

"Have you known them a long time?"

"No. Just since last year."

"Oh." Silver's forehead furrowed. "Well, are they your best friends?"

"They're not even my good friends," I said. "They never were."

Now Silver stopped, still breathing hard. "So why do you sit with them at lunch every day?"

"Because it's better than sitting alone." I shrugged, embarrassed. "Stupid, right?"

Silver was still looking at me, but with an expression I could not read. "No," she said. "It's not stupid at all. Why do you think I sit with all those idiotic boys all the time?"

"What do you mean, idiotic? They're the most popular boys in the whole school. And they're crazy about you!"

Silver rolled her eyes. "Well, I'm not crazy about them. If you want to know the truth, they drive me nuts. Especially Jeremy. He has, like, no boundaries. I can't stand people who think they can just do and say whatever they want because they're popular. It's so dumb."

"So then why don't you sit somewhere else?"

Silver seemed to think about this for a moment, her teeth working her bottom lip. "I guess 'cause no one else has ever asked me. And, like you said, sitting with someone—even if you don't like them very much—is better than sitting alone."

I wasn't sure if anything else Silver said just then would have surprised me more.

Except for what she said next.

"Oh, there it is!"

I looked up. There, like a mirage, was Witch Weatherly's house shimmering faintly between the trees again. I stopped walking and stared up at the chimney. The red shape we'd seen before was gone, vanished like smoke. I glanced around fearfully, peering to the right and then the left, but there was no sign of the terrible bird. I kept looking around. The trees around the house were dense, but not so dense that I would not be able to make out a sudden flash of red when it came out from wherever it was hiding.

"Wren?" Silver whispered. "What are you doing?"

"Just looking." My voice was a squeak.

Silver gestured toward the front door with a nod of her head. "She's probably *inside*. Don't you think?"

"Yeah." I turned my attention back to the house. It somehow looked smaller than it had before; the pointed roof wasn't quite so high, the front window not as wide as I'd first thought. A drooping chimney sat atop the roof, but no smoke curled its way from the inside. The siding was a mess of peeling paint, and a bedraggled line of purple flowers edged the ground next to the front steps.

I could feel Silver looking at me. "You ready?" she whispered.

There was no magic moment then. No rush of courage filled the inside of my chest, and my heart did not slow down from its rapid-fire beating, not even a little bit. This bravery thing was crazy, and still—despite everything I was learning about it—probably the scariest thing in the world.

"Yes," I heard myself say. "Let's go."

Chapter 34

The back of Shining Falls was less than two hundred feet from the front of Witch Weatherly's house, which meant that her "front yard," which consisted of an enormous circular patch of overgrown grass, a few large boulders, and an old, rotting tree stump, stood in between the two. A walking path wound its way through the grass to the front door, and on either side of the house, hundreds of different plants, all in various states of bloom, had been planted. Tall yellow stalks edged the perimeter, while shorter, purple thistle clumped inside. There were blue, bell-shaped flowers hanging off thick green stems, and gigantic white orbs, big as snowballs, hovering atop slender stalks. A scent unlike anything I'd ever smelled before lingered in the air: something like lemon and wood smoke, and maybe a little bit of gasoline, too.

The slats on Witch Weatherly's bottom step made a squeaking sound as Silver collapsed down on it. Her hand was still pressed against her side, and the blue tinge around her lips had gotten darker. I wasn't sure what that meant exactly, but I knew it couldn't be good. I angled my way around her, stepping carefully around a few loose pieces of timber scattered next to the railing. A stool with two broken legs lay on its side, and some of the floorboards on the porch were rotting at one end. I took a step closer to the door and held my breath. The inside of my mouth was so dry that when I swallowed, nothing happened.

"Okay," I whispered. "Here goes." I held my breath.

I knocked twice and took a step back.

"Maybe you should knock a little louder," Silver said. "She probably can't hear very well."

I knew Silver was in terrible pain, but the nonchalance in her voice was irritating me. She wasn't the one up here knocking. She wasn't the one Witch Weatherly would see first when she flung open the door, the one whose throat she would lunge at, maybe with the red raven on her shoulder.

"Wren," Silver said.

I knocked again, a little louder this time, and brought the front of my T-shirt up over my mouth in case a scream decided to emerge without my permission. The doorknob was a dull black thing that looked as if it might fall off, but it did not move. Not even an inch. The only sound was the fleeting chirp of crickets somewhere, and the thunderous roar of the falls in the distance.

Finally, I turned around. "Now what?"

"Look in the window," Silver said. "See if you can see anything inside."

I crept over to the windowpane, my heart thrumming in my chest. The odd shape I'd seen before was gone, but the glass was dirty, the edges smudged with years of grime and soot. I cupped my hands over my eyes and peered inside. A large room, neatly kept, was spread out before me. There was a small fireplace with a wrought-iron stove inside, a wooden, rectangular table pushed up against the wall next to it, and in the corner, a narrow twin bed. Nothing else. No person. No bird. Nothing.

"It's empty," I breathed, stepping back away from the window. "At least as far as I can see."

Silver dropped her head into her hands and leaned to the side until she was propped up against the porch railing. "How about a phone?" she moaned. "Can you see a phone?"

"Silver, I'm telling you . . ."

"Wren, please! Just look one more time!"

I stepped back over to the window and peered back inside. This time, I looked more slowly. There were a few random objects on top of a mantelpiece, but none of them looked like a phone. On the table next to the fireplace was a plate, empty except for a few crumbs, and something that looked like a pair of glasses.

Glasses? Witch Weatherly wore glasses?

The bed in the corner was neatly made, but empty, too. No TV or bedside table. No phone.

"Anything?" Silver asked.

I started to answer when a faint scratching noise on the side of the house made my skin prickle. The flash of red emerged so quickly from around the corner that I didn't have time to scream. Instead, I lunged backward, nearly tripping over Silver, and then scrambled to the other side of the porch on my hands and feet as the form materialized in front of me.

"The raven!" I screamed, finding my voice. The red thing bobbed out farther from the side of the house, hovering now, its wings spread wide. "It's the bird! The raven!" I grabbed on to the railing, and clung to it, burying my face inside my arms. If it was going to come after me, I would not let it near my eyes. No matter what.

A strange sound emerged from behind me, softly at first, and then getting louder. It was Silver. She was struggling to breathe, fighting for her life against an animal that would maim her already-injured self in the worst way possible. I had to help her. I lifted my head and then screamed again as a sound like a whoosh of air burst out behind me. It was followed by the sudden flapping of wings, and then a slapping noise. "Wren!" Silver gasped. "Look!"

"Cover your eyes, Silver!" I shrieked. "Duck your head!"

"No!" Silver made the odd sound again. It almost sounded as if she was laughing. But it was a weird sort of laugh, mixed in with pain and breathlessness, and a little bit of amazement, too. "Look, Wren! You have to see this!"

I lifted my head a quarter of an inch and peeked out from under one arm. Silver was holding something in her hand, tugging on it, and staring up at the sky. What was this crazy girl doing now? First wasps, then hornet-head snakes. She wasn't going to be foolish enough to try to pacify a killer raven now, was she?

I followed her gaze with fearful eyes, my breath coming in raspy spurts, and then sat all the way up.

It couldn't be.

There was just no way.

Silver glanced over her shoulder at me and made the weird laugh sound again. "Look, Wren! It's a kite! Help me! I can't hold on to it!" She tugged again at the string in her hands, and the bright red shape danced overhead, a tattered flag swooping and fluttering in between the brush of trees.

"What are you doing?" I cried.

"It's her kite!" Silver yelled. "I don't want it to fly off! Help me!"

I rushed over and grabbed the string above Silver's hands, pulling with all my might, until the enormous red kite gave up suddenly and collapsed to the ground in front of us. It skittered once, flapping against the ground, and then lay still. I stood there for a minute, just staring at it, not quite sure whether or not to believe my eyes.

It was obviously old, taped and retaped again in some parts, the once vibrant hue now a faded rose color. The edges were worn and tattered, the long tail of it split and whippet-thin from use. But the most peculiar part of all was the outline of hundreds of feathers that had been painted on the sides. In the front, where the ends came together in a little triangle, were two eyes and a beak, painted roughly on the thin canvas.

One by one, my fingers relaxed their hold on the string. *This* was Witch Weatherly's deadly red raven? The one that circled the mountain at all hours, keeping guard over her place? The one that poked out people's eyeballs with its beak, and then ate them?

"I can't believe it," I whispered.

"It's just a kite!" Silver looked at me with enormous, glassy eyes. "It must've been stuck on the chimney when we saw it before and blew off!"

"I can't believe it," I said again. "It's . . . it's not even real."

"It looks real from far away," Silver said forgivingly. "I bet some people saw it and just started thinking the worst."

"Why would she paint feathers on it though?" My head was spinning. "And the beak? And the eyes? It's like she wanted people to think she had a crazy red bird up here."

"Maybe she did." Silver pulled the kite gently along the ground, and then drew it up the steps.

"But why?"

"I don't know." Silver set the kite on the porch behind her. "Maybe it's her way of keeping people away." Her hand was still pressed against her side, and she was breathing hoarsely. "Wren, it really hurts. Did you see a phone anywhere inside?"

"Uh-uh." I shook my head, still trying to wrap my head around the fact that there was no red raven. Or at least, no *real* red raven.

"Well, we have to go in." Silver tried to get up, clutching at the banister with both hands. "She's got to have one in there somewhere, and I have to call someone. I can't take this pain for one more second."

"Silver!" I stared at her, aghast. "We can't just go inside without permission! That's, like, breaking and entering!"

"We have to." Silver's face set itself into a tight grimace. "I'm in bad shape, Wren. It's still bleeding. I can feel it seeping through the sheet." She held up her fingers. They were stained with blood. "And it hurts so bad. It comes in these waves, and sometimes it's so strong I feel like I'm going to faint. I just . . . I can't . . ."

"Okay." I stepped toward her quickly and let her lean into me. The glassiness in her eyes seemed to be getting sharper and her blue lips had started to quiver. "It's okay, Silver. We'll figure something out."

Silver hobbled back up to the door with me. She leaned heavily on my shoulder as I stared down at the shaky-looking knob. "It's not like we're going to do anything bad," she whispered. "We just need a phone, Wren. We have to call for help."

Her words reverberated inside my head as I reached for the knob. Of course we weren't going inside the house to do anything bad. Silver and I weren't bad people. But how were we going to explain that to Witch Weatherly if she came back and found that we had broken into her house?

I pushed on the knob. The door creaked open. A smell like dirt and warm bread drifted out.

"Come on," Silver whispered. "We gotta make this quick."

Chapter 35

We shuffled inside a step at a time. There was a green-and-blue chair just inside the door, and Silver sank into it with a groan. I stood next to her for a minute and looked around. It was hard to see with only the watery dusk filtering through the windows to light the dark floorboards. In fact, I didn't see any lamps or light fixtures at all. A large candle sat on top of the mantelpiece, and I could make out a broom propped up in one of the corners. It looked as if it had been fashioned out of a piece of bark and twigs, the sweeping part tied together with twine. Draped along the wall above it hung a soft blanket of cobwebs.

"Silver," I said. "I don't like this. We shouldn't be in here."

"I know." Silver held on to one side of the chair and looked around. She was starting to breathe heavily again, and her face looked even paler than before. "Let's just find the phone so we can get out of here."

I moved quickly then, hurrying around the strange little room as if I was being timed by an invisible stopwatch.

252

Which in a way, I was. Who knew when Witch Weatherly was going to come back? I had to make the call and get us the heck out of here before she came within ten yards of her place.

"How about over there?" Silver pointed to a large urn standing next to the fireplace. It was almost as tall as me, and capped with a rusty-looking lid.

"In *there*?" I asked, staring at the strange-looking container. "What is it?"

"*I* don't know," Silver said. "But we have to look everywhere, Wren. Seriously."

I tiptoed over to the urn and regarded it for a moment. It had a long, slender neck, like a giraffe, and then curved down into a wide, belly-shaped bowl. Who knew what could be inside? Maybe the remains of small children. Their bones or fingernails.

"Please, Wren!" Silver was getting impatient. "Just look inside!"

I put my hand on the small latch under the cover, and then lifted it slowly. Something tiny flew out—and I screamed, covering my head with my hands.

"It's a moth!" I heard Silver say. "Wren, it's okay! It's just a moth!"

I brought my arms back down and watched the tiny insect as it fluttered behind the musty curtains.

"Look again," Silver pressed. "Anything?"

I peered back inside. But there was nothing at the bottom except ashes and a few twigs. A strange odor made me wrinkle my nose, something like rotten eggs and oranges. "Ugh." I stepped away. "Nothing in there except a really gross smell."

"How about over by her bed?" Silver asked. "My grandma always keeps her phone right next to her bed."

Witch Weatherly's bed was a twin size, much smaller than the one I slept in at home, with a normal-looking sheet, pillow, and blanket. But the wooden headboard at the top of it was not like anything I'd ever seen before. Hundreds of carvings had been etched into the wood; different species of birds, plants, vines, and flowers. There was even a tiny mouse peeking out from one corner, complete with a miniscule nose and whiskers. I ran my fingers over the carvings, marveling at their beauty and complexity.

"Maybe under her pillow?" Silver called.

I lifted her pillow. A small black book lay beneath it, the cover worn and faded to a pale charcoal color.

My blood ran cold.

The Secret Power of Plants was scrawled across the front of it. Beneath the title, in cramped handwriting, someone had added the words "*and Animals.*"

"Wren?"

"It's the book," I whispered, leafing through it. "The one Aunt Marianne told us about." Inside, the pages were filled with pencil drawings of various plants, flowers, and wildlife. There was a picture of a hornet-head snake on one page, a small, daisy-like flower on another. Beneath each drawing, Witch Weatherly had written descriptions of all the living things on Creeper Mountain. I began to read slowly, feeling my hands start to shake.

"Wren," Silver said. "Please!"

I opened my mouth to respond, then froze as the front door banged open like a gunshot.

There, with an enormous stack of wood in her arms, stood Witch Weatherly herself.

Chapter 36

The witch caught sight of me first and dropped her armful of wood. It clattered to the floor, scuttling in all directions like awkward, legless animals. Silver let out a small gasp, and the witch snapped her head around.

"Who are you?" Her voice was raspy, like sandpaper, and her eyes moved quickly between Silver and me. She still held a single piece of wood in both of her hands like a bat, as if we might decide to charge at her at the same time.

I opened my mouth, but nothing came out.

The eyes that glared at me from the doorway were small and black. There was no mistaking the wrinkles around them, or the long hair, white as cotton, partially hidden beneath a triangle of dirty pink cloth. But the rest of her face seemed askew, as if someone had reached under her skin, twisted it a little to the right, and then set it back down again. Her lips looked off center, as if they had been pushed to one side, and her nose was missing the tip, ending abruptly in a strange, blunt piece of skin.

She had, truth be told, one of the most horrifying faces I'd ever seen.

"Who *are* you?" she hissed again, taking a step toward me. Her fingers tightened as she readjusted her grip on the wood. "And what are you doing in my house?"

"I'm . . . I'm sorry." My voice was a squeak. "I'm Wren. And that's my cousin, Silver. We were just . . . looking."

"I can see that," the witch snarled. "What were you looking *for*?"

"For . . . a phone."

"A phone?" The witch stopped in her tracks.

"Please," Silver said, struggling to get out of the chair. The witch turned, raising her stick again. Silver sat back down quickly. "It's not what you think, ma'am. We were taking a walk, and I fell in a hole, and I got hurt. I'm bleeding. Bad. We were just trying to find a phone so that we could call for help. That's all."

Witch Weatherly glanced down at Silver's waist. The dark outline of blood seeped through the thin sheet. "You fell in a hole?" she asked.

Silver nodded. "It was covered on top, with grass and leaves and vines and everything. I didn't see it. There was something sticking out from the side, I think . . ."

The witch nodded, as if recognizing something from Silver's description. "Was there anything inside the hole?" Her eyes gleamed a little as she spoke. "Down at the bottom?"

"No." Silver shook her head and clutched at her side. "No, I don't think so."

The witch grunted and turned back around, looking at me. "Are you hurt, too?"

"No," I whispered.

"Something wrong with your eyes, then?"

I shook my head, confused. "No, there's nothing wrong with my eyes."

"Then why are you poking around in my bed?"

"We . . ." I swallowed. "We thought maybe you had the phone under your pillow."

The witch raised one shaggy eyebrow. "Anybody you know keep a phone under her pillow?"

I shook my head.

"Put that book back," she snapped. "It's personal property."

I'd forgotten I was even holding the book. I slid it quickly under her pillow, hoping she couldn't see the flush in my cheeks.

Her tongue darted out from her mouth, and she licked her lips. "How old are you?"

"Twelve," I answered.

She turned, thrusting her chin at Silver. "You?"

"I'm twelve, too." Silver's voice sounded faint. I wondered what she thought of Witch Weatherly's horrifying face, if she was as frightened as I was.

"Old enough to understand things like trespassing on private property and basic personal privacy." The witch snorted, glaring at me. "Who else is with you?"

I shook my head. "No one."

"You two came all the way up here all by yourself?"

"Yes."

"Why?" Witch Weatherly asked.

Silver and I exchanged a glance.

"Just to snoop, eh?" The witch answered for us. "Surprise, surprise. Just like all the rest of 'em."

"We didn't mean to snoop," I whispered. "Really, we didn't. We knocked, but there was no answer."

"That's because I wasn't *here*." Witch Weatherly arched another eyebrow. "I was down by the falls, getting wood for my fire."

"Is there any way . . ." Silver's voice was hoarse, trailing across the room like an injured butterfly. She held herself up on the edge of her chair with one hand, and waved the other one weakly. "I mean, do you think you could call someone? My side . . . it just hurts so bad."

"And what would you like me to use?" Witch Weatherly demanded. "Smoke signals?"

Silver stared at her, openmouthed. "You don't . . . have a phone?"

"Of course I don't have a phone," the witch said. "I don't have electricity."

Silver's shoulders sagged. For a moment, I thought she might burst into tears.

The witch didn't seem to notice. She gripped the wood again, as if reminding us that she had it—and that she knew how to use it. Her eyes twitched at the corners, and the right side of the old brown skirt she was wearing trailed on the ground.

"Just in case it wasn't clear the first time," she said, "let me inform you again that this is private property, which means that, injured or not, you have no right to be here. Now get out, both of you!"

Something took hold of me then; I'm not sure what. Maybe I was tired. Or maybe I realized how long a day it had really been, how many hours we had been climbing, or how much trouble we'd be in when we got back. Maybe I was worried that Silver wouldn't be able to bear the pain in her side much longer. Whatever it was, I took a step forward.

"We can't go," I heard myself say. "My friend needs to go to the hospital. And you're the only one around. Please, you have to help us!"

The witch's eyes disappeared into two slits. Her stub of a nose flared the tiniest bit. "I don't *have* to do anything," she hissed. "You are standing in *my* house, which means that I can do whatever I want. I already told you I don't have a phone, which means there is nothing else I can do for you. Now, I'm not going to say it again. Either both of you leave by the time I count to three or . . ."

"But she's hurt!" I begged. "Isn't there anything you can do? Wrap it in something? Or help me make a stretcher so I can carry her back down the mountain? Anything!"

"*One*." The witch squinted as she stared at me.

Behind her, Silver swayed in her chair. Her eyes were

as wide as quarters, and the shaking in her lips had moved down to her arms.

"Please." I struggled not to cry. "I'm scared. I don't know what might happen if we try to go back down the mountain all by ourselves."

"Then you shouldn't have come all the way up here by yourselves." The witch pointed a menacing finger at me and took a step forward. "*Two*."

I looked around the room wildly, trying to collect my thoughts.

"But she saved your kite!" I burst out.

For a split second, the witch looked unsure of herself. Her finger wavered and then dropped to her side. She turned around and glanced at Silver. "You saved my kite?" she repeated.

"Yes, ma'am." Silver's voice was barely above a whisper. "It was starting to blow off into the woods, but I grabbed the string." A strange look came over her face then, as if she was confused. "It's on the porch outside, if you don't believe me. I tied the string around one of the banisters, too, so it wouldn't fly off again."

It was the last thing she said. As I watched, she grimaced, then slid off the chair, and like a marionette with disjointed limbs, landed in a heap next to it.

"Silver!" I cried.

A muscle pulsed along the edge of Witch Weatherly's jaw, and her mouth set itself in a tight line.

"Please!" I took another step toward the witch. From this distance, I could see the rippled skin along her neck, thick and uneven, like old lunch meat. My voice quavered. "Please do something. She's my friend! I don't want her to die!"

I clutched my hands together, wringing them in front of me like an awkward prayer. I didn't know what else I could say to convince her to help Silver. *Please*, I thought to myself. *Pleasepleaseplease.*

"She's not going to *die*," the witch said impatiently. "But she obviously needs medical attention." Her blue eyes slid around the features of my face. "I'll see what I can do. And when I'm finished, you've got to go. Both of you."

My head nodded up and down like some kind of windup toy. I didn't care what we had to do next, just as long as she did something—anything—to help Silver.

Chapter 37

I didn't say a word as the witch lifted Silver's shirt and examined her injury. The blood didn't seem to be oozing out quite as fast anymore, but the wound itself looked even worse than it had earlier, like a tiny piece of fruit rotting around the edges. The witch drew her fingers lightly around the perimeter of it and then brought the edges together, as if trying to squeeze it shut. Her nails were long and dirty, and up close, I could see the skin on her hands and wrists. It was deeply rutted, as if it had been clawed off at one time and then grown back unevenly. I wondered just how much of her body had been burned in the fire. It was impossible to know for sure, but just from the exposed sections, I could only imagine it had been a lot.

She stood up after a moment and wiped her hands on the front of her skirt. "Help me carry her over to the bed. We need to make her as comfortable as possible."

I held Silver's legs as Witch Weatherly gripped her under the arms. As we lay her down, a sound like air being forced out of a balloon came out of Silver's mouth, and her fingers twitched.

"It'll be okay." My voice was a whisper. I wasn't even sure she could hear me at this point, but it didn't matter. "You're gonna be okay, Silver. I promise."

Witch Weatherly had gone back across the room and was standing in front of the fireplace, stirring something inside a small pot on top of the stove. From the back, with the handkerchief tied around her head, and the way her old work boots peeked out from beneath her skirt, she could have been anyone, I thought. Anyone at all.

I watched as she bent down and opened the door to the tiny oven. She shoved a piece of wood inside and shut it again. The stove made a little whooshing sound and began to spit and crackle. How was it that she still fiddled around with fire? What was it inside her that made her dare such a thing after nearly getting killed by one? Did it ever frighten her anymore? Had she ever startled awake in the middle of the night, sniffing for smoke, or eyeing the stove from her bed?

She gave a satisfied grunt, and went back to stirring the pot with a long spoon. After another moment, she took the pot off the stove, and moved over to the urn I had peeked in earlier. Opening a tiny door in the front, she scooped out a few spoonfuls of something that looked like ashes. Dumping them inside the pot, she stirred it again and headed back across the room.

I reached back, keeping my hand as close to the wall as possible, and the witch came closer. She stared at me for a moment, and then said, "Move."

I scuttled out of the way, standing at the foot of the bed, as the witch set the pot down on the floor. She pulled up the bottom of Silver's T-shirt carefully, until the entire wound was exposed, and looked at it again. After a moment, she straightened up, walked over to the table on the other side of the room, and put on her glasses. This time, when she returned, she drew up a chair and sat down. She settled the small pot on her knees and drew out the long-handled spoon. A black sticky syrup dripped from one end, and I drew back in alarm as she drizzled the steaming liquid into the gash. Surely Silver would wake up now, screaming in pain. I waited, holding my breath, but except for a slow rolling movement beneath her eyelids, Silver did not make a sound. She didn't even flinch. Even her breathing—slow and shallow—did not change.

"What is that?" I whispered, staring at the black, gooey ribbon still dripping from the spoon.

"Herb glue," the witch answered, without taking her eyes off the spoon. "Calendula, ginseng, aconite, and yarrow. The mountain is full of them."

"What will they do?"

"Stop the bleeding. Act as an antiseptic to kill germs."

I could feel something lifting inside—a flicker of hope. "So then . . . she'll be okay?"

"Probably."

Her voice was noncommittal, as if the state of Silver's health was about as important as a rock, but she also seemed to work with a certain kind of confidence, like she had done such a thing before. When she was finished, she put the spoon back in the pot. Then she took both hands, holding them together loosely as if she was about to say some type of prayer, and settled them on top of the wound. There was a small opening between her thumbs, and she blew through it once, twice, and then a third time. I didn't know if I was watching some type of witchcraft, or if Witch Weatherly was just an honest-to-goodness nutcase, but I didn't dare move.

She sat back finally, her eyes moving down to Silver's wrist, which was still red and raw from the rope-vine. "You use creeper to drag her out of that hole?" she asked, examining it closely.

"Creeper?" I leaned forward in alarm. "What's a creeper?"

"Trumpet creepers," she said. "The long vines with the little red trumpet blooms on the ends? They're all over the place up here, grow like weeds. Where do you think this mountain got its name?"

I moved back again, stunned. I'd always assumed that Creeper Mountain had gotten its name from the fact that Witch Weatherly lived on it. It had never occurred to me that it might be for anything as common as a vine.

She pointed to a pile of logs in the corner held together by a thick cord of twine. "I got creepers put to use all over the place here. They're as strong as any rope. You

266

braid them together and tie them around a grown man's belt, and you could pull him up the mountain."

"That's what I did," I said. "We didn't have anything else to pull her out of the hole, so I twisted some of those vines together until it made a cord and she wrapped them around her wrist."

Witch Weatherly nodded and released Silver's arm. "She should rest." She headed back across the room and set the pot back on top of the stove. "Let her be now. Don't crowd her."

I took a few reluctant steps away from the bed as the witch went over to a cupboard covered with peeling green paint, opened one of the doors, and took out a white sack. She opened the sack and pulled out two small buns. Her glittering eyes flicked over at me.

"You going to sit down for a minute and eat something, or just stand there gawking at me like a loon?"

I hesitated, even as my stomach growled, looking at the buns. I couldn't remember how long it had been since I last ate. The granola bars and cheese sticks hadn't been the most practical—or the most filling—food for the trip. But was I really going to risk eating something here? What if the buns were poisonous? What if this was a trap so that she could sedate me and then cut my throat and . . .

"I have butter, too," the witch said, sliding a plate across the table. She nodded toward a brown earthenware jar with a lid. "And buttercup honey." She split open one of the buns, spread a thick layer of butter on the inside, and then poured a column of honey over the top. It looked delicious.

I didn't move. The buns couldn't be real. Or if they were, they were probably poisonous. Everyone knew Witch Weatherly never went off the mountain. So where did she get things like flour and butter?

"Oh, sit down!" The irritated tone in her voice was back. "You're making me antsy, standing there staring at me like that. I know you want to eat something. You look like a good puff of wind could knock you over."

I moved across the room, inch by inch, until I was standing at back of the chair. The witch had moved over to the stove, where she was busy stirring the small pot again. I held on to the sides of the chair and stared at the roll, as if it might disappear if I looked at it hard enough. I could eat the whole thing in one bite. And afterward I would probably keel over, dead as a skunk.

"Go ahead," the witch said, watching me over one shoulder. "There's more when you're done."

I sat down slowly. It was now or never. I picked up the bun and brought it close to my mouth. The smell of yeast and flour emanated from the soft dough like a faint perfume. I took a bite and chewed. It tasted so wonderful—the bun light and chewy, the honey just sweet enough, combined with the salty butter—that my eyes almost filled up with tears.

As I ate, the witch walked over to the other side of the room and busied herself with something inside a basket.

I could feel her eyes on me as I tore off another piece of the roll and shoved it into my mouth, but she did not say anything. After I finished the second roll, she walked back over to the small stove inside the fireplace. Taking the tin kettle off the top of it, she poured a steaming liquid into two blue mugs. One of the mugs was missing a handle. She brought both of them over, placed one in front of me, and then fished two more rolls out of the sack.

"Eat some more," she said. "And drink some tea. It helps with digestion."

I slurped some of the tea—which was a pale yellow color and tasted sweet—and then sat back against my chair. It was not until I was halfway through the third roll that the witch came over to the table again. She sat across from me, and folded her hands on top of the smooth wood. "Good?"

I nodded.

"All right then," she said. "I gave you something. Now it's your turn."

I sat back, swallowing hard. What did she want? A finger? A lock of hair?

"Do you remember where the pit was that your friend fell into?"

My brain began to race as I thought back, trying to place where we had been. "There was a really big tree near it. A pine tree I think, that was kind of bent over to one side. It was right past that."

The witch's eyes lit up as I spoke, and then seemed to fade again. "And there was nothing at the bottom of it? Nothing at all?"

I looked at her curiously. "What do you mean? What would be at the bottom? Is it a trap?"

"Well, of course it's a trap." She huffed impatiently. "What did you think it was? A swimming hole?"

I was almost too scared to ask the next question. It seemed so obvious. But I wanted to know. A part of me wanted to hear her say it. "What are you trying to catch?"

"Hornet-head snakes," the witch answered. "The buggers. The mountain is overrun with them. Didn't you see any on your way up?"

"We saw one," I answered. "It came pretty close to us, but we didn't move, and it just slithered away."

"You're lucky. I've been bitten twice."

"Twice?" I drew back. "But I thought you died if you got bit by a hornet-head snake!"

"I'm here, aren't I?" She snorted and took a sip of her tea. "But I'm allergic to their venom. When I got bit, I was in bed both times for three days. Second time, I wasn't too sure I was going to make it at all. The more of them I catch, the better. I'm trying to create an antidote."

"An antidote?" I repeated.

"For when I get bit," she said impatiently. "You know, like when you get stung by a bee. The doctors give you an antidote if you're allergic, so you don't die. Same thing."

I thought about the little book again under her pillow. It was probably filled to the brim with stuff about those snakes and their venom. And how to use them to create spells.

"Why would you dig a pit to catch a snake?" I asked. "That doesn't make any sense. Wouldn't they just crawl back out?"

"Most snakes would," said the witch. "But hornet-heads have a terrible sense of direction. Snakes in general have no depth perception, but the hornet-head snake also can't see very well. Those two things combined get them very confused when they fall down a large, dark hole. I stick a snake loop in the side of each pit, too, which they thrash around in for a little while, before they fall to the bottom. Which makes it easy for me to scoop them up in my nets and take them to the other side of the mountain where they won't bother me anymore." She shuddered the faintest bit, a slight rolling of the shoulders. "The fewer hornet-head snakes on this side of the mountain the better. I hate the little buggers. Always have."

I sat there for a moment, rolling the information around in my head. It was like watching the layers of an onion being peeled away; the more things that I uncovered about Witch Weatherly, the more I realized that none of the things I had heard about her were true.

Or at least, not all of them. I had to get to the part about Momma. And I would. As soon as I worked up the nerve.

"Did you haunt the falls?" I blurted out.

"Pardon?" The witch looked at me sharply.

"The falls," I stammered. "Shining Falls. Did you haunt them?"

"Why in the world would I haunt them?" Witch Weatherly curled her flat lips, as if tasting something unpleasant. "And how, pray tell, do you go about haunting anything if you're not dead first?"

"Silver and I saw the lights." I sat up straight. "We looked into the pool at the bottom, and there were lights flashing. Like lightning, but wider."

"That's from the algae that grows on the rocks at the bottom," the witch said. "They harbor a special organism that gives off light. It's called bioluminescence. Look it up sometime. It's not rocket science."

I sat quietly, mulling this over. She sounded pretty convincing. And there was a pretty good chance that she knew what she was talking about, since she'd studied botany all those years ago. Still . . .

"So you girls were just exploring the mountain, eh?" she asked. "Out for a walk?"

I looked down at my hands. "Yeah. Kind of."

"Not much to see up here," the witch offered. "Unless you're looking for hornet-head snakes, of course." She placed her hands carefully on the table before her. "Or me."

I fixed my gaze on a stray crumb in the middle of the table.

"You come up on a bet?" she pressed. "A dare?"

I shook my head.

"Were you supposed to grab something from my house and bring it back down to school? Show everybody, just to prove you'd been here?" Her eyebrows narrowed.

I sat back, scared by the sudden aggressiveness in her voice. "No, nothing like that."

"Then what?"

I opened my mouth to say something about Momma, but it wouldn't come.

"Silver has this history project . . . ," I said instead, taking Momma's bird necklace out from inside my shirt and rolling it along my fingers. "You know, for school. We have to do a report about the history of anything, as long as it's from Pennsylvania. And Silver and I thought that, since you . . ."

I stopped talking as I realized Witch Weatherly wasn't listening to me. Her eyes had dropped from my face down to the necklace. As she looked at it, the color seemed to drain from her cheeks.

"Where did you get that?" she whispered.

My fingers froze around the locket.

"Where did you *get* it?" Her voice was a hiss.

"From my mother."

"Your mother . . ." The witch's eyes moved slowly around the table. "Who's your mother?"

"Greta Baker," I said automatically. "She used to be Greta Woodbine."

The witch's eyes bloomed wide. She opened her mouth and shut it. Once and then again, like a fish gasping for air. "She's alive, then?" she whispered. "She's still *alive*?"

Chapter 38

For a moment, I was too taken aback to speak. "What do you mean, she's still alive?" My voice was a whisper.

Instead of answering, the witch got up from her seat. My eyes followed her as she moved across the room and reached for a small box on the mantelpiece. Her skirt swished around her ankles, and her white hair peeked out from beneath her handkerchief. She came back over to the table and sat down, holding the box between both of her scarred hands. The top of the box looked like a miniature version of her headboard, etched with daisies and petunias, leaves and vines. Her fingers trembled as she lifted the little lid, dipped a hand inside, and then took something out.

I leaned in as she held it out to me, hardly daring to breathe. There, in the middle of Witch Weatherly's hand, was the other half of Momma's bird necklace.

"But . . ." I sat there for a moment, too stunned to move. Then my hands flew up to the back of my neck as I struggled to unclasp the chain, to prove her wrong. But even as I set the medallion on the table in front of us, I could tell that it was a perfect match. Witch Weatherly's half of the medallion had the other end of the bird; its missing tail feathers, and the remaining section of branch it was sitting on. Even the broad, jagged edges were a mirror of the other half—a missing puzzle piece forgotten long ago.

What was going on? I didn't understand. "But this can't be the same necklace. Momma told us that it broke in a bicycle accident. She said she could never find the other half."

"A bicycle accident?" Witch Weatherly shook her head. "I don't know why she'd say that." She sat down in her chair again. "No, I gave it to her a long time ago. All the way back when I lived in Sudbury."

"*You* gave it to her?" I stared in amazement. "Why?"

"She was lonely." The witch stared at a spot beyond me. "She needed a friend."

"She was lonely?" I repeated. "What do you mean?"

Witch Weatherly stared down at her piece of the necklace, as if it might help her get her thoughts in order. "I was twenty-three," she began. "I'd just finished college when I got the news that my father had died. He'd left me the family house in his will, and so I came back to Sudbury and moved in upstairs." She looked up at me and smiled the merest bit. "I've always liked being up high."

I didn't move.

"After a while, I rented the room downstairs to a little girl and her father so I could make ends meet. The little girl had big eyes and brown hair. I would see her from my kitchen window, walking to and from school each day. She was quiet. Never smiled. I think she missed her mother, who had moved away, and her sister, too. Pretty soon, I began to notice that her father, who was a traveling salesman if I remember, didn't come home every night. Then I realized that sometimes he'd be away longer than one night. A few times, it was almost a week. Those nights, I could hear her downstairs, crying in the dark. I tried to go to her, but she wouldn't let me in. She said her daddy had told her never to open the door while he was gone."

I was barely breathing. It was almost impossible to believe that Witch Weatherly was talking about Momma. Or Grandpa William.

The witch opened her hand again and looked down at the medallion. "My father wasn't around very much when I was growing up, either. He gave me this necklace when I was a little girl. It was something he wore in the army, and he thought it would help things if we both wore parts of it. When he died, I took the other half back. But one night, as I heard that little girl crying, I just couldn't stand it anymore. I took my half of the necklace and put it in an envelope with a note that said, 'From Bedelia, upstairs. Try to be brave.' And then I slid it under her door. If she couldn't open the door for me, I at least wanted her to know that she had a friend."

Why hadn't Momma ever *told* me such a thing? She couldn't have forgotten. Had she felt so badly about what had happened afterward that she couldn't bring herself to speak of it?

"We started talking a little bit after that," the witch went on. "Just outside on the porch, a hello here, a good-bye there. She told me her name was Greta and that she had an older sister who lived far away. I met her sister once, if I remember right, and her mama, too. They didn't stay long; just a week or two." The witch's face darkened. "Why someone would split up a family like that is something I'll never understand. Children need their mothers. And their sisters. But that's how it was for Greta. She still never let me inside when her daddy left town, but she'd come out on the porch when I went out to read, and we'd talk some, here and there. She told me once—and I'll never forget it—that I was the only person who'd said a single word to her that day." Witch Weatherly shook her head. "I don't know if I've ever met a lonelier child. I found myself beginning to watch for her, making sure she got down the road safely every morning, and waiting by my windowsill until I saw her after school let out again." Her eyes squinted. "I was glad to be her friend. She was my friend, too, but I don't think she ever knew it."

The witch stood up and walked over to the window. She rolled the bird medallion between her gnarled fingers and gazed through the glass.

"And that was why, when I came home from work one day to find the whole house in flames, all I could think about was her. I'd been experimenting that morning with some nettle leaves, trying to boil them down and make a poultice, and I must have left the stove on. Greta's father had gone off on one of his sales trips, and no one else but me knew she was in there. I heard firemen yelling as I ran through the front door, and a policeman grabbed my arm, but I kicked him right in the groin. My only thought was to get to her. To take her out of that burning building and get her somewhere safe.

"The inside of the house was black with smoke. It crawled inside my mouth and stuck in my throat, swallowing every last bit of air. I could feel my lungs starting to squeeze and burn as I raced from room to room. I screamed until I was hoarse . . ." She stopped here and dropped her eyes. Her mouth was trembling, and she moved a hand to tuck a wayward strand of hair beneath her handkerchief. "And then I heard her. A little voice, coming from the next room. I ran toward it, but just then, the ceiling groaned overhead like the beams of a ship starting to give way. I looked up just as the whole thing fell in on me. And that was the last thing I remembered. Until I woke up in the hospital a few days later. My face and arms were wrapped in bandages, but it felt as if my whole body was on fire. Still, I was awake. I was alive. When a nurse walked into my room, the first thing I said was, 'The girl? Greta? Did she make it?' And the nurse shook her head. 'No girl here,' she said, and walked out of the room."

The witch stopped talking then and gazed at me. The faraway look in her eyes made it almost impossible to decipher what she was thinking. But my own brain was going a mile a minute. Witch Weatherly said she'd heard Momma somewhere in that dark, burning building. Which meant that someone else had gone back inside and rescued Momma—a fireman, most likely. And that, based on three little words that a hospital nurse had said, Witch Weatherly had never known it. She thought Momma had died.

"I'm not sure what happened after that," the witch said. "I was in the hospital for some time, undergoing skin graft surgery and all that. And I guess I sort of shut down. I thought Greta was dead, that I hadn't been able to save her. I blamed her father, I blamed myself, I blamed my crazy fascination with plants and my carelessness with the stove. I wasn't much of a people person to begin with, but after I got out of the hospital, I didn't want to be around people at all anymore. After all my bandages came off, I looked like something out of a horror movie anyway. So I came up here. And this is where I've been ever since."

"But . . ."

"But what?" Her eyebrows narrowed.

"It wasn't the stove," I whispered.

The witch's eyes fluttered, as if she'd gotten something caught in one of them. "Pardon?"

"You didn't set the fire," I said, a little louder this time. "Momma did. On accident. She was there by herself, and she was bored, and she started playing with matches downstairs . . ."

"No." The witch's mouth began to tremble. "That can't be right. It was me. I forgot to turn the stove off."

"Momma said it was her."

"She said that?" The witch's eye twitched again. "To you?"

I shook my head. "To Daddy. She's blamed herself all these years for hurting you. And that's why she broke down."

"Broke down?" the witch repeated.

And then, before I knew what I was doing, I told Witch Weatherly everything. I told her about Momma's gray hair and scaly, patchy hands that came and went every spring. I told her about the years of sadness and Momma's breakdown, and how Dad had taken her to a hospital in Ohio. I even told her about Momma's setback, and how she'd talked about the fire. By the time I was finished, my heart was beating so hard I could hear it in my ears. My hands were shaking and my tongue felt like cardboard. But I was also completely convinced about one thing. Witch Weatherly hadn't cast a spell on Momma or Creeper Mountain. She hadn't wanted revenge or payback. In fact, she'd been hurting just as much as Momma had, because she didn't know the real story, either.

All these years, Momma had blamed herself for the Weatherly house burning down. She even thought she was responsible for Bedelia fleeing to the mountain and becoming a societal outcast. It was heartbreaking to think about. But even more heartbreaking was the realization that Witch Weatherly had carried the same burden. She thought she'd killed Momma, that she was responsible for the death of a child. Both Momma and Witch Weatherly had assumed the worst about each other and had gone and lived their lives accordingly.

It was time to change those assumptions.

It was time to make things right.

"Do you think you'd ever want to come down and see her again?" I asked.

"Oh no." The witch shook her head. "I don't come down the mountain. Ever."

I looked down, disappointed. It would take a lot of convincing to get Momma to come up here. Actually, who was I kidding? She'd never do it.

The witch slid her half of the medallion toward mine. "You give that to her when you get back down the mountain."

I took a finger and moved Momma's half of the medallion until it lined up with hers. There was the little bird, whole now, sitting atop a thin branch with six little leaves coming out of the sides.

"Do you want me to tell her anything when I give it to her?" I whispered.

If I hadn't been sitting there three inches away from her, I wouldn't have believed it. But Witch Weatherly's eyes filled with tears. She shook her head. "That's enough," she whispered.

I glanced back down at the necklace, as if studying it for clues. There, spelled out beneath it was the word—

"*GRIT*?" I looked up curiously. "I always thought it spelled GRETA. What does GRIT mean?"

Witch Weatherly wiped at the tears in her eyes. "It's an old word the guys in the Army used to use," she answered softly. "It means courage."

Chapter 39

Silver stirred across the room just then, almost as if she had heard us talking. Witch Weatherly got up from the table and went over to the bed. I followed. Silver still looked a little wan, but the color was starting to come back in her cheeks and the terrible blueness around her mouth had vanished.

"Hey," I said softly, taking her hand. "How are you?"

Silver blinked a few times, and then tried to smile. But it came out wavy and strange looking, as if her lips had turned to rubber. "I feel weird," she said. "My arms are heavy."

"That's the aconite," Witch Weatherly said. "It helps fight infections, but it can affect your muscles a little. It'll be gone in a few hours." She slid a palm over Silver's forehead and nodded. "Your fever's gone. How does your side feel?"

"It doesn't hurt at all." Silver's eyes widened. "What'd you do?"

"She put this whole mix of stuff on it," I said. "Herbs

and things she boiled on the stove and poured into your cut. It sealed it off, and stopped the bleeding."

"Wow," Silver said softly. "Thank you." She looked over at me with fearful eyes. "How long have I been out? What time is it?"

I went over to my backpack and fished out Silver's cell phone. "Seven thirty," I said, trying to hide the dread in my voice. We were late. Really late. It was impossible to know what Russell was doing right now, or what Aunt Marianne was thinking, but I knew neither of them could be good.

"Oh, we have to go!" Silver tried to get up, moving the covers back with one hand, but her movements were stiff, and she fell back against the pillow.

"You're not going to be able to go anywhere for at least a few more hours," the witch said. "Until that aconite wears off, you aren't going to be able to walk."

"Plus, it's dark," I added.

Silver took a deep breath. "We have to find a way. I'm telling you, Wren, my mother probably officially freaked out at least an hour ago. I don't want to make her wait half the night just to let her know I'm okay. She'll have a heart attack."

"But it's *dark*!" I spluttered out.

"I threw a flashlight in the bottom of my bag." Silver edged herself off the bed, balancing herself with one hand. "We can use that."

"Silver," I tried again. "I really think we should wait until . . ."

"I *have* to get back down there," Silver said. "As soon as possible. Seriously. I'll crawl if I have to. It'll be okay."

"You can take her in my sled," Witch Weatherly said suddenly. "I have a big plastic red one out back that I use to haul wood in the winter. She can lie flat and there will be room for your backpacks, too."

"You have a lot of red things around here, don't you?" I said.

"It's my favorite color," said Witch Weatherly. "Come with me. It's behind the house."

I followed the witch out back and tried not to act surprised at the size of her yard. Something that looked like an old, worn-out garden was on the left side, and there, meandering inside a small fenced-in area, was a small goat. "You have a goat?" I asked, staring at the small animal. It was chewing grass and swishing its tail.

"Of course I have a goat," Witch Weatherly said. "I like milk. And butter." I watched as she emptied her canoe-sized sled of leaves, and then wiped it down with a cloth. It was a good size, with a wide back, and ample room on the sides. Silver might actually be comfortable.

"Do you make your own flour, too?" I asked, thinking of the buns I'd eaten.

"Sure do," she grunted. "There's a whole wheat field over on the west side of the mountain. I harvest it every summer. All right, let's go."

I couldn't believe we were leaving already. And with so much left to talk about. Maybe even to fix.

"You said you don't ever come down the mountain," I said, "but what about last week?"

Her hands stopped moving. "Last week?"

"We were on a horse ride through the pasture at the bottom, and my horse saw your red kite in the trees and got spooked and ran off." I put my hands on my hips. "How'd you get your red kite back if you never go down the mountain?"

The witch held my gaze for a moment, and then made a huffing sound. "I think you've just met your question quota for today, which means that I'm done giving answers. Let's go. Everything's ready."

I stared at her, filled with disappointment. It wasn't like we'd become friends or anything, but after everything we'd just found out about each other, was she really just going to let me go like this? As if nothing had even happened? And what about Silver? She might have been on the mend, but she was still severely injured. And we were three, maybe even four hours from home.

On top of a mountain that was covered with hornet-head snakes.

In the absolute pitch dark.

"So you're not going to . . ." I hesitated.

"Going to what?" The witch looked at me impatiently.

"Walk us back down?" The words came out in a peeping sound.

"Young lady, how many times do I have to tell you? I don't leave the mountain." She raised one eyebrow. "Unless my kite flies off."

"But we don't really know the way!" I pleaded. "And it's so dark!"

Witch Weatherly grabbed the sled rope out of my hand and pulled it toward the front of the house. "You found your way up here," she said over one shoulder. "Which means you can find your way back down. Now let's go."

Chapter 40

We started out slowly. Every few feet, I would glance over my shoulder at the wide silhouette of Witch Weatherly against the light of her fire in her living room. I was surprised by how much I wanted to run back and . . . and what? Say thank you for being so kind to Momma all those years ago? Tell her I was sorry for all the ways we—and all of Sudbury—had misjudged her? She would recoil, probably, look at me strangely. She'd been embarrassed that I'd seen her eyes fill with tears, I was sure of it. And she sure didn't have any patience for my scaredy-cat ways. I wasn't going to push things. Instead, I reached over my shoulder and gave her a tiny wave. She nodded and went back inside her house, shutting the door behind her.

It was a whole different story, being up Creeper Mountain in the dark. A full moon, pale and round like one of Witch Weatherly's buns hovered over the trees, throwing dark shadows over the forest floor. Somewhere in the distance, an owl hooted, and other sounds that I could not place snapped and crackled at every turn.

Sounds that made my whole body shiver and my mouth turn cold.

"I'm sorry you have to pull me." Silver's voice floated up into the darkness; one of her arms was draped over her eyes. "I hope I'm not too heavy."

"You're okay," I said. "Besides, it's all downhill this time." I walked slowly, following the small circle of light that my flashlight afforded, and dragging the sled behind me. I was glad Silver couldn't see my face just now; all the swimming that was going on in my head was sure to have created a very unique expression.

I thought about the spell I'd been so sure Witch Weatherly had put on Momma; it had been real after all. But it hadn't been the kind I was imagining. In fact, it had been the opposite. Momma had felt such guilt about starting that fire. And Witch Weatherly had felt responsible for an actual life! The truth was, they'd both been under a spell and hadn't even known it.

"So," Silver said. "Did you two talk at all while I was asleep?"

"Yes." It was a tiny word that somehow encompassed so many things. A lifetime, almost.

"Like what?" Silver asked.

I stopped walking and turned around. "You wouldn't believe it."

"Tell me," Silver said.

I talked and talked as I pulled the sled, telling Silver everything that Witch Weatherly and I had uncovered—about Momma, and Sudbury, and each other, too. I was pretty sure I would have run into a burning building if I thought Silver was trapped inside, just as Witch Weatherly had done with Momma. Even if it scared me. Because friendships—real ones, anyway—were worth feeling scared for. Sometimes, it was the scary parts about them that led you to the brave ones.

Silver let out a low whistle when I finished. I turned, half expecting to find her laughing in disbelief. "It's unbelievable," she said softly. "All of it. I mean, it's even better than a legend, you know? Because it's real. It's like the realest, most awesome story I've ever heard in my life. Plus, you guys totally bonded."

I thought about this for a moment. Witch Weatherly and I had definitely shared an experience. And for the first time in my life, I found myself thinking about her as the real person she was—a student, probably very smart; a woman, who told it like it was; and most importantly, a true friend—someone who had helped my mother feel less lonely at a time when she felt loneliest. If she had felt guilty all these years, I could only hope that hearing the news about Momma made her feel a little less so. It was all I could give her, the only thing I had left.

"You never got your interview," I said suddenly, remembering.

"You know what," Silver said, "I think I did. It's just not the one I thought I was going up there to get. I think the stuff you found out—stuff that only we know now— well, maybe we should keep it that way. We can think of something else to do for our history project."

I nodded, overwhelmed all over again by how grateful I was to have Silver for a friend. But I was getting tired. She was a little heavier than I expected. I sat down after another few yards. My hands hurt from holding the rope attached to the sled, and my shoulders ached from pulling it.

"You okay?" Silver asked. "Do you think you can make it the rest of the way?"

"Yeah," I said. "I just need to sit a minute."

A snap sounded in the distance, followed by another. I sat up, rigid with fear, and glanced around. By now, it was so dark that it was difficult to see my hand in front of my face. Another crack sounded, followed by the swish of leaves.

"Flashlight," Silver whispered, beckoning with her hand.

I handed her the light and pressed myself flat against the base of the tree. Silver swung the light to the right and then to the left. There was another snap, and then one more, much louder this time than the first. I covered my face with my hands, and held my breath.

"I didn't mean to scare you," said a slightly breathless voice. "I just wanted to give you something."

I lowered my hands, staring at Witch Weatherly, who was now lit up in Silver's flashlight beam, clawing her way through a mess of brambles. She was holding an envelope.

"Boy, you can *move* when you want to," Witch Weatherly said, looking at me. There was a slight edge of admiration in her voice. "I've been following you now for the past hour. Couldn't catch up for the life of me."

"Why didn't you just yell?" I asked.

She glanced around nervously. "Loud noises startle the hornet-heads."

It was as if the spoken word conjured the animal itself. The snake appeared out of nowhere, its small yellow head poking out from a thick clutch of leaves, directly behind Witch Weatherly's left ear.

"Oh!" I took a step back, pointing.

Witch Weatherly froze, her eyes as large as quarters. *Behind me?* she mouthed.

I nodded.

A sound came out of her mouth then, a grunt—no, a whimper—combined with the edge of terror. She fastened her gaze on me and did not blink.

Silver sat motionless in the sled, still holding the flashlight, which lit up the snake in an eerie glow. "Don't move," she whispered. "It worked before. Just don't move anything."

But what had worked for us before was not working now. Instead of slithering away, I watched in horror as the reptile descended slowly along Witch Weatherly's shoulder. Its black tongue flicked in and out as it unraveled its length from the branch. Witch Weatherly was holding her breath. The fear in her eyes was palpable.

Suddenly, I thought of something.

It was a million to one, but I had to try.

I put my hand out slowly, trailing just the tips of them

along Witch Weatherly's sleeve. Fingers loose and wide, knuckles raised slightly. Middle finger lower than first and fourth; thumb extended.

It's just a pencil, I told myself. *It's just a pencil.*

I froze as the animal's yellow head snapped up and then seemed to relax again.

Could I really do this?

I couldn't do this.

There was just no way.

"Wren?" Silver hissed below. "What are you *doing*?"

I moved my hand another inch. I was going to have to flatten my entire hand beneath the snake and then lift it up, threading it lightly through my fingers. Someone else had written about this very thing—and said it worked. Now I was going to have to trust it would work for me.

I slid my hand toward the still-moving reptile. *It's just a pencil. It's just a pencil.* There was no doubt about it; I was going to have to move my fingers quicker than I had ever done before. Twice as fast—maybe even three times. But it was the only way. There was nothing—and no one else.

Pencilpencilpencil.

Gritgritgrit.

Quick as a flash, the hornet-head snake lunged. My fingers moved with a will of their own, sliding underneath and threading the snake between them before I even realized it was done. I held the snake away from my body, moving it gently, quickly between my fingers until I could lightly toss it toward the ground.

The snake stared at me for a long moment, then disappeared back into the tree from where it had come.

Witch Weatherly staggered backward and sat down hard on the ground. Her face was as white as the moon overhead, and her fingers were shaking. "Where on earth did you ever learn how to do such a thing?"

I shook my head, almost as dumbfounded as she was, and then grinned. "Your book!" I was almost laughing. "*The Secret Power of Plants and Animals*! The one under your pillow. It was the first entry."

Witch Weatherly looked confused for a moment, and then she reached inside her jacket. "This one?"

"Yes!" I burst out as the slim volume appeared under Silver's flashlight, the title words scrawled across the front.

Witch Weatherly opened the book and then shut it again, holding it in my direction. "Show me. Read it."

Silver repositioned the flashlight over the witch's shoulder as I read aloud:

"*Hornet-head snakes: Members of the Elapidae family. Indigenous to northern North American territories. Possibly ticklish between the sixth and ninth vertebrae; have a hunch that holding them between loose, relaxed fingers and then moving fingers lightly along these regions may result in animals becoming more calm and easy to handle.*"

She looked up at me. "You tried that after reading *this*?"

"You wrote it," I whispered. "Didn't you?"

"Well, yes," she said. "But I just thought that was an old wives' tale. I've never *tried* it. I wouldn't dare get that close to a hornet-head snake. And I never actually thought it would *work*."

I grinned. "Well, now we know it does."

"Yes," Witch Weatherly said. Her voice had changed. It was no longer raspy, or even old. She sounded relieved. And maybe even the tiniest bit grateful. "Thank you."

"You're welcome."

"Here." She thrust the envelope at me. "Give this to your mother along with the necklace. It might . . . help."

I took the envelope from her slowly.

There on the front, in shaky letters, were the words:

From Bedelia, Upstairs.

Keep trying to be brave.

Chapter 41

We could see the red flashing lights halfway down the mountain, and two policemen with their dogs met us another third of the way down. The policemen took over dragging the sled and called an ambulance, while I raced on ahead, hoping to see Russell. He was standing with Aunt Marianne at the base of the original trail we'd started out on, holding on to her leg.

"Wren!" He broke his hold on her all at once as he saw me and ran, throwing his arms around my neck. "I thought the witch ate you!"

"Oh, Russell." He smelled like turpentine and peanut butter. "I'm so sorry if you were worried."

He pulled away from me. "Did you the see the red raven? Did it peck at you? Did the witch make you paralyzed?"

"No." I shook my head, smoothing his hair off his forehead. "No, she didn't do any of those things."

"Oh." Russell kicked a small clump of dirt. "That's kind of boring, then."

"Aunt Marianne." I stood up as she walked over. "I'm so sorry, we—"

She pressed me tightly to her, not letting me finish, and began to cry. "Oh, Wren. Thank goodness you're all right. Where's Silver? I don't see her."

"They're carrying her down. She fell . . ."

The policemen appeared then, Silver between them on the sled, propped up on her elbows. Aunt Marianne rushed over. "Honey, what happened? Are you hurt?"

"I was." Silver's voice was shaky. "But then Witch Weatherly fixed it up." She looked away as her mother's face turned into a question. "Mom, I'm so sorry I disobeyed you. I promise I won't do it again. I swear."

"You're grounded for a month," Aunt Marianne said, fighting back new tears. "And you too, Wren." She put her arms around both of us and squeezed tight.

"Holy dingbats!" Russell shouted, "You two are grounded for a whole entire month? That's like twenty years in Captain Commando time!"

It might have been, I thought. But then it might not be the worst thing in the world, either.

After all, I would have Silver with me.

Two weeks after our trek up the mountain, Aunt Marianne told us that Momma was coming home. That afternoon. I wasn't sure why, but I felt nervous about seeing her. Not just because of Witch Weatherly's letter, which, Dad had said, was the turning point in her recovery. But because I knew she was different now because of it. And that I was, too. It wasn't just that I'd talked to a witch or climbed a mountain. Mostly, I was different inside, as if a window that had been shut for a very long time had suddenly been opened. I wasn't sure anymore if the new me would fit alongside all the old pieces inside. Mostly, I knew now that Momma and I were not the same at all; we were two very different people.

I was okay.

It was Momma who hadn't been. And now that was about to change.

Silver came up to my room just as I finished packing, and sat down on the edge of the bed. "So," she said, twisting a piece of her long hair. "I guess that's that."

I fiddled with the loose snaps on my suitcase, trying to come up with something to say. We'd been through so much over the past few weeks that it was almost impossible to know where to begin.

"I'll see you in school," I said finally, and then blushed. What a stupid thing to say.

"Will you sit with me at lunch?" Silver looked at me out of the corner of her eye.

"Sure. If you want me to."

"I do. Just us."

I hesitated, thinking about something I'd been wanting to say for a long time. "Thanks for the underwear," I blurted out. "It . . . it really helped a lot."

"Any time." Silver was studying me with a weird expression on her face. "You know, you helped me a lot, too, Wren."

"Me?"

She nodded. "I called my dad last night."

"You did?"

"Yeah. And I left a real message this time. Not just breathing." She reached up, brushing the bangs out of her face. "We'll see if he calls. But I did it. Even though I was scared. At least I did it."

I hugged her then, full of gratitude that I knew a girl like her. And that, despite all the odds, somehow we understood each other in a way that no one else did.

Momma was in the car when Dad came over to the house to pick us up. She looked different walking toward me, her shoulders straight and square, her chin lifted ever so slightly. And there was a light in her eyes that hadn't been there before. The pink blotches on her hands, which her doctors had said were a reaction to all the stress she'd been carrying, were so faint that I could barely see them.

"Momma!" Russell screamed, running toward her. She hugged him tight, even lifting him off the ground so he could wrap both of his legs around her.

I held back, still gun-shy.

She put Russell down finally and looked over at me. "Hi, butterbean," she said, and the sound of her voice rushed over me. I ran to her before I could think another thought, and buried myself in her arms. She cried and held me tight until Dad came over.

Russell squeezed in next to me, and Dad moved in behind Momma. He put his arms around all of us, and we stayed there for a moment inside a long, very warm family sandwich, without saying anything.

"Ready to go home?" Dad asked finally.

Momma stroked my hair, and then leaned over and kissed the top of my head. "I think we are," she said. "What do you think, Wren?"

I couldn't speak. Not just yet. But I nodded.

Yes, it was time to go home.

It felt weird walking into the house again after being away from it for such an extended period of time. The air inside smelled stale and too warm, as if it had been trapped inside a plastic container. There was another smell I didn't recognize, but I didn't give it too much thought until Momma stopped short as we walked into the living room. There, on the wall above the fireplace, was the biggest landscape painting I had ever seen.

Russell dropped Momma's hand and ran toward it. "It's the We Tree!" he yelled. "Look, Momma, it's the We Tree!"

It *was* the We Tree, I realized, as my eyes swept over the low, wide branches of the enormous oak. There were the thick clusters of green leaves, the side of a blue house on one side, even a little river in the distance. All those Saturdays that Aunt Marianne had left the house to "go paint," she'd been coming here. To recreate something they'd lost. Right in Momma's very own living room.

I looked over at Momma. Her hand was pressed against her mouth, and her eyes were filled with tears. I know it sounds strange to say that she looked happy even though she was crying, but she did. She looked happier than I'd seen her in a very, very long time.

I put my arm around her waist and held her tight.

"Welcome home, Momma," I whispered.

Chapter 42

Russell and Momma and I were back at Silver's house a month later for Windy Sunday. It was my turn to make plans. I hadn't told Silver or Aunt Marianne what we were going to do, but I was excited about it. Maybe a little bit nervous, too. But I wasn't afraid. And that might have been a first.

"Can't you even give me a clue?" Silver asked, as we started out across the pasture. "I mean, there's really nothing to do out here unless you've got a horse."

"Yeah," said Russell. "This totally stinks without a horse."

Aunt Marianne and Momma laughed behind us. "A horse?" Momma said. "Don't tell me you two are regular riders now."

"Oh yeah!" Russell shouted. "And not just riding, Momma. Flying!"

Momma laughed again and shook her head. "You'll have to promise me that you'll show me the next time we come."

I watched her, smiling. She was a different person since she'd been home. Happier, lighter. As if something that she had been carrying for years had finally let go. I knew someone else like that, too.

"Wren!" Silver said. "This is driving me nuts! What are we going to do?"

"Just hold on," I said, giving her a poke in the ribs. "You'll see."

"I'm starving," Russell muttered. "I hope you packed pancakes."

We were halfway across the tall grass when I spotted the pink scarf moving toward us. Loose strands of white hair fluttered out from under it like pieces of milkweed, and something red was tucked under one arm.

"Who's that?" Russell asked.

Silver stopped walking.

"Come look." I pulled both of them forward and grinned.

"Who *is* that?" Russell dug his heels into the ground, refusing to budge. "She looks weird."

"It's Bedelia Weatherly," I said, talking to Russell. "And she's not weird. She's nice. She's going to let us fly her kite."

"A kite?" Russell's eyes got huge. "I love kites!"

"How'd you get her to come down the mountain?" Silver's voice was hushed.

"I walked up to her house yesterday, and I just asked."

I looked over at Momma. "I told her there was someone who really wanted to meet her again."

Momma smiled at me.

Bedelia Weatherly came closer. She lifted one hand and waved.

We waved back and began to run.

Acknowledgments

Because of their love, encouragement, and never-ending support, I would like to thank the following people:

My agent, Stacey Glick, who does not know the meaning of the word *no*, and possesses the kind of fierce energy that I can only hope to know one day.

My editor, Jenne Abramowitz, whose enthusiasm and tenderness for this book have brought me to my knees, and whose keen editing skills have made for a better, richer story.

Everyone at Scholastic who has worked tirelessly to bring this book into the world.

My husband and children, whose patience for my need to go off alone and write is one of the greatest gifts I will ever receive.

Thank you all.

Read on for a sneak peek at
CECILIA GALANTE's newest
heart-wrenching novel.

In this big, beautiful world, nothing matters more than family.

Saying good-bye is never easy. But when Jack and Pippa's mother dies, they are faced with the biggest decision of their lives. How far are they willing to go to keep their family together?

The microwave won't work. I push all the right buttons, open and shut the door, even unplug the thick cord in the back and plug it back into the wall again. But the little screen stays dark. None of the green buttons on the side light up either. How am I supposed to make my apple-cinnamon oatmeal?

Jack comes in, scratching his head. His hair has gotten long and shaggy over the last couple of months, and his shorts and T-shirt, which he probably slept in, are a mass of wrinkles.

"The electricity's out," he says, his voice thick with sleep. "You're gonna have to eat something else for breakfast." He goes to the fridge, takes out a half gallon of chocolate milk, and brings the container to his lips.

I watch his Adam's apple bob up and down as he swallows, Mom's voice ringing in my ear: "You put that carton down, Mr. Manners, and get yourself a glass."

Suddenly, a strange look comes over his face as he rushes to the sink and spits out the milk. "Bleechhhh! It's sour!" He wipes his mouth with the back of his hand and opens the refrigerator again. It's dark inside. "No refrigerator, either." His shoulders slump as he walks over to the window and stares out at the lake.

Why is the electricity out? Why doesn't the refrigerator work? I wait for Jack to explain, but he just stands there, looking out the window. I take my bowl out of the microwave and stir the flakes of oatmeal. Maybe I'll just eat it dry. It can't be that bad, can it?

"Who's that girl on the Andersons' dock?" Jack asks suddenly.

I swing my bare feet under the table and take a bite of the oatmeal. It tastes like little bits of paper, and I spit it back out.

"You see her?" Jack asks. I pick out one of the dried pieces of apple and nibble the edge of it. If he'd said something about Mr. Thurber, I would have leapt out of my seat. I don't really care too much about other girls. Except for Nibs.

"C'mere. Pippa. Look, will you?"

I get out of my seat and glance out the window. Some girl is sitting on the Andersons' dock, on the other side of Nibs' house, with her legs draped over the edge. Her hair is so long that it hangs down around both sides of her face like curtains. It's hard to tell from here, but it looks like she's wearing pink cowboy boots.

"Have you ever seen her before?" Jack asks.

I shrug.

"Is that a yes or a no?"

I shake my head no and head back over to the table.

Jack turns around again. He doesn't say anything for a long time. I know he's probably thinking she's pretty and that maybe he'll work up the nerve to go say hi to her. Except that Jack would never do anything like that. The only thing that scares him more than pretty girls is the thought of actually having to talk to one.

I get up from the table and grab one of Nibs' newspapers, which I keep in a pile next to the sink. It's an old one from two weeks ago, but I don't care. This morning's paper is still on the dock, and I need something to read while I eat.

"Listen, Pippa." Jack walks over to the table and leans against a chair. "You and me have to go into town today and get some new clothes for school." He opens a bag of white bread and takes out the last four slices.

I slump down against one arm. I hate shopping about as much as I hate dry oatmeal. Which, looking down into my still-full bowl, is saying something.

"Yeah, well, I feel the same way." Jack shoves bread into his mouth. "But Dad gave me his credit card and said we have to go. He said you could pick out whatever you want. As long as it's not a belly shirt or anything with heels."

I roll my eyes. Like I'd ever wear a belly shirt.

Jack crams the last of the bread into his mouth and looks up at the clock. "It's only nine o'clock now. The stores don't even open 'til ten. We have lots of time. I'm gonna ride down to the junkyard to look for some more wood for the tree house. You go upstairs and get ready. When I get back, we'll go, all right?"

Junkyard, my foot. Jack's already got more wood stacked up in the backyard than he can use in a year. He's going to Finster's Rock, just around the bend in the lake, so he can stare at that girl without her knowing.

The house is so quiet after he leaves that I almost start to cry. I like the quiet outside, with the stillness of the water and the silence of the sun, but inside, all it does is scare me. It's funny how the sound of nothing can be filled with so much something. Whatever something is.

I turn my attention back to the newspaper and read the funny pages. But none of them are funny, so I start leafing through the middle section. Most of the stories, which seem to be about church festivals and something called stock inflations, are boring. Like, *really* boring. I'm not really sure what Nibs always seems so worked up about when it comes to reading this thing. She pores over it from front to back every morning, as if someone's hidden something in there that she's got to find.

Finally, on the third page, there is a story that catches my attention. It's about a man who put on a Spider-Man mask and walked into a bank. He handed the lady behind the counter a note that said he had a gun and that he would use it if she didn't give him all the money in her register. But the lady started to cry, and when another bank person came over to help her, the man got scared and ran out.

I shake my head, rereading the last part again about

him running out. What a dope. Then again, if you're dumb enough to rob a bank wearing a Spider-Man mask, I guess you'd be dumb enough to run back out again without any money.

On the other side of the Spider-Man story is an article about a curly-haired lady who caught a forty-five-pound catfish in Lake Bomoseen. I lean in so I can examine the fish up close. Catfish are ugly, and this one is no exception. Its long whiskers hang down near the woman's knees, and its eyes are as big as pool balls. **WHAT A WHOPPER!** says the headline. The lady, who is wearing a big orange windbreaker and a blue knit hat, is smiling so hard it looks like her face might break in half. I can't really blame her.

Jack will be so jealous. The biggest fish he ever caught weighed six pounds and was about as long as his arm. But then, he's never been much of a fisherman.

I cut out the picture and hang it on the refrigerator.

Jack'll spit when he sees it.

Saddle up for a life-changing adventure.

Joseph Johnson has lost just about everyone he's ever loved. And when a man secretly sells the only family he has left—a fast, fierce pony named Sarah—Joseph will face down deadly animals, outlaws, and the fury of nature itself on his quest to get her back.

scholastic.com

COURAGE1

Stories of family, friendship, and finding yourself... from award-winning author Sarah Weeks!

Sometimes you find a friend where you least expect it . . .

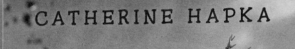

CATHERINE HAPKA

Hear
Dolp